OTHER
MAPS

.||.

The past is not a receding horizon. Rather, it advances one moment at a time, marching steadily forward until it has claimed everything and we become again who we were, we become ghosts when the past catches us.

—Brandon Taylor, *Real Life*

Did you ever get blamed for something you didn't do? After a while you decide you might as well do the things you're blamed for.

—Lisa Moore, *Caught*

The map is not the territory.

—Alfred Korzybski, *Science and Sanity*

OTHER MAPS

a novel

Rebecca Morris

Copy-edited by Elise Moser, Jennifer McMorran
Cover design: Debbie Geltner
Author photo: Petra Niederhauser
Book design: DiTech

Library and Archives Canada Cataloguing in Publication

Title: Other maps : a novel / Rebecca Morris.
Names: Morris, Rebecca (Rebecca J.), author.
Identifiers: Canadiana (print) 20240369467 | Canadiana (ebook) 20240369505 | ISBN 9781773901626 (softcover) | ISBN 9781773901633 (PDF) | ISBN 9781773901640 (EPUB)
Subjects: LCGFT: Novels.
Classification: LCC PS8626.O75783 O84 2024 | DDC C813/.6—dc23

Printed and bound in Canada

Legal deposit – Library and Archives Canada and Bibliothèque et Archives nationales du Québec, 2024.

LLP is grateful to the Canada Council for the Arts, the Canada Book Fund, and SODEC for their support of our publishing program and to the Government of Quebec through the Société du développement culturel and the Programme de credit d'impôt pour l'édition de livres—Gestion SODEC.

Linda Leith Publishing
Montreal
www.lindaleith.com

Table of Contents

Other Maps

CHAPTER 1

Guelph, Ontario
March 2004

Anna gripped the emergency exit handle, fingers flexing against the cold metal bar. The country club ballroom behind her was full of fat cat assholes, sipping their sparkling wine and pretending not to be watching her. None of them would look at her directly but she could feel their eyes tracing her pale dreadlocks, ogling the tattoos that showed at her neck and her wrists.

God, she needed a cigarette. And another drink. At twenty-six, she was too old to be playing the dutiful daughter, obeying every tug on the leash. But as long as she took her parents' money, she belonged to them.

Still, she didn't have to play easy to get. Anna stared out at the snow-covered golf course, a restless itch running down her spine. One push on this door and she'd be outside, plunging through snowdrifts, the freezing wind cutting through her thin dress. Would the alarm sound, once she opened the door? Would anyone come after her? Her mother was across the room, encircled by her equally cold and elegant friends. Anna had been avoiding her all evening, skirting the edges of the room, dodging behind other guests or slipping away into the bathroom whenever Joyce moved in her direction. As for her father, he was at the bar, of course. Single malt in one hand, working his middle-aged charms on a dark-haired woman in a green dress. His tuxedo jacket strained at the seams when he leaned forward, his

1

blue eyes glittering under the soothing balm of female attention.

Basically, this was hide and seek. If Anna got caught by either of her parents, she'd be enduring their lectures, dragged from one tiresome conversation to another, all night long. No, thanks. Wasn't it enough that she'd given up that sweet room-and-board position at a beachside hostel in Costa Rica, boarded a plane in gorgeous thirty-degree heat and flown north to the arctic wasteland that was Southern Ontario in March? She'd put on this prim dress with its Peter Pan collar, followed her parents into this country club ballroom, raised a glass for her father's self-satisfied speech about early retirement. She didn't have to perform for their friends like a fucking monkey.

Anna shifted her weight, feet aching in her borrowed heels. She leaned forward, squeezed the metal bar of the door, braced for that first blast of winter air, then paused as a reflection moved across the dark glass. It was one of the waiters, the good-looking one who'd been shooting her glances all night. He was younger than Anna, with chestnut hair combed back against his head. She turned her head to watch as he slid between guests, refilled wine glasses, dodged a couple of kids playing tag, then met her eye and winked.

Maybe she'd stick around a little longer after all.

She dipped into her beaded handbag for one of the loose tablets along the seam, a mixture of Tic Tacs and Ativan. She tucked the pill into her cheek and it dissolved into a bitter grainy mess that she washed away with the dregs from her glass of red wine. Her fingers tightened on the stem of her wineglass as the waiter approached. Closer, closer. At the last second, she wheeled and reached for his tray.

"I'll take another glass," she said, smiling into the waiter's eyes.

The waiter pulled his silver tray out of her reach.

"We're not supposed to serve you any more."

His gaze moved to her forehead, to the blue stars inked over her pierced eyebrow.

Anna stepped closer.

"Of course. I don't want to get you in trouble." She could see a patch of stubble by his ear where he'd missed a spot shaving. She wanted to lick it, to feel those bristles against her tongue. "Could we find somewhere more private?"

Reflexively, the waiter glanced over his shoulder, towards the hallway to the kitchen. Then she was following him, the door swinging shut behind them as she lifted the tray out of his arms and set it down on a wooden bench by the wall. She took a full wineglass in each hand, laughed when he shook his head and drank them both herself.

The wine wet on her lips, Anna turned to the waiter and touched his crisp white collar. He stepped forward, mouth opening against hers, hands tightening on her ass. Closing her eyes, Anna kissed him back, reaching up to run her fingers through that shiny hair, abandoning herself to the warmth of his body through his cotton shirt, the sliding heat of his tongue, the faint smell of soap on his skin.

She didn't hear the door swing open behind them, didn't register the cloying scent of Opium perfume until a cold hand gripped her arm and spun her out of the waiter's grasp.

"For God's sake, Anna," hissed her mother's voice. "Can't you control yourself for one evening?"

Anna's heart dropped as the waiter backed away, wiping his mouth.

"That's right, go!" Joyce called after him. "I'll be speaking to your manager!"

The wine and the Ativan churned unpleasantly in Anna's stomach. For a moment she thought she might puke, right there at her mother's feet. She fought down the feeling, squeezing the shaft of her metal tongue ring between her teeth.

"Thank God your father didn't see this. He doesn't need your drama. Not tonight." Joyce reached to fix Anna's updo, jamming a bobby pin across Anna's scalp to secure a loose dreadlock. She tugged the pashmina down to cover Anna's tattooed arms. "Show a little self-respect for his sake."

Anna gazed into the middle distance. The wine was sour at the back of her throat but at least the Ativan was starting to kick in, weighing down the lid over her emotions. And this party couldn't last more than another hour or two.

Her mother stepped back, flicked her platinum bob into place and scanned Anna from head to toe before leading her back into the crowded ballroom. A dozen heads turned as they came through the door, a dozen pairs of eyes staring and then dropping away when Anna lifted her chin and raked the room with her most ferocious look, the one that read *do not fuck with me.*

"Here they are," boomed her father as they approached. His cheeks were pink, his forehead glistening. "My two favourite girls."

"This one's still out of control." Joyce intercepted Malcolm's hand as he reached for Anna's shoulder. "I don't know why you insisted on having her here."

"Annie?" So many shades of disappointment in the way he said her name. He gave her a searching look, then shook his head. "Anyway. Look who's here."

He was already smiling again, beckoning to the woman from the bar.

Anna pressed her lips together as the woman exchanged air-kisses with Joyce. What had her mother instructed? *Let us do the talking. The less you say, the better.* That was fine. It was so much easier when she didn't have to talk.

"Joyce, you look fantastic," the woman said. Her face was heavily made up, vaguely familiar. One of her father's old secretaries? "You're simply stunning. I'd never be able to pull off that dress, couldn't keep my figure after my third baby was born."

Joyce's face hardened and Anna looked away, dropping her eyes to the checkerboard inlay on the parquet floor.

"'Freedom 55,'" the woman went on. "What a wonderful theme for a party! I don't think Michael will ever retire. And when do you leave on this fabulous cruise?"

Anna closed her eyes and floated on her sedative cocktail, tapping her tongue ring against the roof of her mouth to count out the seconds. Just think, in a few days she'd be back at Pearson with a one-way ticket to Paris. It would be springtime there, the daffodils pushing through the dogshit. Maybe she could crash at Serge and Phoebe's. Last year, she'd stayed there for a blurry week of late nights and cheap drugs, the three of them stumbling down cobblestoned alleyways and then sleeping it off in their freezing apartment. They knew how to have a good time. Descending into one tiled Metro station after another, emerging across town a whole new person. Every sliding door severing another link to the past.

A touch on her arm brought her back to the present.

"And this must be Annie, the world traveller! So grown up. I haven't seen you since you were a little girl in pigtails." She raised an eyebrow. "Remember me, honey? I'm Janice. You went to school with my son Oliver."

A far-away alarm started to sound in Anna's head.

"Of course she knows you," said her father. "She's just jet-lagged. Annie, you haven't forgotten Janice Sutton?"

The alarm was louder now, clanging, reverberating. The woman tilted her head back, plucked eyebrows nearly disappearing under her bangs.

"Look, he's here with us tonight. Over by the buffet."

Anna saw his profile first, that high forehead and snub nose. Olly Sutton was older, rounder, but the shape of his adolescent face lay just under the surface.

"He's teaching at Laurier, your old high school," Janice Sutton said. "History, mostly. I'm trying to convince him to try graduate school, maybe law or political science. I think he could run for office someday. But you know young people. They've got their own ideas."

Olly glanced over and the years dissolved as Anna met his eyes. The rest of the room went quiet, voices and classical music dropping away. Olly's face blurred and she saw him at seven, twelve, sixteen; the younger versions expanding and contracting into each other, into this present-day smirk.

"Annie Leverett," he drawled, as he reached their group. "I almost didn't recognize you. Back in town for your parents' big party, eh?"

He reached for her, then his hands were on her shoulders, pulling her stiff body in for a hug. Olly leaned forward, whispering: "I can meet you in the bathroom in five minutes. Just like old times, right?"

"You asshole."

With a ferocious burst of energy, Anna shoved him away. Then the nausea was rising up, a blinding rush that couldn't be contained, and she was tilting forward, knees bent, hands against the rough fabric of her nylons, throwing up wine-dark vomit that splashed everywhere.

*

The next morning, Anna woke confused, stiff and aching after a night of terrible dreams. She rubbed her eyes, squinting in the hard morning sunlight as the room came into focus.

A tall bookshelf with pastel rows of Nancy Drew and Baby-Sitter's Club novels. A white wooden desk under the colourful chaos of a bulletin board. Chains of roses cascading down the wallpaper in a pattern she knew too well: pink, pink, pink, cream. Her old bedroom was a time capsule, a dainty confection for a girl who hadn't existed in years. Or—was that true? For a moment, the dislocation doubled back on itself, the years evaporating so that she was still that sixteen-year-old Annie with all this time to live again—then she lifted her hands and saw the tattoos.

Thank God.

She scrubbed at her face as scenes from yesterday's party swam through her mind. When she reached the cloying creepiness of Olly Sutton's arms around her back, Anna bolted out of bed, shoved open the window and spat into the snow-filled eavestrough.

She sat there shivering for a long moment before she pulled on a sweatshirt and lit her first cigarette of the day. She sucked the calming nicotine deep into her lungs, blew plumes of white into the cold morning air and looked out over the pitched roofs and the leafless trees between her and the river, the grey limestone buildings leading up the hill to the Church of Our Lady. God, she hated this city. She hadn't been back since her grandmother's funeral, two years ago. Or was it three? And now she was stuck here for a whole week.

She shook her head and peered down at the garage roof, assessing the distance. She'd made that jump a few times, dropping down to the back patio and slipping out to meet one of the boys who'd come calling for her. It would be slippery today under all that melting snow. Was it worth risking her neck? Risking her parents' fury when they found out she'd disappeared again? Or could she find another way to short-circuit this visit?

*

The grandfather clock in the hallway read ten when she clattered downstairs. Joyce was at the kitchen table, reading *The Globe and Mail* in a shaft of sunlight.

"Is there any coffee?" Anna squeezed the bridge of her nose to quieten her headache. "I slept like shit."

Joyce shook out the pages of the newspaper.

"One night. That's all we asked: one night without drinking." Her voice was icy. She didn't look up. "You'll have to make your own coffee. Your father's been up for hours and I've switched to green tea in the mornings."

"Right." Anna filled the machine's reservoir, dumped grounds in the filter and tapped her foot against the tiled floor as the coffee brewed. "I think I'll leave today," she said, keeping her tone light. "Is Dad around for me to say goodbye?"

"Our flights aren't until Sunday."

"There's no reason for me to stick around so long." She lifted a mug out of the cupboard and looked back at her mother, whose face was hidden under her coiffed blond helmet. "I'll fly standby if I have to."

"Don't be ridiculous." Joyce turned another page. "I won't throw away money to change a perfectly good ticket. Why don't you spend your time clearing out your old bedroom? That room's been going to waste too long."

Anna felt a hiccup of panic.

"I don't want anything from upstairs. You can throw it all out. Give it away." She stirred sugar into the mug and slurped at the coffee, scalding her tongue. "Get Yolanda to do it."

Her mother finally looked up, sliding her tortoise-shell glasses down her nose so Anna could see the anger in her eyes. "Yolanda hasn't worked here in years. You think Raimunda doesn't have enough to do? I'm not paying her to sort through your room."

"Please." Anna's stomach twisted. "I can't stay here."

"Enough drama. You should have done this years ago. We've got garbage bags in the pantry, cardboard boxes in the garage. We'll keep the furniture, but you can empty out your closet and your desk. All your old junk." Joyce tapped her glasses against the newspaper. "It's not as though you've got somewhere more important to be. I know you're not used to thinking of others, but considering that we're the ones funding this self-indulgent lifestyle of yours—"

"Yes, yes, I know." Anna rubbed her forehead, smoothing her throbbing temples. "It's fine. I'll get it done."

*

Back upstairs, Anna opened the door and surveyed the room with distaste. Better get this over with quickly. She took a deep breath, hauled open the closet's accordion doors, shoved half the hangers to one side and glimpsed a crushed velvet sleeve in deep burgundy.

She'd bought that top at Le Château in the old Eaton Centre downtown. Memories swam to the surface: the feeling of sophistication when she'd worn it to school with a black choker. Then the last time she'd worn it, the day she came back to school after—

No. Her mind clamped down.

Anna slammed the closet doors, crossed the bedroom and opened the window again. She lit another cigarette and closed her eyes, listening to the steady drip from the eavestrough at the corner of the roof. Breathed in and out, letting her heart slow. She could get through this. She just needed to start somewhere less emotional. She risked a glance over her shoulder, towards the other side of the room. Desk, bookshelf, unmade bed. And there, under the bed frame, stacks of old board games.

She flicked her cigarette butt into the backyard and dropped to the carpet, peering under the mattress at the colourful cardboard boxes: Monopoly, Life, Guess Who, even childhood favourites like Candyland and Perfection. Anna bent down to examine the boxes. She was sorting through the yellow plastic shapes for the spring-loaded Perfection board when it came to her: What if she treated all this like a game? Turned this task into a series of challenges, with little rewards for every emptied shelf and drawer?

She looked through the boxes, found the Scattergories timer and twisted the round plastic dial to start it ticking.

The day passed quickly after that. In timed three-minute sprints, she pulled postcards and ribbons off the bulletin board, sorted through piles of notebooks, stacks of faded stationery and floppy disks held together with dried-out elastic bands. She yanked clothes off hangers and dumped out dresser drawers, shoving everything into plastic trash bags. In between bursts of cleaning, she went down to the kitchen for bowls of Lucky Charms and Cocoa Puffs cereal, shots of spiced rum from her dad's liquor cabinet.

Only two things made her pause. First was the wooden dollhouse she found at the back of the closet. Her father had built that for her, decorating each room with different samples of wallpaper, wiring switches to tiny chandeliers that still lit up. Most of the furniture was still in place, the father doll sitting in his wingback chair, the mother upstairs in a wooden rocker beside an empty cradle. There used to be a little girl doll too, a long-haired figurine in a flowered dress, but she was nowhere to be found.

The other thing she found was her jewellery box, an old birthday present from her grandmother. That was on a bookshelf, its pale blue leather lid faded from exposure to the sun. When she flipped back its lid, tinkling music started to play and the ballerina shivered to life. Anna poked through the velvet inner compartments. No jewelry, but there, tucked into the base of the box, was a sealed envelope with FOR ANNIE written in purple ink.

Anna picked up the envelope. That looping capital A, the careful hops of the N's, the circle over the I. She knew this handwriting. This came from Helen Wright. They'd been best friends for what, ten years? Until—

The timer went off, making her jump.

Holding the envelope like a live grenade, Anna gave it a little shake, the folded paper inside slipping back and forth. Then, holding it at arm's length, she walked over to the last garbage bag and wedged the envelope inside, beside a pack of Hello Kitty stationery. She wiped her sweaty palms against her jeans and left the room, but at the top of the stairs, something made her stop. Something made her turn back and retrace her steps. Quickly, before her brain could catch up to what her hands were doing, Anna snatched the envelope out of the garbage, thrust her thumb under the flap and tore it wide open.

CHAPTER 2

Helen Wright hung her threadbare winter jacket in her locker in the Bay's employee break room. She pulled on her white lab coat and checked her makeup in the mirror by the door, making sure her birthmark was covered. Of course, when she tilted her head she could still see the raised edges of the port wine stain under the careful layers of concealer and foundation: an embossed border along her right cheek, thick tentacles stretching to her nose and ear and neck.

Helen had been wearing makeup her entire life. She remembered her mother leaning over her stroller, sponging Max Factor pancake makeup over Helen's face to ward off the stares. "It looks grotesque," her father had argued with Linda, while Helen lay unsleeping in her toddler bed, her baby sister snuffling in her crib in their shared bedroom. "All that makeup on a little girl! She looks like a clown."

After he moved out, Helen and her mom worked their way through shelves of drugstore foundations, thick creams that dried out her skin and smothered her pores but created a monochrome mask over her birthmark. No wonder Helen grew out her wavy chestnut hair, taught herself to style it as a heavy, glossy curtain over her patchy makeup. It had taken her years to find the right products and learn to apply them properly, to create this illusion of an ordinary face.

She would have had such a nice face, too, if it weren't for the birthmark; wide cheeks that made her look younger than her age, soft brown eyes, nicely shaped lips.

These days, Helen's skin and makeup routine combined calming ritual and precise science. Her face was—at a glance—perfect.

It's practically invisible, Helen reminded herself, for the millionth time. She shook out her hair, arranging the long shiny dark layers to frame her face. A light touch to blend out her eyeliner, a quick swipe of lip gloss, and she nodded at her reflection, satisfied. Ready to start her shift.

Helen was halfway through inventory, lining up bottles of foundation from lightest to darkest, when she noticed the strange girl at the Dior counter. She seemed to take up an inordinate amount of space, with hair frizzed out in bleached dreadlocks, a body cloaked in a shapeless black coat. She was talking to Carmen, the floor manager for the Bay's cosmetics section.

The stranger leaned across the counter and Carmen crossed her arms, shook her head and then nodded, seeming to relent. She lifted her arm and pointed across the floor, straight at Helen. The stranger turned and Helen glimpsed metal studs puckering pale cheeks, a smudge of blue ink tattooed across her temple.

Thanks, Carmen. Helen swallowed, pasting on her professional smile.

"Façade can help you put your best face forward," she said. "How can I help you today?"

"Helen," said the girl. Her voice was low and husky. She unzipped her coat, releasing a strong smell of cigarettes and revealing a riot of tattoos that stretched along her sharp collarbones, up her neck and into those bleached dreadlocks.

"That's me." Helen touched her plastic name tag and glanced at Carmen, who was huddled with Toni at the Lancôme counter. "Are you looking for something specific?"

"I'm looking for you." The stranger frowned. "You don't recognize me? It's Anna. Anna Leverett."

The hair on Helen's arms stiffened under her cotton sleeves.

"Annie?"

The tattooed girl gave a wry smile and her features suddenly resolved into the face of Helen's old best friend. Helen blinked, seeing Annie at twelve, adjusting puffed blond bangs with eczema fingers. At fifteen, her hair crimped and her eyes lined in pale blue. She heard Anna's muffled laugh as they passed notes between their desks, smelled her baby powder scent as she draped an arm across Helen's shoulders.

Then a final memory dropped into place: Annie pushing past her in the hallway at Laurier High. Her blond hair lank, her face expressionless. No last words, no explanation, just a blank refusal to meet Helen's eyes or return her phone calls. And all those rumours: Annie had been caught drinking at school. Smoking hash. Dealing pills. Giving blow jobs in the boys' bathroom.

The last time Helen saw her, Annie was huddled over a joint with the daytime stoners in Laurier's student parking lot. She hadn't even looked up when Helen called her name.

Now, this new version of Annie was smiling as if none of that had happened. As if she hadn't disappeared ten years ago, as if she didn't look like a completely different person. As if they were still friends.

"I go by Anna now," Annie said. "Look at you, all professional! You finally got rid of the birthmark?"

"It's still there." Helen raised a hand to her cheek. "I'm just better at covering it up."

"Right. Cool." Anna stood back to look at Façade's display. She picked up a foundation compact and clicked it open. Before Helen could stop her, she ran a finger over the makeup and drew a damp beige line across the back of her other hand, blotting out a section of tattoos.

"Don't." Helen reached across the counter and grabbed the compact out of Anna's hand, flinching as their fingers touched. A hundred questions pinballed through her mind. *What happened? Where did you go? Why did you leave me?*

In the end, she reverted to training. "Well? How can I help you today?"

Silently, holding her eyes, Anna dug into a pocket, pulled out a folded envelope and held it up so Helen could see the purple ink.

"What's that? Is that my handwriting?"

Helen put out her hand.

"We have to talk," said Anna. She held the envelope out of reach. "Is there somewhere we can go?"

*

The food court was practically empty. Just a couple of old men sitting in front of the Manchu Wok and a young mother scratching lottery tickets while her baby slept bundled in its stroller.

Helen took a seat at a corner table, waiting with arms crossed while Anna bought coffees at the Tim Hortons.

"I can only take twenty minutes," she said, as Anna slid her paper cup across the table.

"Twenty minutes after ten years?"

Helen bit back a retort. She watched this new Anna fiddle with her coffee, her nicotine-yellow fingers pulling the plastic tab off the lid, tearing it into little brown shards and lining up the bits of plastic.

Helen clicked her own plastic tab neatly into place in the designated slot. She couldn't stop glancing at Anna's face, at the purple shadows under her eyes, the faded scar on her chin. All those piercings: she counted four, no, five metal hoops and studs puncturing the sallow skin of Anna's face. Uneven dreadlocks, some wrapped in wire or strung with wooden beads. And her tattoos! Nobody in Guelph had tattoos like these. That spray of blue stars on her temple, the tangle of images emerging from the tattered neckline of her grey sweater. When their eyes met, Anna grinned.

"You like?" She pulled at the neck of her sweater to expose the top half of a tree. Animal silhouettes clung to the branches, all with big round watching eyes. "I can strip down later if you want, give you the grand tour."

Helen blushed. "How many do you have?"

"I haven't kept track." Anna took a sip and pushed up her sleeves to show off the images on her arms; some faded and fuzzy, most new and sharp. Words and symbols, stylized objects, and skeletal creatures. Between her wrist and her elbow, Helen saw Viking runes, a black sparrow, a grinning Mexican skull, and a tiny spouting whale.

"How did you choose them? Do they all stand for something?"

Anna traced a finger along the sparrow's outstretched wing. "They're like a map," she said. "Where I've been. What happened along the way."

Here be dragons, Helen thought. "You must have been everywhere."

"Pretty much." Anna rotated her wrist, making the images shift and settle. "But these are the people and places I want to remember."

"Am I on there?" The words were out before Helen could stop them.

Anna stopped smiling.

"No." She pulled down her sleeves and sat back in her plastic chair. "There's nothing and nobody from Guelph."

"But you've moved back?"

"Jesus, no," Anna said. "My parents flew me in for my dad's big retirement bash. Got to keep up appearances, right? That's how I knew where you worked. My mother buys her two-hundred-dollar seaweed face creams in this mall. Anyway, I'm here to talk about this." She dug the crumpled envelope out of her pocket and dropped it onto the table.

Helen unfolded the note and scanned her own round adolescent scrawl.

"I left this with your mom," she said, looking up. "She said she'd give this to you. I came by your house, too. I called a bunch of times, but you never called me back. What else do you want me to say?"

"Read it," Anna said. "Go on. Read it out loud."

"I don't—"

"Please?"

Helen sighed.

"Dear Annie," she read, in a flat voice. "I miss you. I hope you're okay. I don't know why you won't talk to me anymore but I'm really sorry if I did something wrong. I keep hearing crazy rumours about you but I don't believe them. I just want to know what's going on. I'm always here if you want to talk. You'll always be my best friend. Love, Helen."

She lay the note on the table between them and looked up.

"I never got it," said Anna.

"What?"

"Your note." Leaning forward, Anna placing her index finger on the paper. There was a gothic G tattooed between her first and second knuckles. "I found it yesterday when I was cleaning out my old room. You gave it to my mother?"

"Yeah. I thought—" Helen started, then changed her mind. "Nothing. Never mind."

"What?"

"There was that party."

The air between them seemed to ripple.

"Oh yes." Anna leaned back, crossing her arms. "Here we go. I thought you didn't believe the rumours?"

"I didn't! I don't." Helen wrapped her fingers around her cup, squeezing until the cardboard buckled. "But you changed, after that. Everything changed. None of it made sense."

"Oliver Sutton's New Year's party."

"Exactly."

"Come on. You know what went down, after you ditched me."

"I never ditched you. *You* were the one who disappeared."

"Whatever."

"You did!" Helen said. "There were those drinking games in the kitchen. I went to the bathroom and when I came back, you were gone. I looked everywhere. Finally, I called my mom to come pick me up. I didn't even stay until midnight."

"Poor you."

They stared at each other.

Helen thought back to that party. They'd got ready together; Helen in a long blue dress, Anna more casual in jeans and a sweater. They'd snuck shots of vodka from Anna's father's liquor cabinet, swished with Scope before he drove them over to Olly's house. At first, it was an adventure, hanging out with the cool kids, pulling each other from room to crowded room. Then Annie disappeared.

The next day, Helen called her house, but Annie's parents wouldn't tell her anything. "She's resting," her father said. "She's grounded," said her mother. Neither of them would answer Helen's questions or put Annie on the phone.

After the holidays, the rumours started right away, but Annie's desk sat empty for nearly three weeks. It didn't take long for a group of popular girls to swarm Helen after gym class, peppering her with questions.

"Where's your friend?"

"Did she tell you what she did?"

"*So* disgusting. I'm not surprised she won't show her face."

Helen clutched her gym clothes to her chest. "I haven't talked to her," she insisted to Jennifer, Sarah, and Laura. "I don't know anything."

After that, the whispers were everywhere. *Annie got totally hammered at that party. She was like a porn star, couldn't get enough.* Of course, Helen didn't listen. She knew the rumours weren't true. *I heard she was desperate. Followed Olly around all night like a puppy dog.* Helen kept her head down, hurrying between classes, waiting for her friend to come back and clear everything up.

"What actually happened?" Helen stared across the table at Anna. "I heard…I don't know. Crazy shit."

She'll do anything with anyone.

"I don't know what you heard."

"So many things. Some of them definitely weren't true. That whole idea that you were chasing after Olly, that you wanted to impress him…you didn't even care if we went out that night! I was the one who wanted to go to a real New Year's party." Helen looked down. "I always wondered if that's why you stopped talking to me."

"I don't even remember that," Anna said. "Hey. It wasn't about you, all right? I was going through a bad time. I just assumed you'd written me off. Like everyone else."

"We were best friends! It was you and me, against the world. Then you left, and it was just me."

"I didn't just leave. Laurier kicked me out."

"That's what happened?"

"One of the gym teachers, that one with the moustache? I forget his name. He caught me with a grade twelve kid in the boys' locker room. The school freaked out. They told my parents they didn't have the resources to deal with me."

"But before that." Helen swallowed. "At the party. What really happened?"

Anna tilted her head.

"I got drunk," she said. "Really drunk. I blacked out. The next morning, I woke up in Olly's bedroom. All my clothes were in a pile on the floor. Except my sweater. I never found my sweater." She tugged absently at the silver ring in her eyebrow. "It was clear I'd had a big night. Like, sex definitely happened. I got dressed and went downstairs. Olly was in the kitchen. He told me what I did. *Who* I did. Asked if I was up for round two."

She made a face. "You know, I saw him this past week-end, at my dad's party. He's still a sleazebag."

"Oh my God." Helen touched Anna's arm. "I'm so sorry."

Anna jerked her arm away. "There's nothing to be sorry *about*. I don't remember any of it."

"But obviously something happened!"

"You've never blacked out? It happens to me all the time. A few too many drinks, and that's it, I'm gone." Anna snapped her fingers. "But I don't always *look* gone. The lights stay on but nobody's home. I'm still talking, walking around, even fucking. I just won't remember anything, later."

"But still. Some of those rumours were made up."

"Exaggerated, maybe."

"And you don't know what actually happened, at that party?"

"*Everyone* knew. The whole school."

Helen stared at her.

"What about your parents? What did they say?"

"You think I told them anything? Like what? Sorry, Mother, sorry, Dad. I let a bunch of guys fuck me last night. You okay with that?"

"You were blacked out!"

"Yeah, I also stayed out all night. I nearly gave my mother an aneurysm," Anna said. "Lesson learned. I shouldn't have had so much to drink."

"I don't know. It doesn't make sense. Just because you got drunk, you wouldn't turn into some kind of nymphomaniac."

"How would you know? Maybe life isn't a Disney movie, Little Miss Follow-the-rules, Don't-rock-the-boat, Colour-inside-the-lines."

Helen winced, lifting a hand to her cheek.

"I'm not talking about that. But you and this whole fucking town, you're all so judgemental. It's just sex, okay? It's not a big deal."

"It was a big deal back then."

"Good thing we're not sixteen anymore!" Anna said. "And so what, if I don't remember the details? It was one night. I had lots of crazy nights, after that. And mornings, and afternoons. As I'm sure you heard. Even if you *didn't believe the rumours*." She flicked at the folded note with her finger.

Helen pulled back the note and smoothed it out. The paper was soft under her damp palms.

"We were only fifteen."

"You were fifteen. I was already sixteen."

"We were just kids." Helen closed her eyes and thought again of that party, of her confusion as she pushed past drunk classmates, through crowded rooms. She thought of the Annie who came back to school, trudging down the hallways, vacant and indifferent. How could she not know what happened? How could she not want to know?

She looked up. "You should find out."

"What?"

Helen felt breathless. "You've only got Olly's version. But we knew everyone at that party. There must be other people who could tell you what happened. You could find out the truth." She pointed a wavering finger at Anna, her ribcage expanding as if she'd swallowed a balloon. "You could stay, and we could find out."

Anna stared at her. For a moment, her brash new persona seemed to waver, so that Helen caught a glimpse of the old Annie underneath: puzzled, thoughtful, considering. The last ten years dropped away, and this girl across the table was the Annie Leverett who'd taught her all the secrets in the original Super Mario, who sang the harmonies to "A Whole New World," who let Helen do her makeup before they set off, giggling, for Olly Sutton's New Year's party.

Then the new Anna smirked, and the old Annie was gone.

"It's not worth it." She swept her hand over the table, sending the torn-up bits of coffee lid fluttering to the ground. "That's ancient history."

"Really? But—"

"Anyway, I'm flying to Paris on Sunday. I just wanted to tell you I finally got your note."

"Better late than never." Helen's arms felt heavy as she pulled out a pen and printed her phone number on the note, blue ballpoint under the purple ink of her old signature. "Here. I'll give you my number, in case you change your mind."

Anna shook her head. "Why does this matter so much to you?"

"Why?" Helen pushed the note across the table, thinking of all the what-ifs and should-have-beens. "I missed you," she said. "I always wondered what happened to you. And if you stayed, we could find out."

"Whatever," Anna said. She took the note, crumpled it up and stuffed it into the pocket of her jeans. She tugged her coat off the chair and shoved her arms into its giant sleeves. "It was good to see you, I guess."

"Sure. Likewise," said Helen. She dropped her empty coffee cup into Anna's, then they walked away in opposite directions.

*

That evening, Helen stood in her apartment's kitchen, brewing tea as she talked to her mother on their nightly phone call. Outside the window, the snow-laden maple in the backyard made her think of the tree tattoo on Anna's chest. She kept seeing Anna's face under that cloud of witchy blond hair, the piercings and tattoos shifting as she laughed and frowned across the table. *I don't remember any of it. I woke up in an empty room. Sex definitely happened.*

"How was work?" Linda asked. "Did that shipment come in? The one you were excited about?"

"What? Oh, the powders. Yeah."

Helen stared out at the maple tree. She glanced down at the broken appliances in the neighbour's yard, then up at the sky filled with shreds of pink and orange. Where was Anna now? Was she staying at her parents' house? Would Helen see her again?

"Helen, honey. Did you hear what I said?"

"What?" Helen blinked, looked down and added sugar to her tea. "Sorry. I'm distracted."

"You're as bad as Gord," Linda said. She was probably sitting at her own kitchen table, in the Toronto condo she shared with Helen's stepdad. Linda would be drinking her own cup of tea, a herbal mix Gord made with the mint and chamomile he grew on their balcony. "You know his new receptionist quit? Said she's allergic to dogs. I mean, why would she take a job in a vet clinic? So now he's doing all the filing until he finds someone else."

"Mm-hm." Helen looked down, swirling the tea in her cup.

"So what's wrong? Is it something at work?"

"Sort of. I was working the counter, this afternoon. Annie Leverett came by to see me."

"Annie Leverett! I didn't know you were still in touch."

25

"We're not. I hadn't seen her in ages."

"She had some health problems, didn't she? How is she doing?"

"She's..." Helen heard the echo of Anna's laughter. *Laurier kicked me out.* "She's okay, I guess. She looks really different."

Helen turned at the sound of the fridge opening and saw her roommate bending over, peering inside. Thom was wearing his blue and white Leafs jersey with thick headphones hooped around his neck. He tucked a two-litre bottle of Coke under his arm, closed the fridge door and stood on tiptoe to grab the Tupperware container from the top of the freezer.

"Hey," Helen called to Thom's disappearing back. "I was saving that!"

"Saving what?" Linda asked. "What happened?"

"Thom took the last piece of my apple cake."

"Is that what you're making for my birthday this weekend? Apple cake?"

"You know that's a surprise."

"Any special ingredients I should pick up?"

"If you're asking for a hint, forget it." Helen set her mug in the sink and opened the freezer to forage through boxes of Lean Cuisine. "Okay, what should I have tonight? Chicken parmesan or mushroom risotto?"

"Risotto sounds good. Did I tell you Julia's bringing Glenn to Toronto this weekend?"

"For your birthday? Why?" Helen picked up a fork and stabbed air holes through the shrink wrap. "Isn't this supposed to be a family event?"

"She says she's got big news. I think she might have heard about that job placement she wanted. Or another scholarship."

"Great." She punched the buttons on the microwave. "Fantastic."

"Now, Helen."

"It's fine." She crouched down to watch the rotating tray. "More great news for Julia. I'm so happy for her."

*

That night, Helen lay in bed, staring up at the ceiling. She'd spent the whole evening pushing away thoughts about Annie. Not the tattooed stranger she'd become, but the girl who'd stayed up past midnight on sleepovers to whisper-sing along to *The Little Mermaid* on VHS. The best friend who'd drawn smiley faces on the back of Helen's hand, who'd packed extra Pop-Tarts in her lunchbox so Helen didn't have to eat Gord's rock-hard homemade granola bars.

After supper, Helen reorganized her sweater drawer, ran a bubble bath, sorted through her makeup collection and planned the next day's look: metallic lavender eyeshadow, pale glossy lips. None of it helped to blot out the tiny blue stars tattooed across Anna's temple, the surge of disappointment Helen had felt when she walked away.

When her bedside clock showed 12:30, Helen pushed back the duvet. She got out of bed and padded along the wooden floorboards of the hallway.

"Thom? You awake?"

She knocked on the door to his room. When she heard his murmur, she eased the door open and slipped inside.

CHAPTER 3

Anna sat cross-legged on her bed, playing clock solitaire. She dealt out the cards facedown, twelve piles to make the numbers on the clock and a thirteenth pile in the middle. She turned over the top card in the middle stack: a seven. She moved it over to the seven o'clock position, flipped the next card and followed the cards around the dial: Three. Jack. King. She hissed out her breath, slapped the king down in the middle and kept playing.

Eight. Queen. Ten. Four. Another king.

Her grandmother had taught her this game. Her grandmother Annette, who hated board games but loved cards. She always kept a pack of them in her purse, had taught Anna to play crazy eights, gin rummy, euchre and about ten different variations of solitaire. Or no, she'd called it *patience*. "An only child should know how to play patience," she'd told Anna. This was the version Anna liked best. Clock solitaire. Perfect for killing time.

Nine. Jack. Ace. Three. Ten. King.

Anna set her cigarette on the edge of the gold-rimmed Wedgwood saucer she'd swiped from her mother's collection of antique china.

One more king, and she'd lose the game.

Seven. Six. Three. Ace. Anna had been playing for over an hour. She didn't want to go downstairs, where her parents were packing for their cruise. She didn't want to go out and run into anyone she knew, all those nosy neighbours and old classmates. Or random townies with their disapproving glares. Better to hide here in her emptied-out room, where the only items left from her childhood were the boxes of board games stacked on the desk.

Five. Nine. Three; that was the last card on the three o'clock stack. She tidied the edges of the pile and kept going. Six. Queen. Eight. King.

Game over.

Anna sighed and tossed the card on the pile.

Today was Friday. Only two more days until she'd board that plane to Paris. Serge and Phoebe's number was disconnected but it didn't matter, really. She'd find a hostel. Worst case, she'd catch a couchette heading south, maybe towards Nice or Rome or Barcelona, whatever train was leaving first. She wasn't picky.

She gathered the cards, shuffled, laid out a new game. She couldn't wait to get out of here. *You should stay.* Helen didn't know what she was asking. Stay in Guelph? Everyone hated Anna here. They looked down on her, called her a slut and a fuckup. Why would she stay?

Don't you want to know what happened? And then what? What would that possibly change?

Anna turned over the first card: a king. She shook her head and kept playing.

*

By mid-afternoon, the flowered wallpaper was closing in and Anna was sick of losing. She figured she'd go for a couple of loops around the block. Maybe walk down to the river and test the ice. As she slid on her boots in the front hall, though, her mother called down from the top of the stairs.

"Annie, you're going out? If you're heading downtown, could you stop by the bank? We've ordered some foreign currency."

Other Maps

"The bank?"

"Never mind." Joyce appeared on the stairs with her arms full of silky tropical dresses. "I'll do it myself. I'm leaving for my hair appointment in a few minutes. Your father's already out so the door will be locked when you get back. You remember the code for the alarm?"

"Is it still my birthday? Eleven-thirteen?"

Joyce blinked down at her. "I suppose it is. Anyway, we're going to have dinner with the Vetrones. You'll have to fend for yourself."

Outside, the light glared bright against patches of snow, with gusts of cold wind that swirled the dust from the sidewalk and snatched at the smoke from her cigarette. Anna circled the block a few times before trudging up the hill towards the local park.

Ahead of her, a man climbed out of an orange pickup truck. He was wearing a long blue parka and a black tuque with an absurd oversized pompom. His gait was familiar as he crossed the street, with a bounce like a gazelle tripping over its own long legs. Could that be Johnnie Campbell? He'd walked in that distinctive way since he shot up to his full height in ninth grade.

Anna stopped, ready to turn around, when Johnnie took a seat on a park bench and lit a cigarette. No, a joint. The scent of weed blew back to her, making her sniff the air greedily.

"Hey!" Anna called. "Johnnie!"

Johnnie looked back at her without recognition. "Yes?"

He stood up and put his hand behind his back, like a kid who'd been caught sneaking a cookie.

Anna stepped onto the frozen grass. "Let me give you a hint," she said, as she approached. "You puked on my winter boots, back in grade six. You claimed you had the stomach flu."

"Holy shit." Johnnie's grey eyes opened wide. "Annie Leverett?"

She bobbed a curtsey. "In the flesh."

"Jesus, you look different. I haven't seen you since—" He broke off and gave an all-over shudder, like a dog shaking off water. He held out the joint. "You want some?"

"I thought you'd never ask." She took a long pull, holding the fragrant smoke deep inside her lungs. "Johnnie Campbell," she said, as she exhaled. She nodded at the Guelph Public Works badge sewn to the front of his parka. "Working for the city?"

His eyes widened further. "I'm on break."

She laughed, sitting down beside him. "I'm not going to rat you out."

"This is just my day job. I work for my uncle on weekends. He's a balloon pilot, over near Kitchener."

"A balloon pilot!" Anna snorted. "Very practical."

"I want to take over his business in a few years."

They passed the joint back and forth.

"So what's going on?" Johnnie asked. "You've moved back to Guelph?"

"God, no. Just visiting."

His eyebrows went up. "You live around here? In this neighbourhood?"

"Not me. My parents."

"Nice houses around here."

"The houses, yes. Not the people."

When they finished the joint, Johnnie stood up and dusted off his jeans. He held out a gloved hand to help her up but Anna ignored it, squinting hazily up at him.

"Thanks for sharing."

"Anytime."

Anna smiled. Behind him, the sky was a bright cloud-less blue.

"You're nicer than most of them."

"Nicer than who?"

"All those assholes we went to school with. Olly Sutton." Again, Anna's mouth filled with bile as she said the name. She spat onto the frozen ground and wiped her mouth with her sleeve.

"Yeah, well." Johnnie looked away. "I was never cool enough for that crowd."

Anna tilted her head farther back, scrunching up her eyes against the sun. "You're cool enough for me." Suddenly she wanted to unzip that blue coat and press herself against the body underneath. "How long is your break?"

"Technically it's over. I've got to finish loading those sticks." Johnnie nodded at the orange pickup parked at the edge of the park, its cargo area piled with long branches.

"My parents' house is just over there. There's nobody home." Anna stood up and stepped towards him, touching the badge on his jacket. "You want to see it?"

Upstairs, in her old bedroom, Johnnie whistled as Anna stripped off her shirt.

"Jesus, that's a shit-ton of tattoos. I've only got two. One on my back and one here." He pulled up the edge of his sweater and touched a jagged-edged star on his ribcage.

"What is that? A ninja star?"

"It's for Metallica. But I'm getting it changed. I can't support them anymore after their bullshit with Napster."

Anna tugged at his sweater, lifting it over the soft white skin of his belly. "Take this off."

"Are you sure?" Johnnie laid a hand over her fingers. "You know, I had the biggest crush on you, back in middle school."

She laughed and pulled his face down to hers, running her thumb against the dark scruff on his chin.

"Stop talking." Anna kissed him, tasting weed. "Just take off your clothes."

*

Afterwards, they shared a cigarette. Anna lay on her side, staring out the window at that clear blue sky. Sex was definitely better than solitaire. When Johnnie shifted on the mattress, she rolled over to face him.

"We've never done that before, have we?"

"What? No."

"You're sure?"

Johnnie blushed. "I think I'd remember."

"You'd be surprised."

She closed her eyes as his fingers traced up and down her arm. She was still pleasantly high, almost relaxed enough to fall asleep. Before that could happen, she got up and went to the bathroom to piss. She sat on the toilet, smiling to herself, flexing her bare toes against the heated tile floor.

When she came back, Johnnie was sitting cross-legged on the floor in his underwear. He'd taken Hungry Hungry Hippos out of its box and was placing handfuls of white marbles in the middle of the board.

"I thought you had to get back to work?"

"I've got time for one round." Johnnie pressed the lever to make the green hippo lunge forward, its plastic mouth opening wide. "I love this game. I had it when I was a kid."

"Everyone had this game," said Anna. But she sank down onto the carpet across from Johnnie. "One round. Then it's time for you to go."

They played about eight rounds, in the end. The last one was a complete free-for-all, both of them giggling wildly as they pounded on their respective hippos' levers, using their other hands to scoop wayward marbles back onto the board. Finally, Johnnie leaned back and raised his hands.

"I give up! You win!"

Grinning, Anna snapped up the last few marbles with her orange hippo. Johnnie climbed to his feet, adjusting the elastic of his tighty-whities. He held out his hand. This time she took it, letting him haul her to her feet.

"You want to do this again sometime?" Pulling on his jeans, Johnnie raised his eyebrows at the game, then at the bed.

"I'm flying out on Sunday."

His face dropped. "Oh."

"Let's not make this a big deal."

"Right. Of course. No problem."

She followed him downstairs, watching as he zipped up his coat, stepped into his work boots and pulled that ridiculous woolly hat over his ears. He looked down at her hopefully.

"Do you know when you'll be back in town?"

"God, who knows." She waved him out the door. "But thanks for the good time."

*

After Johnnie left, Anna took a beer from the fridge and drank it in the empty kitchen, staring out at the covered

34

pool in the backyard, at the lights in the neighbours' windows. She thought about Helen frowning across the Formica table in the mall's food court. *You should stay.* Helen was still so earnest, so idealistic. It was kind of sweet. When was the last time someone had asked Anna to stick around? But honestly, what did Helen imagine would happen if Anna stayed in Guelph?

Stay. We could find out the truth.

In truth, Anna was glad that she didn't remember much about that party, that school year, that whole messed-up time in her life. She didn't like the parts she did remember.

She'd finally gone back to Laurier in late January of 1994, three weeks after the holidays. Joyce had talked to the school, told them there'd been a family emergency, made sure Annie received "incompletes" instead of "fails" on her report card.

This was the first Monday after exams, the start of a new semester. A fresh start for Annie as well, she hoped. Back then, she still thought things could go back to how they used to be. *I bet nobody remembers that party*, Annie told herself, as she got dressed for school. That wonderful burgundy Le Château top in crushed velvet over her favourite pair of faded jeans, rolled at the ankles. The jeans were looser than they'd been in December but fine when she cinched in the waist with a woven leather belt. Annie brushed her shoulder-length hair until the blond shone like spun gold, dabbed on strawberry-flavoured lip gloss and vanilla perfume from the Body Shop.

Things felt different from the moment Joyce dropped her off. Every single student turned to stare as Annie trudged through the snow up to the main door. Alone or in groups, everyone was leering, smirking, whispering, watching as Annie edged down the hall to her locker. She was trying to remember her combination when someone bumped into her and she whirled around to confront a huddle of innocent-faced girls.

"Slut," one of them hissed, under her breath.

That was the first time that Annie was called that name, but certainly not the last. The long low-pitched L like a growl, the sharp snap of jaws on the T.

Her own breath got faster as she turned back to her locker, spinning the metal dial, her fingers trembling as she lined up the numbers and yanked on the combination lock. Annie looked in the mirror, as if she might see something on her face that explained the stares, some new growth or discolouration like Helen's birthmark. But only her own panicked face stared back at her.

The teachers were brusque but kind enough. They didn't seem to notice the snickers, the lewd gestures, the way Annie's classmates edged away like she was infected with some disgusting but fascinating new disease. Annie tried to ignore them. She held her head high and pretended she didn't see the glares, hear the sniggers, feel the phantom brush of fingers against her jeans when she bent to pick up the pencil case that someone "accidentally" shoved to the ground.

At recess, Annie barricaded herself in a bathroom stall. Fighting back tears, she listened to the girls at the sinks as they embroidered the story with salacious new details:

"I heard she screwed two guys at once, while the rest of them watched."

"I heard she asked them for money first."

"No way, Annie doesn't need money. She did it for free!"

"Maybe she's the one who paid them!"

Heart pounding in her ears, Annie squeezed her eyes shut, praying for them to shut up and leave. When the bell finally rang, she went straight to the office and told them she was sick. They let her call her mother. Annie lay on the plasticized cot in the nurse's darkened office until Joyce came to pick her up.

Helen didn't understand. The truth was that there was no going back to the Annie she'd been before. It was better to leave the past behind, those details shrouded in mist. Keep moving forward. Take the taxi to the airport with her parents on Sunday, strap herself into her airplane seat and fly far, far away.

*

It took several more beers and a couple of Joyce's Ambien for Anna to get to sleep that night. The next morning, she woke to her father knocking on her door.

"Anna? Are you in there?"

Groggily, she sat up in bed as he opened the door.

"Hey kiddo," boomed Malcolm. He was wearing a cream Aran sweater, as if he were ready to captain a fishing boat. "You joining us for brunch?"

"Only if she's ready in five minutes," came Joyce's voice, from down the hall.

Anna groaned.

"What time is it?"

"Almost ten. The club does a waffle bar on Saturdays. You always liked waffles." Malcolm stepped into her room, surveying the mess of clothes strewn across the carpet. "You can finish packing when we get back."

"What would she pack?" Joyce appeared in the doorway, her head tilted as she inserted her pearl earrings. "She's got one backpack with all her worldly possessions."

Anna swallowed past her dry throat. She pictured the club's dining room, full of the same pale staring faces as the retirement party. Would Olly's parents be there again? Would Olly? She pictured his sneer from the other night, felt his hands squeezing her shoulders. *Just like old times.*

"No thanks," she said. "I'm not hungry."

"What did I tell you?" Joyce turned away. "You should have let her sleep."

"You're sure?" Malcolm drummed his fingers against the wooden door. "The taxi's coming early tomorrow. I thought we could have one more family meal before we go our separate ways."

"Yeah." Anna rubbed her face. Again, she heard the echo of Helen's voice. *You've only got Olly's version of what happened.* She saw Helen leaning forward across the food court table. *You could stay, and we could find out the truth.*

"About that," Anna heard herself say. "About tomorrow. I've changed my mind. I'm going to stick around Guelph a little longer."

There was a moment of silence.

"You're joking." Malcolm squinted at her.

"I mean it." Anna sat up in bed. "You can cancel my ticket. You need someone to watch the house for you, right?"

"The Vetrones are watching the house." Malcolm said. "You've told us for years that you hate being here. Too many triggers, you said."

"What's that?" Joyce reappeared in the doorway, fingering the oversized button on her pale-yellow blazer. "We all leave tomorrow. The flights are booked."

"You can't force me to get on a plane."

"She can't stay here, Malcolm." Joyce's hand rose to her throat. "I don't want her here alone. I wouldn't be able to sleep at night. We'd have to cancel our trip."

"Now, honey." Anna's father turned to his wife. "Let's not exaggerate."

Anna looked back and forth between them. "I want to spend time with Helen Wright. She's a positive influence." She squeezed the blanket in a tight ball in her lap. "You've seen me this week. Things are different, under control."

"Helen?" Joyce's eyebrows flickered. "With the birthmark?"

Malcolm shook his head. "I don't want you relying on someone else to make good decisions for you."

"It's out of the question," said Joyce. "And we're going to be late. We'll lose our reservation."

"It would only be a few weeks." Anna stared into her father's blue eyes. "Isn't it better than leaving the house empty?"

Malcolm scratched at his cheek, leaving pink marks on the freshly-shaved skin. "You should have said something earlier. Given us time to talk it over."

"I know. I'm sorry." Under the blanket, Anna dug her nails into her knees. "But I'm not getting on that plane. You can let me stay in this house or I can book a hotel. Either way."

"Malcolm!"

"Dad?" She held his eyes.

"It's hard to know the right call here." Malcolm sighed and looked down. The light from the hallway glittered against his hair, picking up the silver in the blond. More silver than Anna had noticed before. "I tell you what. I'll discuss it with your mother, over brunch. We'll let you know what we decide."

✻

"We have some conditions," her father told her, later that afternoon. They were in Malcolm's study and he was packing up his photographic equipment, nestling his telephoto lenses into their special padded compartments. "We worry about you, Annie. It would be so easy for you to slip back into bad habits. Especially here, where you'll have old friends pressuring you—"

"That's the whole point of staying. To break my bad habits." She scuffed at the pattern on the carpet with her socked foot. "Helen was never into the party scene."

Malcolm picked up another lens and checked the caps on both ends.

"No parties. No drugs, nothing dangerous or illegal. No strangers coming in and out of our house." He looked up at her. "We can't put your mother through any more heartbreak."

"Of course not."

"She wants you back in a support group. NA, AA, something professional. I know addiction is a disease. I'm not blaming you, Annie. But we need you in treatment."

"Of course. Absolutely."

She looked up at the map on the wall, the blue and white stretched canvas perforated with pins showing all the places Malcolm had been. Mostly business trips around North America and Europe, with a few scattered pins marking Caribbean resorts.

"I'm serious, Annie."

"I'll make an appointment with Dr. Stewart first thing tomorrow."

"Good." He snapped the case shut and picked up a black folder from his desk. "Here's a copy of our itinerary. I want regular contact, Annie. Not just when you're in trouble; every week. There's a satellite phone on board. You'll need to check the time difference before you call."

"Got it." She bit the inside of her cheek to keep from smiling.

"I've told the Vetrones next door that you'll be staying for a few weeks. They'll be watching out for you."

She looked down at the patterned carpet and nodded.

"We're trusting you, Annie. Don't let us down."

*

The next morning, Anna got up early to say goodbye.

Her father handed suitcases to the driver waiting outside. "Remember what I told you," Malcolm said. He held out a gloved hand. For a moment, she thought he wanted to shake, then he pulled her in for a hug. "Be smart."

"Stay out of trouble," said Joyce. Her painted lips were dry and hard as she kissed Anna on each cheek.

Her parents climbed into the taxi, the doors slammed, and the car engine started. Anna stood holding her breath, waiting for them to turn around, to march back into the house and say *We're not going anywhere.* But they went, they were gone. She was all alone in their empty house.

She pushed the front door closed and pirouetted right there in the front hall, the stone floor cool and smooth under her bare feet. *We knew everyone at that party.* Helen had been easy to find. And Johnnie Campbell had shown up practically on her doorstep. Anna could probably find another half dozen old Laurier classmates at the bars downtown on Friday night. *There must be other people who could tell you what happened. You've only got Olly's version.*

41

Olly Sutton looming over her at her father's retirement party. *I can meet you in the bathroom in five minutes.*

Anna shivered. Had her parents turned down the thermostat? She pulled one of her mother's fur coats out of the hall closet and put her arms through its dead, heavy sleeves. It might be better to track people down one by one, before they could compare notes and change their stories. She rubbed her face against her shoulder, pressing her cheek into the soft white fox fur. *I'll give you my number, in case you change your mind.* It might be even better not to do this alone.

*

Before anything else, Anna kept her promise to her father.

"Dr. Stewart retired last year," said the receptionist, when she called. "But Dr. Hussein is taking new clients. She's working our walk-in clinic today, if you want to come see her."

Dr. Hussein looked like she was fresh out of med school. She was a tiny woman with curly dark hair pulled back in a loose bun.

"Anna Leverett?" she said, looking up from her clipboard. "Take off your coat, please."

"Not a lot of Husseins in Guelph," Anna said. The waxy paper rustled under her jeans as she hoisted herself onto the table.

"I'm from Etobicoke." Dr. Hussein unwound the stethoscope from her neck.

"Are people assholes about your name? Since 9/11?"

"Some. Deep breath, please," the doctor said, pressing warm fingers against Anna's throat, under her jaw. She moved through the examination, pausing to write quick notes on her clipboard. "What brings you here today?"

Anna put on her most responsible expression.

"I need to renew my prescriptions."

"Ah." There was a pause as the doctor flicked through her chart. "You've got quite a history. And you haven't been here for a few years, have you?"

"I've been out of town. And yeah, I had some issues when I was younger."

Dr. Hussein glanced down. "I see several in-patient stays, the Homewood, CAMH. You've had substance problems? Mental illness?"

"Not anymore." Anna kicked her boots against the side of the table. "Now it's mainly anxiety. That's why I need the Ativan."

"Have you considered antidepressants? They can help with anxiety."

"I've tried them. They don't help. Celexa, Zoloft, lithium—"

"That's an antipsychotic."

"Look." Anna clasped her hands between her knees and leaned forward. "They threw around a lot of diagnoses. One shrink thought I was bipolar, another had me admitted for anorexia, which I never had, by the way. I used to be kind of messed up. But I'm fine now. I'm just here to renew some basic meds. Ativan, Ambien, Percocet—"

"What's that treating?"

"I dislocated my knee a few times, stretched out the ligaments. It still hurts."

Dr. Hussein nodded. "I'll give you the Ativan and the Ambien, but not Percocet. That's a controlled substance." She pulled a prescription pad out of her pocket.

"I have a lot of pain."

"Physiotherapy." The doctor ripped the papers off the pad and handed them over. "Advil. You don't want to risk an opiate dependency, trust me. Now, what about birth control?"

"That's not a concern."

"If there's any chance you'll be sexually active, risking pregnancy—"

"Didn't you see my chart? I got my tubes tied when I was nineteen."

"Nineteen?" Dr. Hussein frowned down at the chart. "That's very young."

"Old enough to know that I'm never having kids." Anna slipped off the table, fanning herself with the prescriptions. The Percocet was a disappointment; she should have asked for Vicodin. "Thanks for the renewals. It was nice to meet you."

"You too. By the way," said the doctor, as she opened the door. "Have you got a therapist in town? I can recommend a few names, if you need someone to talk to."

"I'm fine. But thanks."

"Come back if you need anything. And one more thing: Cut back on the smoking."

Dr. Hussein sounded so maternal that Anna felt a twinge in her chest. Then she was out the door, pulling out her smokes and heading for the pharmacy around the block.

CHAPTER 4

Helen spent that same weekend in Toronto for her mother's birthday. She took the GO bus in on Friday, which gave them a whole peaceful evening before her sister Julia arrived from Ottawa with her boyfriend. Gord made homemade pizza, the three of them played Scrabble, and then Helen and her mother watched the fourth episode of the BBC *Pride and Prejudice* until Linda fell asleep over her rug-hooking project.

"Mom," said Helen, pressing pause. "Mom! Why don't you go to bed?"

"Maybe I will." Linda yawned, gathering up her yarn and hooking supplies and placing them beside her Ikea armchair. "Your bed's all made up in the spare room."

Helen smiled up at her. "Thanks. Have a good night."

"You too. Oh, I meant to ask; what happened with your friend?"

"My friend?" As if she had so many. "You mean Annie?"

"You said she came to your work. Is she looking for a job?"

"I have no idea."

"It must have been nice to catch up." Linda pushed up her glasses and rubbed her eyes. "When you see her again, tell her I say hello."

"She was only back for a few days." Helen turned off the TV and set the remote on the coffee table. "I doubt I'll see her again."

*

On Saturday afternoon, the whole family sang "Happy Birthday" to Linda as Helen carried in the cake.

"Oh, Helen," said Linda, pushing back her wooden chair as Helen set the cake down in front of her. The light from the candles flickered in the oval lenses of her glasses. "It's beautiful. And my favourite colour!"

"It's a triple-chocolate torte with raspberry ganache." Helen had circled the edge of the cake with fresh raspberries, pressed berries into a careful "52" in the centre of the pink glaze. "Happy birthday, Mom."

"Thank you, darling." Linda held back her greying curls to blow out the candles.

"What makes it triple chocolate?" Gord asked. He was the other baker in the family, although he tended towards sourdough and whole grain instead of sugar and refined flour.

"Cocoa powder, baking chocolate, chocolate chips." Helen grinned. "Actually, with the chocolate curls on top, we could call it quadruple chocolate."

Gord shook his head. "You've outdone yourself. Shall we take a picture? With the cake in front?"

"I want all four of us together. Come stand here, Julia." Linda beckoned to Helen's sister, sitting across the table with her boyfriend. "Glenn, would you mind taking our picture before I cut the cake?"

Gord held out his Canon.

"It's set on automatic. Just press the button to let it focus."

Julia turned her head and said something to Glenn in an undertone. She'd bobbed her dark hair Amélie-style and looked infuriatingly sophisticated in her simple black turtleneck, without a trace of makeup.

Glenn stood up along with Julia, his easy smile exposing the gap between his front teeth. Good-natured, broad-shouldered Glenn Starkey. He'd started dating Julia after high school, but Helen had known him since kindergarten. Sometimes she still saw the mischievous five-year-old smiling out of his grown-up face.

As Glenn took the camera, Helen found herself thinking again about Anna. Glenn had been friends with Olly Sutton, hadn't he? Maybe he'd even attended that party. Either way, he would definitely remember Anna. Before she was kicked out, Annie Leverett had become a punchline at Laurier, a running joke among their classmates. Not that Helen was planning to bring her up tonight. She thought of Anna's laugh when Helen asked if she was staying in Guelph. The way she'd shrugged off Helen's concern. *That's ancient history.*

"Wait." Julia held Glenn's arm. "Let's use the tripod. Glenn should be in the picture too."

"It's a family photo," said Helen.

"I know," Julia said. "That's why I want him there. We're getting married."

For a second Helen almost laughed. Married? Then her stomach turned over as her mother's hands flew to cover her mouth, as Linda fluttered out of her chair, the birthday cake forgotten on the table behind her. Gord stepped forward too, wrapping Linda and Julia in an embrace, shaking Glenn's hand, pulling him into a hug.

Linda turned to Helen, her eyes shining with tears. "Can you believe it?" she mouthed, and Helen couldn't, she really absolutely couldn't fucking believe it, but she got to her feet anyway.

"Congratulations."

She gave her sister a brief hug, then Glenn. He smelled clean and sporty, like Irish Spring soap. Helen felt her cheek slide against his sweatshirt and jerked back.

"Ugh, Glenn, I'm sorry." Her face went hot as she eyed the beige smear of makeup on his sweatshirt. "I can wash that for you."

"Don't worry about it," he said, looking over at Helen's mother and sister, who were leaning together in a tight embrace.

"Married! I can't believe it." Linda's voice was muffled against Julia's shoulder. "I didn't think either of you would ever get married. I thought you'd be a high-powered career woman. Married, so young!" Abruptly, she dropped her gaze to Julia's belly. "You're not? Oh, Julia, are you…"

"I told you she'd say that!" Julia laughed and reached for Glenn's hand. "Mom, I'm not pregnant. And obviously I'll still have a career! And twenty-four's not as young as you and Dad. Weren't you twenty-one?"

Helen's stomach tightened, but Julia kept talking.

"We figured, why wait? I'm graduating next year, Glenn's just got his articling placement, then he'll be looking for a job. And if we get married on New Year's Eve, everyone should be available—"

"New Year's Eve?" Helen said. "Next year?"

"This year. My dad's a deacon at his church in Guelph," Glenn explained, draping an arm around Julia's narrow shoulders. "He's already talked to the minister. And we'll hold the reception at the Guelph Marriott. We checked, it's available."

"There's a wedding planner at the hotel," said Julia. "She'll take care of all the details. We just have to show up."

"But Helen can help too." Linda said. "She's already in Guelph. And won't she be maid of honour?"

Helen almost laughed at the absurdity of this suggestion. Maid of honour? She and Julia could barely stand being in the same room. She glanced at her sister and was shocked to see her hesitating, weighing the pros and cons.

Helen stared at her, trying to catch her eye. *Say no! Don't do it!*

But Julia wouldn't look at her. "Certainly she will," she said at last, in her formal addressing-a-courtroom voice. "Helen?"

A hysterical giggle built in Helen's throat. *Objection*! She wanted to say, before she caught the hope on her mother's face. She swallowed the laugh and nodded.

"Certainly."

"Right on, right on!" Gord said, clapping his hands. "What do we say, time for a toast? I think there's some twelve-year-old Glenlivet left. I'll just check the kitchen."

"New Year's Eve!" Linda said, as Gord left the room. "That only gives us nine months to plan! We should write out a guest list. Send your Save-the-Date cards this week."

"I'll just send emails." Julia picked up Gord's elderly grey cat and cuddled him to her chest. "We want to keep this small. Low key."

"Small? My whole family will come from Nova Scotia. That's sixty people right there. What else do we need to think about? Food, music, flowers..." Linda counted on her fingers. "And your dress! Do you know what style you want? Can I help pick it out?"

"I was thinking about that." Julia stroked the cat's bony spine. "I'd love to wear your old wedding dress, if you kept it. The lacy one. With the long sleeves."

Helen scowled. "You're unbelievable."

"What's wrong with that dress?" Glenn asked.

"Nothing," said Linda, after a moment. "That was the dress from my first marriage. To the girls' father." She looked down, took off her glasses and cleaned them with the hem of her blouse.

"Nice, Julia," said Helen. "Very sensitive."

"He lives out west, right?" Glenn looked at Julia. "What am I missing?"

Julia sighed. "Just some long-ago drama that Helen never got over."

"Drama?" Helen said. "He abandoned us. Left mom with two little kids. The guy literally disappeared. Then he finally called, weeks later, with a bunch of bullshit excuses: *I'm not cut out for this kind of responsibility, I'm moving to the mountains to find myself.* I'm supposed to get over that?"

"He's apologized a hundred times!" Julia snapped. The cat jumped off her lap. "It was the seventies, people did that shit back then."

"He fucked up mom's life!"

"Well, and she'd never have met Gord if Dad hadn't left. It all worked out."

"Mom," said Helen, turning to Linda. "Remind me. How many years did it take him to start paying child support?"

"Oh my God," said Julia. "If you'd just grow up and talk to him, tell him what you need, he'd be happy to help you out."

"I have a job. I pay my own way. I'm not letting him buy me off, like some people—"

"Enough!" Linda stood up. "Julia, that dress is long gone. We'll find you something new. And Helen, this is your sister's wedding. She can invite whoever she wants." Her eyes were hard. "I'm sorry, Glenn. Helen and her father have a complicated relationship."

"It's not complicated. He's just an asshole."

Helen shoved back her chair and walked to the window. She leaned over the jungle of plants on the sill and stared down into the dark courtyard below.

"All right." Gord's voice broke the silence. "We're out of whisky, but I found something better." Helen turned to see her stepfather brandishing a bottle of champagne. "I got this from Howard, next door. Who's ready for a toast? Or do we start by taking that picture?"

"Whatever Mom wants," Helen said, forcing a smile.

"Picture first," said Linda. "Go fix your makeup, sweetheart. Gord, can you set up the tripod? I'll dig out the champagne glasses."

In her parents' tiny bathroom, Helen unzipped her cosmetics kit with shaking hands. Trust Julia to upstage Helen's masterpiece of a birthday cake. And what was that bullshit about Linda's old wedding dress?

Helen dabbed concealer over the visible sections of her port wine stain. Gord used to joke that her birthmark formed a map of Switzerland, that Linda must have binged on Swiss chocolate during her pregnancy. Gord was the only one who could tease her like that, as if her birthmark was an adorable quirk instead of a disfigurement. No one had ever actually said it out loud, but she knew that her birthmark was part of the reason her father had abandoned their family.

She stroked powder along her cheeks and down her neck, her heart rate slowing as the ritual worked its magic.

"Finally!" Julia muttered, when Helen got back to the dining room.

"Some of us like to put a little effort into our appearance."

"Girls," said their mother wearily. "I'm glad that Helen wants to look her best. Gord, are we ready?"

"Ready. I'm setting the timer. Everyone in place?"

Gord touched a button on the camera on its tripod, moved to stand beside Helen and gave her arm a supportive squeeze as the shutter snapped open and closed.

*

Helen went straight to work on Sunday afternoon, so she didn't get Anna's message until after 8:00 p.m.

"Someone called for you," Thom said over his shoulder as she dropped her bag in the hallway. He was on the sofa, playing a first-person shooter. "Wants you to call her back."

When she saw the phone number scrawled on the pad of paper, Helen's heart started to bang in her chest. Everything else flew out of her head: the tension with her sister, the lingering nausea from eating birthday cake for breakfast, the humiliating sales meeting with Carmen ("Meeting quota isn't enough," her boss had lectured. "Anyone can make quota. We need you to go above and beyond. We need team players, Helen. The company's needs come first.") Everything washed away in a sudden flood of adrenaline.

Helen dialled the number and held her breath.

"Anna? Hello?" Helen could hardly hear her over the guitar-heavy music in the background. "Hey, it's me. It's Helen."

"Helen! Hang on, let me turn this down." The music fell away. "Hey. I wasn't sure you'd get my message. Your boyfriend sounded pretty wasted when I called."

"Thom? He's not my boyfriend. Just a roommate."

"It took him about five times to get my number right."

"Yeah, that's Thom. I thought you were leaving today?"

"I decided to stick around. Take advantage of the empty house. Did I tell you my parents are cruising around the world?"

"They're what?"

"On a boat. Get your mind out of the gutter, Wright!" Anna laughed her new throaty laugh. "A hundred and fifty days on a boat. Can you imagine? They won't be back until September. So I thought about what you said. And I thought, fuck it, maybe I'll stay. Try and uncover the mysteries of my past." Anna laughed again. "How does that sound? You're still in?"

Helen hesitated. "You mean, about the party? Finding out what happened?"

"Exactly. Shake some trees, see what falls out. So what are you doing tonight? We could get a drink, make some plans—"

"Tonight?" Helen sank down onto the chair by the little kitchen table. "I don't know, Anna. I just got home from work. And it's been a crazy weekend."

"One drink. I'll come pick you up. We'll go wherever you want. Unless," Anna's voice changed, "unless you don't want to be seen with me? If that's what's going on, just say so. I don't have time for bullshit."

"That's not what I'm saying!" Helen rubbed at her eyes. "I just can't do tonight. But maybe tomorrow? What if you came over here in the afternoon and we went through my Laurier yearbooks? Just as somewhere to start."

There was a pause.

"You kept our old yearbooks?"

"Yeah, of course. But that's just an idea, we can do something else."

"No, that's smart. That sounds good. Give me your address."

CHAPTER 5

Anna got lost on the way to Helen's apartment.

"I'm on Alberta Street. In the Ward, near Tytler School," Helen had told her. "If you're coming from your parents' place, you should take York Road."

"I'll find it," Anna assured her, then she spent twenty minutes driving in circles, cursing the area's illogical layout. The Ward was full of hidden switchbacks and high industrial fences, its streets more like alleys which zigged and zagged at odd angles. Finally, after she'd missed the turnoff for the third time, Anna pulled into the Esso on the other side of Wellington.

She scanned the shelves for a map, then got in line behind an old lady counting change and a young guy in a camo jacket with a thick blond beard. While she waited, she unfolded the paper accordion and traced the streets of downtown Guelph with her index finger. She'd just spotted Helen's street when someone nudged her arm.

"Your turn," said the bearded guy, in an undertone.

Anna looked up.

"This ain't a library." The middle-aged man behind the counter was scowling at her from under his baseball cap. "You paying for that?"

She nodded her thanks to the young bearded guy, who paused and met her eyes, first with sympathy, then with something else. Anna's breath caught. She knew this guy from Laurier. But what was his name?

"Ma'am, you're holding up the line!"

The guy—Calvin?—smirked and pushed through the door as Anna slapped her Visa card onto the counter and punched her PIN into the machine. She looked out the window as the guy—was it Cam?—climbed into the passenger side of a shiny black pickup with an oval decal. When the machine beeped, she snatched up her map and bolted for the door, reading the truck's white decal: *Camilleri Construction*. Which meant—

"Hey! Your card!"

Anna hurried back for her Visa as the man behind the counter shook his head.

"Fucking druggie homeless kids."

She glared at him and pushed through the door. As she stepped outside, the pickup gunned its engine and its stereo blared a crunchy skate-punk guitar riff. Their names dropped into Anna's head as she caught their profiles, laughing together. That was Ricky Camilleri driving, wearing a douchey backwards baseball hat. Next to him was Chris Cavanagh with the overgrown beard. As they peeled out of the gas station, Chris lifted his hand in a mocking salute.

Anna answered with her finger, raising her hand as they drove away. Then she climbed back into her parents' car, dropped the map on the seat beside her and sat gripping the leather steering wheel. She squeezed her eyes shut, wishing she'd brought an Ativan, trying to get her breathing under control.

Chris Cavanagh. Ricky Camilleri. Both were a few years older; they'd have been in grade twelve or thirteen when she was in grade ten, although Ricky's younger sister had been in Anna's class. That smirk on Chris's face brought her right back to the halls of Laurier. All those stares from guys trying to catch her eye, their low and insinuating voices whispering her name: *Hey Annie, c'mere, I got something to show you. I heard you*

*like to party, Annie, I hear you like it dirty. I hear you're
all broken in.*

It didn't matter what she wore: turtlenecks, baggy
sweaters, patched jeans. It didn't matter if she brushed
her hair or washed the sleep out of her eyes, if she came
to school zonked on her mother's Xanax or stone-cold
shivering sober. When she walked down the hall, crowds
parted and re-formed behind her, the girls glaring or
looking away, the guys all crooning her name: *Annie.
Hey, Annie, don't be such a tease. We know what you did,
that you're up for it. Want to do it again?*

She did her best to ignore the taunts, but she kept
replaying that moment she'd walked into Olly Sutton's
kitchen on New Year's Day.

"You're finally up!" He'd turned to face her with that
wide predatory smile. "You made a lot of guys very
happy last night. You must be exhausted." And then,
when Annie stared back at him: "Don't you remember?"

"What are you talking about?"

"Don't play dumb. You were the star of the show."
Olly reached out and grabbed her breast through her
thin T-shirt.

"Stop!" Annie pushed him away. "What does that
mean?"

She was dizzy, still half-drunk, but a terrible certainty
was growing in her mind. She'd seen the blood on the
sheets, the bruises on her thighs. Her entire lower body
burned and throbbed so much that it hurt to stand, to
pull up her underwear, even to walk.

"You know exactly what I mean." Olly stepped closer
and leaned in, his hot breath on her neck. His hand was
back, squeezing, twisting. "What do you say, are you up
for round two? Or is it round nine or ten? I lost count."

She'd been back at school for a week when Olly cornered her outside the art room, in front of the display cabinet decorated in red and gold for Chinese New Year. The Year of the Dog.

"What's wrong?" Olly asked, looming over her. "Why won't you talk to me?"

A hot bubble of nausea rose in Annie's throat. She ducked her head, tried to edge away, but he blocked her from leaving, putting an arm on either side of her shoulders.

"Don't act so innocent." Olly leaned closer, his Polo Sport overpowering the hall's mushroomy reek of acrylic paint. "I thought we were friends now."

"Leave me alone!"

Other students were walking by, but they just shook their heads, averted their eyes. "She's such a slut," said a girl's voice.

"Just touch it," Olly said. "It'll only take five minutes."

When Annie tried to push past him, Olly caught her hand and moved it downward, pressing it into his jeans.

"What's the big deal? You still think you're too good for me? You already let me fuck you. Me and all my friends."

Olly's words broke something inside Annie. Maybe he was right. What did it matter? What did any of this matter?

Olly found her again the next morning, at recess. Then at the back of the library, during lunch. Then she followed him into the boys' bathroom on the third floor. He wasn't alone, that time.

They were all so grateful. They were mostly fast, too. Sometimes they gave her things, as payment for her favours. Not money, she wouldn't touch their money, but Tim Hortons gift cards, rolled-up joints, assorted pills. They'd bring freshly baked macadamia nut cookies from the cafeteria, dropping these on her desk along with a wink, with a note suggesting a time and a place.

It wasn't that bad, after the first few times. It was nice to be wanted. Annie went mostly numb, but she learned to find the satisfaction in these brief encounters. It even got to be fun, sneaking around. Before everything spiralled out of control.

*

Helen lived in a red brick house that had been subdivided into apartments, so rundown it seemed to be wilting into the earth. Anna bounced on the spongy wooden floorboards of Helen's porch, examining the peeling paint on the front door, sedimentary layers of green and black and brown. She touched and broke a delicate curl of dried paint, tossed it into a snowdrift, and rang the buzzer.

Almost immediately, she heard footsteps inside, then the door swung wide and there was Helen's familiar face with its thick layer of foundation. Her brown hair was in a ponytail, and she wore a striped apron over jeans and a sweater.

"Are you okay?" Helen's smile dropped. "What's wrong?"

"Nothing. I got lost." Anna trailed her old friend up the staircase, running her hand along the velvet bumps of the old flocked wallpaper. "Isn't this kind of a rough neighbourhood for a girl like you?"

"A girl like me?" Helen laughed over her shoulder. "I've been here almost seven years. It's cheap. And we've got a big kitchen." At the top of the stairs, Helen pointed out wall hooks in the dimly lit hall. "You can hang your coat here."

"Do you remember Ramona Camilleri?" Anna asked, as she followed Helen into the kitchen.

"Ramona? We were in Girl Guides together. Why do you ask?"

"I just ran into her brother."

"Ricardo. He used to drive us to meetings. I don't know him very well."

"Well, he certainly remembered me."

Anna looked around. One kitchen wall was dominated by a pegboard hung with saucepans and baking pans. A tan-coloured fridge hummed off-pitch and the linoleum floor was an ugly jigsaw of different patterns, brown and orange checks patched with tiles of greenish-grey. Despite the cold weather, the window over the sink was wide open.

"Sorry," said Helen, when she saw Anna shiver. "I have to leave that open when I use the oven or the smoke alarm goes off. I'm making sugar cookies."

"For me?" Anna felt absurdly touched. "That's nice of you."

Helen waved this away.

"I bake all the time."

"Very Martha Stewart." Anna sniffed the vanilla-scented air, taking in the spotless counter, the mixing bowls draining in the rack. She nodded at the hockey calendar on the fridge. "You're a sports fan?"

"That's Thom's."

"Oh, right. Your roommate. What's he like?" The slow deep voice on the phone had conjured a heavy guy with a thick beard, reeking of pot smoke.

"Kind of a nerd. He works at a computer repair shop."

"And he's into hockey?"

"Yeah." Helen said. "You can meet him, if you want. So when did you see Ricardo?"

"Just now. At the gas station. Him and his buddy, Chris Cavanagh." She shivered again. "There are lots of Laurier people still here, I guess."

"For sure." Helen checked the oven, pulled out two trays of cookies and slid them onto the stovetop. "We'll give them a minute to cool," she said, fanning the trays with a quilted oven mitt.

"Are there some for me?" A male voice asked from the doorway behind them.

Anna turned to face the roommate. He looked more normal than she'd expected: medium height, brown eyes in an unremarkable face.

"Helen makes the best cookies," Thom said. He leaned across the sink to bang the window closed, then pulled the frayed sleeve of his grey hoodie over his fingers and took a cookie.

Helen sighed. "Anna, Thom. Thom, Anna."

"The famous Thom," said Anna. "You're taking good care of our friend here?"

"She takes care of me!" Thom elbowed Helen, who stepped back in embarrassment. When he focused on Anna, his eyebrows went up. "Geez, that's a lot of ink. You know, I was planning to get a Leafs tattoo this year if they won the cup, but the Flyers knocked them out in the semi-finals. Such a heartbreaker."

"I'll bet." With great effort, Anna resisted rolling her eyes.

"So you two were friends in high school?" Crumbs flew out of Thom's mouth as he talked. "You're not what I expected. I don't think Helen's in your league anymore."

Helen raised her chin. "What's that supposed to mean?"

"Don't get mad. I just think you've got a city mouse, country mouse situation here." Thom held Anna's gaze for another second, then shot Helen a crooked smile. "It's not an insult. I'm just saying you're not a party girl."

He reached for another cookie, but this time Helen blocked his path. Thom feinted left and then right, but Helen held her ground. She wasn't smiling anymore.

"All right, folks. Break it up." Anna cocked her head. "I want to catch up with Helen."

Thom froze and stood back, looking sheepish. He raised his hands. "I'm not stopping you."

"Let's go sit in my room," Helen said. She picked up an old-fashioned flowered plate, piled it with cookies, and passed it to Anna to carry. "Come on. Follow me."

*

The walls of Helen's bedroom were painted a pale yellow, the same shade as the lumpy duvet on the bed. Everything else was white: the metal bed frame, the bookshelf, the mirrored makeup vanity stacked with rows of bottles and tubes. Even the framed print on the wall of Van Gogh's *Sunflowers* coordinated with the colour scheme. It was like standing in the middle of a giant egg.

"Is there something going on between you two?" Anna asked, once the door was closed. "There was a bit of a vibe."

"Me and Thom? Nothing. He just drives me crazy sometimes."

"Uh huh." Anna studied Helen, who wouldn't meet her eyes. "So it's just the two of you here? How did you wind up living together?"

"It's a long story."

"We've got time." Anna sat on the bed and took a cookie from the plate. "Fill me in."

"It's really not interesting." Helen sat down beside Anna, crossing her legs. "I used to live with my friend Crystal. We had classes together, at the university, so when Mom and Gord moved to Toronto—"

"They did?"

"Yeah, when my sister finished high school, they sold their house and moved away. Now they're in a co-op in St. Lawrence Market."

"I can't believe your hippie stepdad gave up his garden." Anna shook her head. "Remember when I convinced him to let us try out his new tent in your backyard?"

"It was me you had to convince! He was happy to have us out there. He probably thought it would get me into camping."

"And then the mosquitoes were so bad that we couldn't sleep?"

"God, that was terrible." Helen laughed. "Yeah, my mom's got a job at U of T. Gord's opened his own vet clinic in Toronto. They seem happy there."

"And your sister?"

"Julia?" Helen wrinkled her nose. "She's in Ottawa, in law school."

"She was always winning awards in school, right?"

"Oh my God, always. Little Miss Perfect. Did you know she's getting married?"

"No! Isn't she, like, fourteen?"

"She's only two years younger than us."

"Jesus. Married at twenty-four? The same guy for the rest of your life?" Anna shuddered. "Kill me first."

Helen took another cookie. "My mother is thrilled. She guilted me into being Julia's maid of honour, like that's supposed to bring us closer together."

"At least you'll get to wear a big ugly dress." Anna said. "Okay, they all abandoned you. How does that lead to your roommate?"

"Crystal was dating Thom back then. He had some issue with his lease, so he moved in too, over the summer." Helen looked down and smoothed out the duvet. "Then Crystal was swept off her feet by this exchange student in her women's studies class. She and Thom broke up and she followed this girl back to Australia. Thom took over her lease."

"Wow. That's some soap opera drama."

"I guess." Helen shifted on the bed, pushing away the plate of cookies. "Anyway. I never actually finished my degree."

"Well, I didn't finish high school. You're still one up on me."

"Oh, man. Sorry. I didn't mean—"

"It's fine." Anna shook her head. "Old news." She got off the bed and moved to Helen's vanity, where she started picking things up and putting them down. A bottle of nail polish. A makeup brush. A silver-tubed lipstick.

"Okay," Helen said, after a minute. "Did you want to look at those yearbooks, or..."

"Yeah. Absolutely." Anna pulled the cap off the lipstick and twisted the base to make the pink bullet appear. "I mean, it can't hurt."

"And you don't...did you say..." Helen hesitated again. "When we were talking, before, you said you don't remember much, from that party."

"I was blacked out."

Anna set the lipstick down and sat on the padded stool in front of the vanity.

"Right. Yeah. But you said Olly talked to you, the next morning."

"He…" Anna frowned, thinking again of teenaged Olly Sutton leaning across his kitchen counter, leering as he fondled himself through his sweatpants. *You made a lot of guys very happy last night.* And then, "It's hazy. I don't think he gave me names."

"That's okay. It's fine."

"I know I hooked up with a lot of guys, but I don't remember many details. Like, of that whole year. It's weird, right?"

Helen blinked. "Yeah."

"But it's fine." Anna took a deep breath. "It shouldn't be that hard to find out what happened. People love talking about me."

"Process of elimination. Who was there at the party, who remembers what."

"Guess Who!" Anna said. "You know. That game with the little cartoon faces, on the plastic frame, and you fold down all the ones that don't…like, does your guy have a hat? Or does he wear glasses? You know?"

Helen was staring at her.

"I'm not crazy, I'm not saying we have to build a game board. Although that might be cool."

"Sure." Helen finally cracked a smile. "Okay."

"We just don't have to make this so serious."

"We don't have to do this at all," said Helen. "We can just hang out."

"Nah. It's cool, playing detective. You've got me curious."

Anna rubbed at her eyebrow, hooking her finger through the metal ring and tugging gently at the skin. She thought of Olly at her parents' soirée, tightening his arms around her. *Just like old times.*

"Well, then. I was thinking. We need to make a list."

"That's so organized! Starting with Ricky and Chris?"

"It's your list," Helen said, after a pause. "But it was mostly people from our grade at that party. Let's just look through my yearbooks. See what we see."

Helen went to her shelves and shifted a stack of fashion magazines, piling them on the floor beside books with titles like *The Art of Makeup, The Beauty Bible, The Makeover Manual.* Then she pulled out a familiar maroon Laurier yearbook.

"Grade ten, right? 1994. Here we go."

Anna sat beside her on the braided rug and took the yearbook out of Helen's hands. It flopped open at a page filled with pictures of athletes, where someone had traced hearts around the face of a tall, dark-skinned boy in a gold and burgundy football uniform.

"Oh my God." Giggles rose in Anna's throat. She looked at Helen. "You used to stalk this guy. What was his name, Dan…?"

"Dave Patel."

Helen reached to turn the page but Anna turned it back.

"You had the whole school mapped out. You made us take these crazy long routes to the cafeteria so you could walk past his locker."

"I was ridiculous." Helen pulled at the page, but Anna held it flat.

"At least he didn't hang out with Olly Sutton. Didn't they have some feud?"

"They had a fight in grade nine, in that park behind the school. Someone called the cops."

"Yeah." Anna examined the picture. "Dave Patel. He was pretty cute." She looked up, into Helen's eyes. "I never hooked up with him, you know. I wouldn't do that to you."

Helen slid the page out from Anna's finger.

"It wouldn't have mattered. He never noticed me anyway."

"Aww." Anna put an arm around Helen's shoulder and gave her a gentle shake. "The one that got away."

"I still see him around. I think he did engineering at Waterloo."

"So maybe you've still got a chance."

The next page showed a picture of two boys in baggy skateboard pants, both holding acoustic guitars. Anna tapped the one with blond hair curtaining a narrow face.

"Him. He was in our year, wasn't he? And he hung out with Olly?"

"Wayne Reilly." Helen peered down at the photo, pulled a notebook onto her lap and wrote down his name. "He's a cop now. Not OPP, just local Guelph police. And you know about Phil?"

She pointed to the other boy in the photo, the one with a mop of curls.

"Phil...?"

"McKinley. He was in that band, back in high school. They played at assemblies?"

Anna frowned. "I guess."

"He's famous now! He's in this band called the Midnight Choir. They opened for Nickelback last summer!"

"Are they good?"

"I think so. Thom likes them."

"Phil McKinley. Wayne Reilly." Anna nodded. "Okay. Add them to your list."

She flipped more pages filled with half-remembered faces and stopped at a collage of candid shots. A pyramid of popular girls in bathing suits on the dock of somebody's cottage. A pair of twins with faces painted in the school colours, yellow and maroon. A room in a wood-panelled basement with Olly Sutton, Phil McKinley, and others holding plastic cups in a sloppy salute. Anna pointed to the blond guy perched on the end of the couch.

"Him. Starkey. What's he doing now?"

Helen started to speak but Anna's ears filled with a rushing sound, her vision going white at the edges. That couch. That group. She leaned closer, pressing her finger against the image.

"That's the party," Anna said, heart leaping in her chest. "Oh my God, is that me? There, at the edge of the picture. That's me in my green sweater."

Anna brought her face down to the page, focusing on the small blank face of the girl in the green sweater, nearly buried under the group of laughing boys. God, she looked young. She leaned in closer and closer, staring until the colours blurred together.

"Anna. Hey, Anna. It's okay." Helen's hand slid in front of her face to block the page, so close that Anna's eyelashes touched her palm when she blinked.

Anna reared back, sucking in air. She slammed the yearbook closed and dropped it on the braided rug. She climbed to her feet, rubbing her sweaty palms down the front of her jeans, fumbling for her cigarettes. "Can I smoke in here?"

"Sorry," said Helen. "We have a balcony—"

"No." Anna's heart was pounding. Helen's yellow bedroom felt small and airless. "I need to get outside. I've got to go."

"You're leaving?"

"I'll call you. We'll do this later. Okay?"

Anna was already opening the bedroom door, moving down the hall.

"Hang on," said Helen, following her. "Do you want to take the yearbook? Or some cookies?"

"No!" Anna grabbed her coat off the hook. "I'm fine. I'll see you soon. I just have to go."

CHAPTER 6

After Anna left, Helen wasn't sure if she'd hear from her again. She'd looked so distraught at the sight of that picture in the yearbook. How strange it was, watching her unravel in real time, the bravado and amusement falling away to leave that awful blankness that Helen remembered from high school.

But then, Helen was used to people leaving. *They all abandoned you,* Anna had joked, but really, it happened too often to be funny. People moved away and Helen was left behind. Helen's parents: first her father, then Linda and Gord. Anna herself, of course. But there was also Melissa, the coworker-turned-friend who'd climbed the corporate ladder up and away to Montreal. And Crystal, running after her red-headed Australian crush. If Thom hadn't stepped in to cover that half of the rent, what would Helen have done? God knows she didn't have money to spare.

After Anna took off, Helen told herself not to get upset, not to get invested. Instead, she did what she always did when someone left: she took refuge in routine. Got up in the morning, did her makeup and went to work. Came home, ate dinner, talked to her mom, went to bed.

But then, a few nights later, Anna called again.

"Helen!" She yelled, over deafening music in the background. "What are you up to? I'm at this hilarious club downtown, it's got an actual cowboy theme!"

"Club Denim." Helen smiled, despite herself.

"Yes! Where the old Odeon used to be. Come and meet me! We'll practise our line dancing."

"It's ten o'clock." Helen looked down at her flannel L.L. Bean pyjamas. "I've got to get up early tomorrow! Some of us work for a living."

"I'll come by your work. What time are you done? Three? I can do three."

"Let's meet by the Tim Hortons," said Helen, thinking of Carmen's disapproving glare.

But Anna surprised her again, turning up at the counter as Helen was finishing her shift. She plunked herself down on one of the stools, the metal wires in her dreadlocks shimmering in the overhead lights.

"The mall cops kicked me out of the food court," Anna said, yawning. She reached behind the rack of lipsticks and picked up the photo, the one showing a barefaced Helen with her birthmark on full display. A jaunty caption was printed along the top of the frame: *Ask me about my personal experience with Façade cosmetics!* "Why do they have this picture of you here?"

"It's our sales protocol," Helen said. She took back the photo, wiped off Anna's fingerprints and set the frame back in its place. "Sharing our stories. It's not a big deal."

"They only hire people with birthmarks? What about her?"

Anna nodded at Helen's coworker, who was counting bills at the cash.

"Barb?" Helen dropped her voice. "She's got scars from an accident. We're a specialty counter, we hire people who use Façade products. It makes sense."

"Doesn't it piss you off, having that photo out where everyone can see it?"

"It's in my contract." Helen printed her initials at the bottom of the hours sheet. "Okay, let's go before

Carmen sees you. She hates when we socialize at the counter."

＊

"You missed out last night," Anna said, as Helen followed her to a white Range Rover in the parking lot. "Thursdays are Garth Brooks night. That place was hopping. Apparently, Guelph's got a lot of wannabe cowboys."

"It's the Aggies. The agricultural college, up at the university," Helen said, climbing into the leather seat. She tucked her bag by her feet, conscious of the yearbook packed behind her sandwich container. "This is a nice car."

"My mother would be pissed if she knew I was driving it." Anna lit a cigarette and steered them out of the parking lot. "So, where're we going? Back to your place?"

"I think Thom's there," Helen said. "Let's find somewhere downtown."

Helen stared out the window, only half listening as Anna launched into another story about her night at Club Denim, about some cowboy hat she'd acquired from a drunken frat boy. At the next traffic light, a bus pulled up beside them, so close she could have reached out and touched its dirty aluminum side.

Helen chewed at the inside of her cheek. When the light turned green, she took a deep breath and turned to Anna.

"I was surprised when you called."

"You were?" Anna laughed. "Why? I said I would."

Helen shifted in her seat. "The other day, at my place, you got so upset over that picture. In the yearbook."

"That just caught me off guard." Anna said. "No, I told you. I'm sticking around. I want to fill in the blanks. Did you know he's teaching at Laurier now?"

Helen's stomach dipped as the car bumped over a pothole.

"What? Who?"

"Olly Sutton," said Anna. "His parents still live in the same house. I went by there, yesterday. His dad was shovelling the driveway."

The car accelerated down the hill.

"I keep thinking about what you said," Anna went on. "How we've only got Olly's version. And maybe it's all true, you know? Maybe teenaged me got drunk and pulled a Girls-Gone-Wild. I just want to know what happened."

Helen gripped the sides of her seat as Anna rocketed through a yellow light.

"We'll find out," she said, feeling breathless.

"Oh yes," said Anna. "You and me, on the case. Solving the mystery. Was it Colonel Mustard in the bedroom with a rope? Or Miss Scarlett, in the kitchen, with a candlestick?"

There was another intersection ahead, another light turning yellow. Helen tensed, bracing for impact. "Anna. Slow down!"

Anna hit the brakes and the SUV fishtailed in the snow, skidding to a stop a few feet from the bumper of a rusty Ford pickup. When the light changed, they crossed the bridge over the frozen river in silence.

Helen's heart was hammering in her chest. She looked over at Anna, at her fingers clenched on the steering wheel, her ragged bitten-down nails.

"We have to be systematic," Helen said at last. "I brought my yearbook. We can look at that picture again, start with that. We don't have to do anything crazy."

*

By the time they pulled into Café Royale's parking lot, Helen had regained her composure.

Café Royale was really a diner, not a café; a boxy, black and white restaurant serving gelato, espresso, sandwiches. At night the place was lit up like a fishbowl, illuminating every customer behind floor-to-ceiling windows. Helen hadn't been here in years. As soon as they pushed through the glass doors she remembered why she'd avoided the place.

Laura Sanders was behind the counter, rearranging muffins on the wooden display shelf. Laura had gone to high school with Helen and Anna. She was one of the always-put-together popular girls, always sporting the right hairstyle, the right clothes, the right friends.

"Shit." Helen stopped on the doorstep. "Can we go somewhere else?"

Too late. "Helen Wright!" Laura called over to her. "Oh my God, hi!" Her red hair was caught in two long braids, like a stylish Pippi Longstocking.

"Hey, Laura." Helen's eyes dropped to the bulge in Laura's apron. "You're pregnant?"

"Due in July." Laura starfished a proud hand over her bump. "I know, I'm huge. I wasn't this big the first time around. People keep asking if it's twins."

"Congratulations," Helen said weakly.

"Thanks. It's so funny, I was just talking about you last week. My sister-in-law had a baby, and he was born with this terrible…," Laura dropped her voice and traced a wide circle around her face, "birthmark. So, of course, I thought of you. They're still doing tests, making sure it won't affect his eyes or his brain or anything. I mean, does yours…?"

Wordlessly, Helen shook her head.

"That's lucky, right? My poor little nephew looks so bad, with this awful red splotch across his face. But I was telling them all about you, about your mom coming to talk to us in grade school so we'd know you weren't contagious. You didn't get rid of it, did you?" Laura leaned across the marble counter. "No, I can see the edges. But you look great. I know you tried to cover it in school but honestly, that never really worked."

Helen looked away, wanting to disappear, to shrink down to nothing. Everyone in the café could hear them; that man at the end of the counter, those old ladies by the window. All of them listening, watching, judging. Helen felt breathless and sweaty, as if Laura had just shoved her under a spotlight, as if she'd scraped off Helen's makeup and exposed her to the whole world.

Then Anna stepped up beside her.

"What the actual fuck," Anna said, "is wrong with you, Laura?"

"Excuse me?" Laura's gold hoop earrings swung. "Helen and I are old friends. What's your problem?"

"My problem?" Anna's voice was hoarse. For one giddy moment, Helen imagined her vaulting over the bakery counter, wrapping her hands around Laura's pale throat. "First, you were never her friend. Yeah, we all remember you and Jennifer and Sarah with your bitchy jokes. That time you covered Helen's locker with *Phantom of the Opera* stickers? Fucking hilarious."

"What? How do you—"

"Don't you remember me?" The studs in Anna's face glinted as she pulled back her dreads. "Annie Leverett?"

Laura's face went blank with shock.

"Yeah. And Helen's a paying customer. Show some respect. How would you feel if you went to her work and she commented on your fat ass and your ugly hair? You say you want medical advice? Go to a doctor. You want Helen's expertise? Make an appointment and pay for a fucking consultation, like everyone else. Right, Helen? What do you say, should we leave? Ask for the manager? Lodge a complaint?"

"No, no," said Laura. Her face had gone red, clashing with her ginger hair. "Sorry, Helen, I'm not...I was just excited to see you. I didn't mean to overstep. Mike always says my mouth works faster than my brain."

"That's okay," Helen heard herself say, from a long way off. "There are lots of treatments for your nephew. More than when we were kids. There's a pediatric dermatology clinic at Sick Kids in Toronto. They're great. Have your sister-in-law ask for a referral."

"Who's Mike?" Anna asked.

Laura's eyes darted between them. "My husband."

"Michael Whitburg," Helen said, remembering. She looked at Anna. "From Laurier. Big football player."

"The Mike from our year?" Anna's smile dropped away. "He was friends with Olly?"

"Olly Sutton? For sure. Mike's in real estate now," said Laura. "Mostly in the South End. If you're looking for an apartment, he could find you a good deal."

"Mike Whitburg," Anna repeated.

"Right. What can I get you?" Laura asked. "Whatever it is, it's on the house. My treat."

Helen smiled into Laura's anxious eyes. "Can I get a coffee?"

"Espresso for me," said Anna. "A double. And maybe throw in a couple of those chocolate cookies."

*

"I forgot she worked here," Helen said, still buzzing as they found seats by the window. "Man, you put her in her place."

"You can't let people talk to you like that," Anna said. "You've got to call them on that juvenile bullshit. Jesus. Laura Sanders."

"I can't believe she didn't recognize you!"

"You didn't either." Anna stirred sugar into her espresso. "I can't believe she's having her second kid already."

"Crazy, right?" Helen broke off a piece of chocolate cookie and took a bite. "I knew Mike was in real estate, though. He's got ads on bus stop benches around the mall, this cheesy picture of him in a tuxedo."

"The mall?" Anna lifted a stained cloth bag onto her lap and pulled out a haphazardly-folded street map. She pushed the cups and plates to the side and spread the map over the table.

"What is this?" Helen asked.

"Isn't it obvious?" Anna planted a finger on the map, held the cap of a red Sharpie in her teeth and yanked, releasing an acetone stink. She made a red X on Stone Road Mall and looked up, smiling around the cap. "You think Mike Whitburg was at the party?" she asked, indistinctly.

"That smell gives me a headache." Helen plucked the cap out of Anna's mouth and handed it over.

"Wait." Anna leaned in again and circled the intersection of Gordon and Paisley, right over Cafe Royale. "That's for our little friend Laura." She recapped the marker. "Aren't you impressed that I'm keeping track?"

Helen leaned in and touched the thick red lines around Anna's house.

"What are these for?"

"Every street I go down, I go over with the Sharpie."

"Wow." The streets of Guelph were scattered with little symbols. Helen's apartment was marked with a square, but there were other marks, here and there: circles, triangles, a star. "How do you remember what they all mean?"

"Come on. What else do I have to do?"

"Okay, yeah." Helen said. "But if you want to get more focused; I brought my yearbook. I don't know if Mike Whitburg was at the party, but he's not in that photo."

Helen pulled out the yearbook, spread it over the map and flipped through the glossy pages. There they all were, piled up on the couch: Anna, Olly Sutton, Phil McKinley and Glenn Starkey, plus a few other boys whose names she'd had to look up.

Anna pulled the book towards herself. "I still can't believe there's a fucking picture of that night in the yearbook." She twisted a blond dreadlock around her finger, winding it up, then unwinding.

Helen looked at her. "I know."

"Okay." Anna shook her head and started printing their names in the empty space by Highway Seven. "I'll track these guys down. Make them talk."

"You're writing over the Mustang Drive In," Helen said, reading Anna's spiky capital letters upside-down. S-T-A-R-K—"Wait!"

Anna stopped.

"Can you close that marker?" Helen said, stalling. She wanted Glenn Starkey at the bottom of Anna's hit list. "I was thinking about this picture. Because...didn't people talk about photos? After the party. I thought it was just another rumour, but maybe…"

"Someone took pictures. Of what happened, you mean? Of me?"

Anna stared at her.

"Maybe. I don't know. But this guy, Sean?" Helen tapped the face of the only Asian guy in the picture, then turned a couple of pages, to the club section. "He was one of the yearbook editors. Maybe he knows if there are more pictures?"

Anna reached for her coffee. She wrapped her yellowed fingertips against the porcelain and stared down into her cup for a long minute. Then she took a drink.

"Okay." She picked up the marker. "Is it 'Sean' with an S or an SH? And where would I find him?"

"That's easy. He writes for the Guelph Mercury. Their office is downtown, across from the Church of Our Lady." Helen leaned over the map and pointed. "It's just a few blocks away."

CHAPTER 7

A few days later, Anna was out by Waverly Drive when she spotted the black Camilleri Construction pickup truck in front of a split-level ranch. She circled the block and pulled over on the other side of the street, studying the house's cream siding, its dark brown roof and matching shutters. Two unhappy-looking lion statues guarded its front steps and a snow-filled fountain in the middle of the lawn was topped with a concrete Botticelli Venus on the Half-Shell.

Anna opened her map over the steering wheel, pushing her aviators onto her forehead. Ricky Camilleri had been a big man on the Laurier campus. Maybe he'd have some insights. But was this Ricky's house? Or was he part of a construction crew here?

She drummed the Sharpie on the paper. *Nothing ventured*, she told herself, when the house's garage door clunked and began to lift. She tucked her dreads up under her woolly hat, opened the car door and zipped her coat up to her chin.

A petite young woman with black hair scraped back in a ponytail emerged from the garage, pushing a green bin that was almost as tall as she was. Anna quickened her pace. Ramona Camilleri had slimmed down since high school, when she'd had chubby cheeks and a laugh like a chipmunk. Now her eyebrows were thinly drawn lines and she wore a set of pink scrubs topped with a grey Mickey Mouse cardigan.

"Hi," Anna said, approaching as Ramona trundled the green bin down the driveway, leaving deep ruts in the slush. "Does Ricky live here?"

Ramona stopped. "Annie?"

"Yeah. Hey, Ramona. I was—"

"I thought you died."

"What?" Anna stepped back.

"I heard you OD'd in some halfway house in Montreal."

"Nope," said Anna. "But thanks for your concern."

Ramona straightened up, pulling her cardigan sleeves down over her hands. "My brother doesn't live here anymore."

"Okay. Well—"

"He's almost thirty years old. Why would he still live at home?"

"Don't you?" Anna asked, before she could help herself.

"What if I do?" Ramona's face went almost as pink as her shirt. "At least my parents didn't kick me out."

"Easy, Ramona." Anna shook her head. "What did I ever do to you?"

"You're a fucking skank," said Ramona. "Peter Martelli broke up with me because of you."

"What?" Peter had been short, curly haired, always cracking jokes. "I don't remember that."

"He dumped me right before my birthday." Ramona glared at Anna. "I had to go alone to my sweet-sixteen party!"

"You're mad about a high-school break up?"

"He said you showed up at his house in the middle of the night, knocked on his window, and when he opened it, you seduced him. You're such a whore."

"What?"

"Just leave, okay? I don't want to talk to you. Neither does my brother."

"Ramona, I didn't—"

"Get off this property!" Ramona grabbed the handle of the green bin and made a little rush forward, like she was going to run Anna over. "Leave us alone! Get out of here!"

*

That night, Anna called Helen to debrief. She was on the cordless phone in her parents' room, trying on some of the clothes her mother had left behind.

"Was Ramona always crazy?" Anna asked, tugging on a silky blue sleeveless blouse and turning to check the mirror. "She basically chased me off her property with a shotgun. And even if I did hook up with Peter Martelli, her story made no sense."

"Isn't Peter gay?"

"Is he?"

"That's what I heard," said Helen. "Maybe that's why you don't remember. Maybe he made it up, as an excuse."

"Oh my God. This shit is bananas, B, A, N, A, N, A, S," Anna sang, stripping off the blue top. "Hey, I'm going out tonight. You want to come with me?"

"It's after nine!" There was a metallic crashing sound. "Sorry, my bowls won't fit back in the cupboard. Where are you going?"

"I'm working my way through the bars downtown." Anna held up a chartreuse boat-neck top. "You can show me where the cool places are."

"Yeah, right," said Helen. "Why were you talking to Ramona? I thought you were going to see Sean about the yearbook?"

"I'm pursuing multiple avenues of investigation." Anna pulled a lacy white camisole over her black sports bra and checked her reflection; very Courtney Love.

"But how am I supposed to find out what happened if people were making shit up?"

"That's why you should focus on Sean," said Helen. "You know he was at that party. Go talk to him tomorrow."

*

The next day, Anna dropped the yearbook and her crumpled map into her bag before she left the house. She was locking the front door when she heard her name.

"Annie! Hey, Annie!"

A girl in a pink velour tracksuit was waving from the porch next door.

"Hey, El," said Anna, relaxing. "Long time no see!"

Elettra Vetrone leaned over her porch railing, grinning. Anna used to babysit Elettra back when she was a tiny pre-teen obsessed with horseback riding. When Anna had to make her dinner, they'd walk to the corner store for boxes of mac and cheese, which Elettra ate with salsa and bacon bits. Elettra must be in her twenties now. She was tall and leggy, her shiny dark hair curling around her shoulders.

"I heard you were back," El said. "Mom said she was supposed to be watching your house."

"And now she's watching me?"

"Exactly!" Elettra laughed. "You've been travelling, right?"

"Uh huh. How about you?"

"I just finished my last year at Queen's. I'm going to Italy this summer with friends, then hopefully I'll be at UBC in September. I'm waitlisted for their med school."

"That's amazing." Anna smiled at her. "Good for you."

"Thanks." Elettra glanced over her shoulder, then jogged down off the porch in her tan leather Uggs. "Hey, you got any coke?"

Anna blinked. "What?"

"I've got zero connections in this city. But maybe you could hook me up?"

"Sorry. I stay away from illegal shit these days."

"Okay." Elettra shrugged and retreated to her house. "Well, see you around."

Anna stared after her, hitched her bag up her shoulder and set off down the hill towards the centre of the city. She was on Eramosa when a pickup truck slowed beside her, its engine vibrating through the soles of her Doc Martens. She raised her middle finger without breaking stride, then lost patience and spun around.

"What?" she snarled, squinting at the orange public works truck. "You need something?"

Johnnie Campbell stuck his tousled head out the window.

"I thought you were leaving town?"

"I changed my mind." Anna eyed him, his dark hair receding from his temples, the friendly curiosity in his face. She stepped closer and rested her hand on the edge of his window. "You looking for another round of Hungry Hungry Hippos?"

Johnnie laughed, a little shamefaced. "I'm supposed to be working."

"And yet, here you are," said Anna. "Got any more weed?"

"Sorry. Not today. But I can give you a lift?"

"A lift." Anna looked down the street, considering. "Yeah, okay. Can you give me a ride downtown?"

She climbed into the passenger side of the truck, sweeping a pile of loose papers off the seat and onto the floor of the truck. The dashboard was sticky with coffee stains and dried crumbs.

"Where are we going?" Johnnie glanced over as he put the pickup in gear. "Anywhere in particular?"

"We can drive around for a bit," said Anna, leaning back in the seat. "But I'm heading to the Guelph Mercury building. You remember Sean Wu? Apparently, he works there."

"Sean Wu from Laurier?"

"Yup." She looked out at the brick houses as they crested the hill. "I heard he might have some photos. From a New Year's party."

When he didn't respond, Anna glanced over and saw an ugly flush creeping up his neck.

"What?" she said. "Do you know what I'm talking about?"

Johnnie twisted uncomfortably.

"I don't know. I saw some Polaroids, but…"

Anna turned sideways in her seat.

"Polaroids." She stared at his reddening cheek. "You saw these when? Back in high school?"

"Yeah."

"Did I look like I was having fun, at least?"

Johnnie hesitated.

"I don't know if it was really you," he said. "I mean, it was hard to see faces."

"Fuck," Anna said. She suddenly felt like she couldn't breathe, like she might puke. She tilted forward, folding in half until her nose touched the denim of her jeans, trying to catch her breath.

The truck jolted and then veered as Johnnie pulled over to the side of the road.

"Jesus, Annie. Are you okay?"

"I'm fine." She sat up, fumbled for the enamel pill-box in her coat pocket and wedged an Ativan under her tongue. She stared out the truck's bug-spattered windshield, feeling the tablet dissolve. "Mm-hm."

"You don't look fine."

"Well, I am. Or I will be." She bared her teeth, attempting a smile. "I forget sometimes, that's all. What a shithole this place is. Full of shitty people."

"Yeah," said Johnnie. "Sorry, yeah."

"Do you know who's got them now? These Polaroids?"

"They're probably long gone. You wouldn't want to see them, anyway."

"Maybe not."

"Hey," said Johnnie. "Do you want me to take you home?"

"No. I need to get this over with."

Johnnie drove the rest of the way in silence. By the time they passed the Church of Our Lady, the meds had slowed Anna's heart to a controlled thump. As he pulled into a parking space, she cracked her knuckles and reached for his zipper.

"Hey!" Johnnie jumped as if he'd been scalded. "What are you doing?"

"Saying thank you." Anna shrugged and pulled her hand back. "But if you're not interested—"

"I'm working! And I have a girlfriend!"

"Calm down!" She laughed. "How come I didn't hear about this girlfriend before?"

Johnnie looked away. "That was an error in judgement."

"Gotcha. I've made a few of those myself." She opened the door and looked back over her shoulder. "Thanks for the lift. Feel free to drop by sometime, to smoke some weed, play some games. Whatever."

As Johnnie's truck pulled away, Anna crossed the road to the newspaper office. A silver globe the size of a beach ball bulged out of the Guelph Mercury's sign, shiny hammered-metal continents glinting in the afternoon sun. Inside, her footsteps echoed off the grey marble walls as she marched up to the receptionist sitting behind a boxy beige computer. There were potted plants on either end of her desk, a bushy fern and something with thick yellow pistils poking out of spiky red flowers. The woman stopped typing as she approached.

"Hi," said Anna. "I'm here to meet one of your reporters. Can you buzz me in?"

The receptionist steepled long fingers under her chin. Her nails were painted like Easter eggs, each one a different combination of pastel stripes and zigzags.

"Do you have an appointment?"

"I'm here to see Sean Wu. He's an old friend." Anna said. "Could you tell him Annie Leverett's here to see him?"

"I don't think we have a Sean on staff." The woman was typing again. "Maybe he's freelance."

"He's a reporter." Anna wanted to reach across the desk, grab a fistful of the woman's frizzy curls and force her to meet her eyes. Instead, she pulled an arrow-shaped leaf from the plant and ripped it down the middle. "Could you check your computer?"

"If you don't have an appointment, I'll have to ask you to leave."

Fingers sticky with sap, Anna looked up at the staff directory on the wall, shiny bronze names mounted on a wooden panel. The last name on the list was Xuan Wu.

"There." She pointed. "That's the name. Wu."

The woman squinted. "Oh, you want Shoo-enn," she said, exaggerating the syllables. "Why didn't you say so? I'll see if he's available."

Sean Wu jogged down the stairs a few minutes later. His cheekbones were sharper, his olive skin clear of acne, but otherwise he could still have been sixteen years old, stripped out of his skater shirts and baggy jeans, dressed up in a blue button-down and a narrow pair of black pants.

He pushed through the glass doors and strode towards her.

"Annie Leverett," he said. "I heard you were back in town."

"I go by Anna now." She jutted a thumb at the staff directory. "You changed your name too?"

"It was always Xuan. I got sick of teachers butchering the pronunciation. It was easier to be Sean, growing up." His dark eyes were guarded. "What's going on?"

"I wanted to ask you some questions. About..." she stopped. Had Sean—no, Xuan—seen those Polaroids? What did they show, anyway? Not her face, but her tits? Her ass? Sixteen-year-old Annie in various positions with various guys? She shook her head. "About high school stuff. Can we talk?"

Xuan hesitated, checking his watch.

"I'm just finishing a piece. Can you give me half an hour?"

"Sure. I can wait here, or..." Anna could feel the receptionist's glare. "Let's meet somewhere else. I'll buy you a coffee."

"How about Café Royale? Do you know where that is?"

Anna huffed out a laugh.

"Sure. Yeah. I'll meet you there."

＊

She walked over slowly, muttering his name out loud, practising: "Shoo-ennn." They'd gotten along fine at Laurier, hadn't they? He'd been in some of her classes, but she didn't think she'd ever met him at the back of the library, jerked him off in one of the locker rooms. But there was so much she didn't remember.

The bright sun made it difficult to see inside Café Royale's window, so she couldn't tell from the outside who was working behind the counter. Anna opened the door and breathed in the smell of coffee and baked goods, the faint chemical undertone of cleaning products. Sure enough, there was Laura Sanders, wiping at the counter in wide aggressive circles.

"What do you want?" Laura asked, narrowing her eyes. Anna grimaced.

"Hello to you too. Can I get a coffee?"

"Not an espressssso?" Laura said, dragging out the sound.

"Jesus Christ." Anna shook her head tiredly. "Just a regular coffee."

"There's no other coffee place?" Laura slammed a paper cup on the counter and yanked the carafe out of the machine. "You had to come back here?"

"There's such great service here."

"Two dollars. Take it and go."

"Just a minute." Anna looked in her bag, taking her time digging out her wallet. "Do you have change for a fifty?"

"Are you—" Laura bit off her words and stabbed at the buttons on the cash register. Her cheeks flushed as she shoved the money across the counter. "Here."

Anna tilted her head. "Now, how much should I tip you?"

"Can you just leave?"

"Can you be a little more polite?" Anna held up a quarter. "I'll make it worth your while."

"I know what you're doing. But it won't work."

"What?" Confusedly, Anna thought of Johnnie, of Helen, then of the Polaroids. "What are you talking about?"

"Hitting the bars, picking up guys. And driving around. Spying on people."

Anna relaxed.

"You've been keeping tabs on me?" She widened her smile, showing her teeth. "Are you jealous I'm out having a good time while you're stuck at home, gestating?"

"Screw you." Laura tossed her long red hair. "You think you're so tough, just because you came back looking like a circus freak. But you haven't changed."

"Oh, I've changed. I don't put up with as much bullshit as I used to." Anna grabbed the paper cup. "Anyway, I can't stand and chat. I've got another guy to meet."

She found a seat outside on the patio, where the aluminum chairs were warm in the spring sun. She lit a cigarette, lifted her boots onto the seat of another chair and closed her eyes. This was better. Fresh air on her face, the rustle of traffic in the background. She could almost forget where she was, what she was doing here.

"Hey, Annie." She opened her eyes to see Xuan standing over the table. He brushed off another chair before taking a seat. "I can't stay long. I'm on deadline."

"Oh yeah? What are you writing?"

"A concert review." His fingers tapped the tabletop. "What do you need?"

"I want—" Anna started, but Xuan interrupted, looking up past her shoulder.

"Hey, Laura. How you doing?"

"Hey, Sean. Nice to see you. I'm good." Laura approached the table and ran a hand over her belly, smoothing the white fabric of the apron. "Well, tired. You know."

"How's Mike? I haven't seen him at the Y lately."

"His knee's acting up. They told him no more basketball until he sees the specialist."

"You mean he's sick of getting his ass kicked." Xuan smiled at Laura, then glanced at Anna. "You heard she's married to Mike Whitburg? High-school sweethearts."

"Oh, I've heard."

Laura ignored her. "What can I bring you, Sean? Something for lunch?"

"Just coffee for now."

Anna lifted her paper cup. "I'll take another one, too."

Without answering, Laura grabbed the cup out of her hand and flounced away.

"Jesus." Anna shook her head. "Speaking of high school."

"Laura's all right."

"She's so fucking condescending! And not just to me. I was in here with Helen Wright. Remember Helen? And Laura treated her like absolute garbage. It was unreal. Like, obviously Helen's sensitive about that birthmark, she spends all this time and energy trying to hide it, and here's Laura, going on and on about it, talking as loud as she can. Just humiliating her." Anna cracked her knuckles. "Laura embodies all the worst things about this town. And now she's popping out kids, perpetuating her line? It's fucking brutal. People like me, people who don't follow the herd, who've got the balls to do anything different: Game over."

Something loosened behind Xuan's eyes. "Try being Chinese and queer." He reached out for the pack of smokes on the table. "Do you mind?"

"Go ahead."

"Anyway, you show up here looking like that, what kind of welcome do you expect?"

"It's just ink. I'm not a fucking leper." Anna sat back in her chair. "So, you're gay? Since when?"

Xuan laughed. "Since always."

"Hey, remember Peter Martelli? Is he gay too?"

"Oh yeah."

"I knew it!" Anna smacked the table. "And are you out? Like, does Laura know?"

As if on cue, Laura reemerged, balancing two coffees on a metal tray: a white ceramic mug for Xuan, another paper cup for Anna.

"This isn't very eco-friendly." Anna lifted her lid, eying the frothy brown liquid. "Did you spit in mine?"

Xuan laughed and shook his head as Laura stalked away.

"You're just making it worse." He lifted his cup. "Mike knows, so I'm sure Laura does too. Some of the guys were a bit weird when I first came out, but most people are cool."

"And you never wanted to leave Guelph? You don't mind the minority-in-a-small-town thing?"

"I went to university in Toronto. Tried life in the big city. But you know, it's expensive. And then my mom got sick, so I moved back home."

"Is she better? Your mom?"

"Pretty much. It was breast cancer. She had a double mastectomy, chemo, the works." He crossed his legs and tapped the cigarette against his shoe, the ashes falling delicately to the pavement.

"I'm sorry. That sucks." She swallowed. "My mother had health issues too."

Xuan nodded. "Cancer?"

"Nothing like that. But still scary."

For a moment, she saw Joyce lying in bed with her blond hair spread across her silk pillowcase, purple smudges under her sunken eyes. Some of those episodes would have been bed rest; others recovering from yet another lost pregnancy. Anna remembered raised voices behind closed doors after Malcolm's business trips, then a new bracelet or necklace shining against Joyce's cotton nightgowns. Sometimes, if Annie was quiet enough, Joyce would pull back the covers and let her curl up beside her, close enough to hear the quick thready rhythm of her pulse.

"Well, then you know. It made me want to stay close to home. And then I met someone, so you know. Guelph's not all bad." Xuan smiled. "Sometimes things work out."

"Sometimes." Anna took a deep breath. "Well, listen. I wanted to ask you about our high-school yearbook. You were the editor, right?"

"One of the editors."

"Right. So there was this New Year's party in grade ten. At Olly Sutton's place." Her throat felt like it was closing up, but Anna pulled Helen's yearbook out of her bag, laid it on the table between them and flipped to the party photo, the heap of drunken grinning boys on the couch. "Look. This is from the party. That's me, right there, in my green sweater. And there's you." She slid her finger to the only Asian face in the group. "The thing is, I blacked out that night. I don't remember anything."

"Nothing?" Xuan's voice twisted in skepticism. "That seems—"

"Nothing. I swear, I have no memories from that night. I know what everyone says I did, but I'm looking for actual proof."

He looked at her.

"You mean the Polaroids."

"I heard about those. But are they really from that night?" Anna mashed her cigarette into the metal table. "I mean, look at these guys, in this picture." She stabbed her finger on each of them in turn. "Olly Sutton. Phil McKinley. You." Xuan made a noise and she spoke faster. "Glenn Starkey. Geoff Fraser. Plus there were others at that party." She looked at Xuan, searching his face. "I know I got around, okay? But that party...it was my first time. I just want to know what happened. You're saying you're gay. But what about then? Were you...involved? Do you know what went down?"

Xuan sucked in his breath. "I didn't have anything to do with girls. That party...I was there for a few hours. And of course I heard, afterwards...what happened." Gently, he closed the yearbook. "I'm sorry. The story I heard. I don't know if I even believed it, exactly. But those Polaroids..." He shrugged. "Everyone saw them. Guys passed them around. We were assholes. It was high school."

She stared into his brown eyes and nodded once, sharply.

"Fine. Yeah. But I need to know. Who fucked me? Was I into it? This whole idea, that there are photos out there. It's crazy, right?" She shivered. "I was thinking. Whoever took this yearbook picture, all of us on the couch. Maybe they took the Polaroids too?"

"That's a different kind of camera."

"You're sure?"

"A hundred percent. Show me that photo again." Anna flipped open the page and he pointed. "See, it's a rectangle. A four-by-six. Polaroids are square."

"Still. Can we find out who gave this picture to the yearbook?"

"People dropped them off. It could have been anyone."

"Not anyone. Someone who was there." Anna glared at him and rapped the yearbook with her knuckles. "Can't you help me look? Or are you trying to protect your buddy Olly?"

"Hey, Olly Sutton is a homophobic asshole. Most of those guys are decent, but he's a prick."

"So. Will you help? Or not?"

Xuan sighed. "I don't know. I've maybe got a few boxes of yearbook things at my mom's house. I could look through them—"

"There you go. Do that." Anna crossed her arms, anger cutting through the fog like a searchlight beam. "I'm not leaving town until I find out what happened. And if it turns out they were lying, Olly and all these other assholes, out there living their cozy lives...well, then fuck them, I'm coming for them all."

CHAPTER 8

"She'll have lots of options for flowers," Helen's mother said, her voice tinny through the phone's external speaker. "I thought midwinter meant we had to use roses. Not that there's anything wrong with that, but would they really suit Julia? Anyway, it turns out almost everything is still available. Lilies, tulips, orchids—"

"Poinsettias?"

Shutting her left eye, Helen bent towards the bathroom mirror and buffed silvery pigment over her eyelid. *Oyster*, this colour was called.

"Too Christmassy. We're going for a New Year's theme. I think black and white is too formal, but maybe we could put winter berries in the bouquets?"

Once the shading on both eyes was even, Helen swirled her brush against the next colour on the palette, a darker grey labeled *Dove*. This went over the silver in a sideways V along her upper lashline and her eyelid crease. Then it was blend, blend, blend.

Her mother had thrown herself into planning this wedding. Helen had been an eight-year-old flower girl when Linda married Gord, but that had been low-key, nothing like this New Year's extravaganza. Helen remembered clutching a bouquet of pink carnations during a quick afternoon ceremony at the courthouse. After he'd put the ring on Linda's finger, Gord had knelt on the carpet to present her and Julia with their own tiny amethyst rings. Helen still kept hers in a ceramic dish on her vanity, along with her collection of Nova Scotia seashells.

While her mother rambled on, Helen examined the magazine photo of Britney Spears propped behind the sink. Tonight was her first night out with Anna and she was replicating Britney's pale smoky eyes: layers of silver blending into icy blue eyeliner, sparkling white to highlight the inner corners. Dramatic but sophisticated.

"Come on, you have to come dancing sometime!" Anna had wheedled on the phone earlier. "You need to have more fun. The Trasheteria's got an eighties night tonight!"

"I hate dancing." Helen had nestled deeper into her corner of the couch with her mug of tea. Outside the window, tree branches swayed in the strong wind. "I only dance when I'm drunk, and I can't get drunk tonight. I'm working tomorrow."

"You're always working!"

"Yeah, it's called a job."

"Okay, what about that bar beside the Trash. Jimmy Jazz. Are you up for that? No dancing, just drinks. I'll give you all the deets on Sean Wu."

Helen picked up a turquoise pencil and traced her lower eyelid. Too intense? Maybe a lighter blue? She turned her face from one side to the other, considering.

"Helen?" Her mother's voice was impatient. "What do you think?"

"About what?"

"About pinecones?"

"Well," she hesitated, smudged the blue with a fingertip and added a touch of pearl to the inside corners, "they're nice?"

"Gord thought they'd be too rustic."

Helen sighed. "Why aren't you talking to Julia about this? She's the bride."

"What about those Save-the-Date cards? Did you get them in the mail? Yesterday you said you were finishing them up."

"I'll finish them tomorrow."

In fact, the unopened boxes of cards were still sitting on the kitchen table. Helen had gotten as far as printing the Excel spreadsheet and scanning the guest list before she shuddered and pushed it away. If those East Coast aunties and uncles with their unwanted opinions weren't bad enough, she'd spotted Oliver Sutton's name in the wedding party. Apparently he was closer friends with Glenn than she'd realized. And then, worst of all, Shane Wright and Karen Chang, her asshole father and his second wife. Helen had only met Karen once, at Julia's high-school graduation. She remembered stilettos, red nails, shiny black hair. Classic evil stepmother.

Helen let out her breath. "Mom, are you truly okay with Shane coming to this wedding?"

"Oh, Helen." Her tone was strained. "Your father's not such a bad guy. And you know he's close with Julia. I hope you'll be civil."

"No guarantees."

"Did you hear he's walking her down the aisle?"

"What?" Helen was suddenly breathless. "What about Gord?"

"Julia wanted your father."

"Of course she did." Helen flicked mascara along her lashes. "You know, those Save-the-Date cards weren't cheap. I had to buy eight boxes, plus fifty dollars' worth of stamps."

"Well, keep your receipts. You'll get the money back."

"I doubt it. Unless...is he paying for the wedding, too?"

Linda didn't say anything. Which said everything.

"Fuck! I mean, sorry, Mom. I have to go. I'll call you tomorrow." Helen pressed the button to hang up, resisting the urge to throw the cordless phone into the bathtub. "Fuck!"

"You almost done in there?" Thom called from the hall.

Helen slicked on one last coat of lipstick and opened the door.

Thom's eyes widened. "You're going somewhere?"

"I'm meeting Anna for drinks at Jimmy Jazz."

"Really." He rubbed the back of his neck, inside his Lollapalooza sweatshirt. "Don't you think she seems like bad news?"

"Why? Because of how she looks? You had blue hair when I first met you."

"She's very intense."

"You don't even know her."

"I guess not." Thom tilted his head. "Jimmy Jazz? Would you mind if I tag along? There's good music there on Monday nights."

"This is supposed to be girl-bonding time."

"You'll barely notice me, I promise. I'll just sit in the corner and have my beer."

"Fine," she said. "But can we go soon? I'm desperate for a drink."

*

At the bar, Helen didn't see anyone she knew, except over by the window, where Hakeem Washington was sitting with a group of other Black guys. He'd been at school with Helen since elementary, the only Black kid in their grade. He'd gone by "Henry" back then. He'd changed his name in grade eleven, showing up that September in a dashiki shirt with his hair grown into an Afro. She gave a little wave and Hakeem raised his drink in greeting, then turned back to his friends.

"Let's sit at the back, near the stage," Thom said. "I'll get drinks."

Helen ducked under the trailing leaves of a hanging plant and slid onto the wooden bench. She folded her coat and looked out the window at Jimmy Jazz's bricked-in patio. It was a rundown secret garden, charming despite the smoke-stained bricks and the old cigarette butts in the potted plants. Last summer, she'd sat out there with a bunch of college kids to celebrate Melissa's twenty-fifth birthday.

Helen looked up as Thom slid their drinks onto the table; his pint of dark beer, her bottle of Corona, half-choked with a wedge of lime.

"Cheers." He wiped his mouth. "No sign of your friend?"

"She said eight o'clock."

Helen crossed and uncrossed her legs under the table, pressing damp palms against the rough denim of her jeans. Finally, Anna made her entrance, breaking into a wide smile when she saw Helen. She pulled off her coat to reveal a shapeless grey sweater and jeans with cob-webby rips in the knees.

"Corona. Classic." She picked up Helen's beer and took a drink. "What're you drinking, Ted?"

"It's Thom." Thom cleared his throat. "This is the dark ale they've got on tap. Can I get you one?"

"I buy my own drinks." Anna said. "Be right back."

Thom slumped in his seat. "I was trying to be polite."

"Don't get weird on me." Helen poked his belly, soft under his sweatshirt. "I thought you were here for the music?"

"I am. He's just about to start." He gestured towards the stage, where a pale musician in a red bandana was tuning his guitar.

Anna came back with a gin and tonic and tapped her glass against Helen's bottle.

"Salud!"

"Cheers!" Helen said, then lowered her voice. "Did you bring your map?"

"To a bar?" Anna sat forward. "That reminds me, I have to tell you what happened with Kyle Bernier. He was a total nerd in high school, so he didn't know anything about the party, but I've never seen such an enormous—"

"Stop! No gross details!" Helen put her hands over her ears until Anna sat back, laughing. "You were going to tell me about Sean."

"Well, that's not his name anymore. Or it never really was. He's Shoo-enn. It's Chinese, spelled with an X. Second, he's gay."

"What? Really?"

"Lives with his boyfriend. Who's also from Guelph, but a couple of years older. So, you know. We bonded over our outsider status."

Helen laughed. "It's not the same."

"Sure it is. Girls, guys. I don't discriminate."

"Wow." Helen digested this information. "Okay, wow."

"Anyway. We caught up, played twenty questions, talked about the yearbook." Anna stared past Helen's shoulder.

"What?" Helen twisted in her seat, but there was nothing there. "What is it?"

"The rumours were true. There are pictures. Some asshole documented the whole night with a Polaroid camera."

Helen stared at her. "Oh my God."

"I know." Anna sat back on the bench and pulled her cigarettes from her pocket. "Gross, right? Someone made some good old-fashioned child pornography, starring me."

"Someone? He didn't say who?"

"He says he doesn't know."

"So what do we do? Go to the cops?"

"Cops? Fuck, no. And anyway, where's the evidence? No, Xuan's going to look through his old yearbook stuff, see if he can find any more pictures. At least, he says he will."

"Would those be at the school?"

"No, his mom's place. But…," Anna tilted her head, "we could do that too. You and me, go back to Laurier, to the yearbook room. Maybe they've got some kind of archive?"

"You want to go back?" Helen asked. "With Olly teaching there?"

"Olly." Anna did something complicated with her fingers, making the cigarette disappear and flick back into sight. She shook her head. "Man, fuck that guy."

"You can't smoke in here." Thom said, pointed at the wall over her head. "There's a sign."

"I'll be done by the time they notice."

Thom opened his mouth, but Helen spoke quicker.

"Could you get me another beer, Thom? I'll pay you back."

When he left the table, Anna flicked ash towards his empty seat.

"The famous Thom."

"You're freaking him out."

"He's very easily freaked out." Anna leaned back, lifting her heavy boots onto the bench. "I don't get what you see in him."

"What do you mean? He's just my roommate."

"Right." Anna smirked. She made a circle with her fingers and pistoned the cigarette in and out. "Your roommate."

"Anna!" Helen's face went hot. "How did you know?"

"It's completely obvious. But whatever, I don't judge."

"We don't talk about that, okay? Don't—"

Thom was back at the table, sliding another Corona to Helen. "I ordered shots," he said, staring at Anna. "Tequila. That cool?"

"Totally. Love it. Let's party," said Anna.

Helen gulped her beer. Jimmy Jazz was suddenly too dark, the music too loud. She tried to get Thom's attention, then Anna's, but they were staring at each other as the waitress approached with a tray of tequila shots. Before Helen could hand out lemon slices, Anna and Thom were already throwing back their shots, banging their empty glasses onto the table.

"Keep up, girl," said Anna, shoving a tequila shot towards Helen.

Helen was already lightheaded, but she drank it down. Almost immediately, the waitress came back and Thom distributed more little glasses, lining them up as Anna drummed on the table. Rapidly, glaring at each other, they took their third shots, then their fourth.

"Anna. Hey, Anna," said Helen. She had to change this vibe, fast. "Did you see who's here from Laurier? Hakeem Washington." Her stiff lips stumbled over his name. "At the front, at one of the tables by the door."

"Oh yeah?" The tiny blue stars on Anna's temple flashed in the dim light as she bolted to her feet.

Helen twisted to watch her go, then looked down. Somehow, she was holding another shot. "This is not a good idea," she said, then threw it back.

Then Anna was back, squeezing Helen further down the bench. "Hakeem got hot! You didn't mention that!"

"You talked to him?"

"He says he did the Muslim Brotherhood thing, back in high school. Totally straight-edge; no drinking, no parties. Says he never even looked at my pictures."

"What pictures?" Thom asked.

"Nothing," said Helen. She lowered her voice for Anna. "The photos, Olly's party...I don't think Thom has to know anything."

"I don't give a shit what he knows."

"Okay." Helen swallowed. "Maybe we should slow down, though."

"Just one more." Anna held up a finger, grinned and took another glass from the tray.

Thom laughed too and raised one finger, then another, and another. Helen shut her eyes. When she opened them again, she was alone at the table. There was only one glass left on the tray.

"Tell Thom to drink it," she said aloud, to nobody. Unsteadily, she stood up and headed to the women's bathroom. The door wouldn't open. She wove her way to the bar.

A glass appeared, brimming with ice cubes. Helen held it with both hands and sucked at the surface, peering through the crowd. Was Anna outside smoking? There was Thom, at the end of the bar, talking to a pretty girl with short blond hair. As she watched, the girl laughed and put a hand on his arm.

Helen swallowed hard and looked away. She took a breath, irritated with herself, with Thom. Of course he could do what he wanted. If he wanted to hit on some girl wearing cheap sparkly eyeshadow and a low-cut shirt, that was completely fine. She didn't even care.

She tottered back to their table, drank off that last lonely shot and coughed at the acrid taste. She sank onto the bench and closed her eyes. No, that was worse. The room was vibrating. Over at the bar, Thom leaned close to the girl, a stupid smile on his face. She should talk to him. She stood up, but her stomach seemed to stay behind, lurching sideways. Oh no. She ran to the bathroom and banged on the door. After a moment, Anna emerged, followed by Hakeem. Both of them adjusting their clothing.

Helen squeezed past them and into the stall, just in time. The tile was cold on her knees, watery vomit burning her nose as she threw up into the disgusting toilet, surrounded by crude graffiti. Someone else knocked on the door as she crouched, head whirling, retching. Finally, she wobbled to her feet and rinsed her hands in the sink, looking away from her reflection in the mirror: her lipstick gone, her eyeliner smudged so her face looked strange and lopsided.

When she got back to the table, Anna was alone. Her smiling face wavered and doubled in the darkness as Helen collapsed onto the seat beside her.

"It's a good thing you puked," Anna said. "You looked green as hell."

"The bathroom?" Helen heard herself say. The bench seemed to be rising and falling beneath her. She laid her head onto the wet tabletop, willing the spinning to stop. Then Thom was beside her, his hand warm on her shoulder.

"She doesn't look good."

"She's fine. She just threw up." Anna said. "Don't worry, I'll get her home."

"I've got it. There are taxis outside," said Thom. "Come on, Helen. Up you get."

He helped Helen to her feet, sliding an arm around her waist as she staggered through the bar. Out on the street, she looked around blearily. "There's no cabs."

Thom rolled his eyes and pointed at the green and black taxi by the curb.

"Don't let her throw up," the driver barked, as Thom bundled her into the back and climbed in beside her. "It's fifty bucks extra for cleaning if she throws up."

"I won't throw up," Helen mumbled, trying to cross her fingers. She pushed the button to lower the window, wanting the clean night wind against her face. "Thom. I'm sorry."

He made a disgusted noise. "I told you she was bad news."

CHAPTER 9

The next morning, Anna woke up to the phone ringing. Eyes still closed, she rolled onto her back and fumbled for the receiver.

"Oh my God," Helen's voice whimpered into her ear. "What happened last night?"

Anna opened her eyes.

"Are you okay?"

"I feel like death. I've never puked so much in my life."

"Drink water," said Anna. She turned on her side and pulled up the covers, shielding herself from the sunlight peeking through the curtains. "What time is it?"

"Almost ten. I called in sick. Can I come over?" Helen's voice was piteous. "Thom's putting together a bookcase and I swear he's being extra loud just to spite me."

"Sure, swing by," Anna said, yawning. She hung up and fell back to sleep.

When the doorbell rang, she stumbled downstairs and opened the front door to Helen, who wore dark glasses and a trench coat.

"You don't look that bad," Anna said. She waved to Mr. Vetrone, unloading bags from his BMW, then stepped back to let Helen in. "Did you have fun last night?"

"Not exactly." Helen took off her sunglasses, revealing a gory starburst in her left eye. "Look at this. I don't know what happened."

"Ooh, you burst a blood vessel. How much did you throw up?"

"A lot." Helen trudged into the living room, where she wilted onto one of the white leather sofas. "How are you okay? You drank way more than me."

"I don't know. Practice?" Anna yawned. "You're a lightweight."

"I'm never drinking again. Ever." Helen groaned, pulling up her feet and lying on her side.

"Next time we'll go dancing. Without your killjoy boyfriend."

"Roommate."

"Fuck buddy." Helen shot her a look, but Anna grinned. "Hey, we're grownups. Fuck who you want. You ready for coffee?"

"Can I use your bathroom first?"

Anna started the percolator, lit a cigarette, and set out boxes of cereal: Lucky Charms, Cocoa Puffs and Cap'n Crunch. When the coffee was ready and Helen still hadn't reappeared, she called down the hall.

"All right in there?"

Finally, the toilet flushed and Helen emerged, hand pressed to her head. Anna held out a mug.

"Here. I can add some Bailey's, if you want?"

Helen shuddered. "God, no." She took a sip, then looked up at Anna, eyes wide. "Did you really hook up with Hakeem Washington?"

"Did I?" Anna flashed to the night before. She remembered sitting on Hakeem's lap, leading him to the bathroom. "Yeah, I guess."

"Will you see him again, do you think?"

"We didn't exactly exchange numbers." Anna finished her coffee, hoisted herself up on the counter and poured herself another shot of Bailey's.

Helen grimaced. "Thom says you're bad news. A bad influence."

"Why do you care what he thinks?"

Anna took a sip of the sweet liqueur and looked down at Helen, with her busted-up eye, her face covered with thick makeup. She looked so concerned, so pitiful, that Anna started to laugh.

"What?" Helen looked indignant.

Anna tried to stifle her giggles. "Just…your face! You look…" She dissolved into laughter. "Oh my God, Helen, you're so…"

"Are you high? Did you take something before I came?"

That made Anna laugh harder. She doubled over, trying to catch her breath. "Sure, I'm high. High on life," she wheezed, between gasps. She laughed until she was wiping away tears. This was that feeling she'd been missing, the feeling of floating just a little bit off the ground, of pure affectionate joy. She took a deep breath through her nose, coughed, and laughed again. "Come on up," she said. "The view is fine."

"You're crazy," Helen said, but she was smiling.

"You say that like it's a bad thing." Anna lifted the bottle of Bailey's and this time, Helen held out her coffee and let her add a shot. They clinked the cups together. "Aren't you glad I'm back?"

*

As April folded into May, Anna filled in her map. She snaked the Range Rover up and down the streets of Guelph, past the tall brick houses of Exhibition Park, through the bourgeois postwar subdivisions by the university. She stopped at Helen's old house near the yellow stone ruins at Goldie Mill Park, let the engine idle outside the Suttons' gabled Tudor while she squinted through the windshield, brooding. Which window looked out of the bedroom where she'd woken up after the party? Was the hot tub still in the backyard? When Olly's mother came outside with gardening gloves and a rake, Anna gunned the engine and drove away.

The snow melted, joggers took over the streets and her map grew heavy with ink, the paper tearing in neighbourhoods where the streets were too close together. The symbols multiplied over the downtown core as she ran into different Laurier classmates: Josh Tatlock behind the counter at the Royal Bank, Pam Tzavaras and Ayako Hayashi working at opposite ends of the old Eaton Centre, Ben Guthrie on the street by the naked family fountain. None of them helpful. "No time to talk." "Sorry, don't remember." "Why are you asking me?"

Finally, she crossed paths with another guy from the yearbook photo: Evan Cohen, dressed in a shirt and tie, walking his schnauzer at twilight through Exhibition Park.

"Evan?" Their eyes locked and Anna skewed to a stop on the pine-needle-covered gravel. Evan wore glasses now, thick plastic frames over deep-set blue eyes. "Evan Cohen?"

Evan stared at her, his expression curdling into revulsion. Then he looked away, tugging his dog in a wide circle off the path. As he passed, he turned his head and spat on the damp earth as if he was warding off a witch.

Anna sucked in her breath.

"Fuck you too, Evan!"

Stiff-legged, she walked to one of the park's concrete benches. She scuffed her boots in the dirt and stared, unseeing, at the kids in wet snow pants playing over by the slide. As the cold seeped through her jeans and the spring twilight closed in, Anna thought about the red lines on her map, the triangle she'd draw in this park, the white streets still haloing Laurier. She knew where she had to go next.

*

As soon as she stepped onto school property, Anna felt like she was moving through a dream, like she might glimpse Phil McKinley smoking with his pals in front of his beat-up minivan, or Olly Sutton throwing a pass up the football field as the spirit band played the school song. Crossing the student parking lot felt like hovering above herself, overlooking the grid of spaces where she'd followed various boys into various cars.

When she pulled open the door by the auditorium, the school smell washed over her, a familiar mix of sweat, paper, and cleaning supplies. Still, she was filled with a dreamlike calm. This didn't feel real. Anna was a spy, a ghost, a memory. The hallway stretched out, narrower but longer than she remembered, lined with grey-painted metal lockers. Her footsteps echoed back to her as she moved past the first classroom, where a ponytailed teacher stood pointing at the blackboard with a piece of chalk. The teacher looked younger than Anna, barely older than the teenagers slouched in their seats.

For the first time, it occurred to Anna that some of her old teachers might still be here. It had only been ten years, after all. But she wasn't that worried. She'd probably slip in and out of the yearbook room without anyone seeing her at all.

She paused where the hallway split, trying to recall the school's layout. The yearbook office was by the English classrooms, wasn't it? Upstairs.

By the auditorium, Anna glanced at the display case and did a double take at the framed poster on display: Phil McKinley, spotlit and sweaty, wearing an unzipped leather jacket and faded jeans, caught mid-strum on a shiny red guitar. The picture was signed with a black Sharpie scrawl and the label underneath said *Philip McKinley, Class of 1997*. Her mind filled with a sudden up-close vision of Phil's face pressing against hers, his mouth open in a stifled gasp. Anna shuddered. Had he made a personal appearance here at the school, performed in the auditorium with his big-shot band?

Up on the second floor, she quickened her pace, glancing into classrooms as if she might glimpse the girl she'd been, sketching diagrams of animal cells beside teenaged Helen with her patchy concealer. Or the doped-up mess she'd become, trading hand jobs for pills in the back of the library.

Anna shook her head. She had to stay focused, even if the air felt thicker as she got closer to the end of the hall, harder to breathe, harder to push through. The yearbook room was up ahead. Her pace slowed; she'd nearly reached the door when she heard heels click-clacking behind her.

"Can I help you?"

Anna turned to face a grey-haired woman in a skirt suit. The past telescoped into the present as she recognized an old English teacher. But what was her name?

"Hi!" She mustered a smile. "I'm an old student, from back in the nineties. You're Mrs…?"

The teacher hesitated. "Mrs. Cruikshank," she said.

"Mrs. Cruikshank! I think you taught me in grade nine? I'm Anna, Annie Leverett. We acted out scenes from that play, something about 'the kindness of strangers'?"

"*Streetcar Named Desire*. Do you have a visitor's pass?"

"I just dropped by."

"Hmm." Mrs. Cruikshank's mouth turned down.

"I've been away for a few years," Anna said, speaking faster. "But I've been talking to Sean Wu. Remember him? He used to edit the yearbook. We wanted to find some old photos—"

"I'm sorry." The teacher's eyes lingered on her tattoos. "Abby, you said?"

"Anna."

"I'm sorry, Anna, but you can't just wander the halls. We don't allow that."

"I'd only be a minute. Just to look through the archives—"

"No." Mrs. Cruikshank seemed to grow taller in her heels. "You can speak to the principal if you want, but he's very busy." She checked her watch. "Come with me, please. The bell's about to ring for lunch."

Anna's shoulders dropped. Her body felt heavy as she trailed Mrs. Cruikshank down the hall, past the staircase she'd come up, towards the main entrance of the school.

When a familiar electric chime sounded, students began pouring out of the classrooms. They filled the hallway, waves of young bodies jostling past Anna with barely a glance, bringing back that feeling of unreality, making her feel invisible. Mrs. Cruikshank greeted a group of girls, reprimanded a tall boy running towards the stairs. They were nearly at the end of the hall when Anna glanced into a classroom and felt a dull pulse of shock. There was Olly Sutton behind a desk, clean-shaven, wearing a collared shirt and tie.

Anna froze so abruptly that a student bumped into her from behind.

"Keep walking, please."

Mrs. Cruikshank touched her arm. Anna took another step, then ducked through the crowd of students, into Olly's classroom.

"Hey, asshole."

"Annie," he said, raising his eyebrows. "You came by for a visit?"

"Hardly. You think I want to see you?"

Mrs. Cruikshank was back at Anna's side. "I found her in the hall. She wanted to go through the yearbook files. Looking for photos, she said."

"Oh really?" Olly's smile widened. His eyes shifted to Mrs. Cruikshank. "Annie used to be a Laurier girl. Did she tell you, Renée?" He closed the textbook on his desk, tucked it under his arm and ambled over. "Poor Annie's been through a lot. Drugs, mental health problems, all sorts of things. She dropped out, I think. Or was she asked to leave?"

Anna pressed her lips together.

"I'm going down for lunch," Mrs. Cruikshank said. "You'll see her out?"

"No problem. You go ahead." Olly stretched out his arm and Anna tensed, but he only reached past her and snapped off the lights. He looked at Anna as Mrs. Cruikshank click-clacked away down the hall. "You want to close the door so we can talk?"

Anna crossed her arms, blocking the open doorway.

"I'm not leaving."

Olly looked up at the clock on his wall. "I've got class again in forty-five minutes."

"I meant Guelph, asshole."

"Yeah, I heard you've been making the rounds." He shifted the textbook under his arm. "I wondered when it would be my turn."

"Fuck you!"

"You did that already." He stepped closer, dropping his voice. "You fucked pretty much everyone, before you flamed out and ran away. And now, what, you think we've all forgotten what a mess you are?"

"I'm not leaving," Anna was trembling now. "Not until I find out what really happened."

Olly shrugged. "Stay, go, do whatever the fuck you want." He leaned in, so close she could smell his after-shave. "No one cares. You don't matter to anyone."

There were footsteps in the hallway and she turned to see a group of lanky teenaged boys. "Hey, Mr. Sutton," one of them said as they passed.

"Hey, guys. Hope you've been studying for my test." Olly looked back at Anna. "You can find your own way out. And don't come back here, Annie. Not unless you want to be charged with trespassing."

CHAPTER 10

Helen lay back in her chipped enamel bathtub, trying to focus on the article in her magazine: *Ten sex tricks every woman needs to master*. Rain rattled against the window as she turned the page, squinting up at the racy line drawings. How come Thom's *Maxim* magazine never taught him to be better at sex? He didn't have any sophisticated moves. Yesterday, she'd come home in a shitty mood after Carmen scooped her on a sale with one of her oldest customers. She'd barely got in the door before Thom sidled up behind her, wrapped his arms around her waist and breathed onto the back of her neck. Five minutes later, they were in his bedroom with his hand down the front of her jeans, his fingers pushing past the elastic of her underwear.

"Hey, do you think," Helen murmured as she moved against his fingers. "Could you go down on me? It was a rough day. Would you mind?"

Thom's fingers stilled.

"I'd rather not." He glanced at his bedside clock and withdrew his hand, wiping it against his sheet. "The guys are coming over. You always take such a long time, you know?"

Helen swallowed her frustration. "Fine. No big deal."

"Can we still…?"

"Sure, yeah. Just get the condom."

They'd been sleeping together for five years. The first time had been only a couple of weeks after Crystal moved out. Thom had been moping around the apartment, renting action movies and drinking too much.

One night, he convinced Helen to watch *Armageddon*. Right as Bruce Willis pressed the button to blow up the asteroid, Thom rolled over and kissed her. Her mind had gone blank as he pawed at her breasts. When he pulled back, brown eyes questioning, Helen managed a nod and they stumbled down the hall to her room. It was over quickly. The next morning, she soaked the smear of blood out of her sheet before Thom even came out of his room. She stared at herself in the mirror, surprised she didn't look different, more adult.

Now, Helen flipped past the sex articles and sank lower, so that only her fingertips were out of the water, her nails the same pale lavender as the bubbles. She'd painted them last night, hiding in her room when Thom's buddies came over to watch the hockey game. At halftime, they'd crashed down the hallway, making her door shudder as they scuffled in front of the bathroom.

"You got enough makeup, Thom? Want a touch-up?"

"Holy shit. Your roommate's seriously addicted."

"Can you blame her? You've seen what she looks like!"

Why were his friends such assholes? Maybe Thom was an asshole too and Helen just couldn't see it. Still, she kept sleeping with him. They'd stopped a few times over the years, while he dated other girls. Each time, Helen learned he'd broken up with his girlfriend when he came scratching at her bedroom door. Each time, she let him in. It was Thom or nobody. Was she supposed to choose nobody?

She could hear his voice in the other room, distorted through the water and the cast-iron tub. Then a girl's voice, laughing and indistinct.

Helen sat up so quickly that the magazine dipped into the bath. She brushed the foam off the darkened paper and dropped the magazine beside the tub. Who was here? Someone from his work? That short-haired girl he'd flirted with a few weeks ago at Jimmy Jazz?

Then the voices stopped and the apartment was silent. Helen slid back under her bubbles. Was Thom kissing that girl? Leading her into his room? She imagined them stripping, sliding between his sheets. The only sounds were the rain on the window, the waves on the side of the tub as Helen sank deeper, slipping her hand between her thighs.

Abruptly, the bathroom door rattled and Anna burst into the room.

"Hey!"

"Anna!" Helen bolted upright, rearranging the bubbles so she was covered up to her neck. Anna was wild-eyed, her smell of cigarettes and body odour overwhelming the vanilla-scented candles. "What happened?"

"I just came from Laurier. I was looking for the year-book room, right, when this dried-up hag of an English teacher starts lecturing me about how inappropriate it is for me to be there. Then, next thing I know, I'm face-to-face with Mr. Olly Sutton."

"You saw him?"

"I was in his classroom! He made me sound like a fucking criminal in front of this other teacher. But like, with this fake sympathy. 'Poor Annie, she had so many problems.' As if he's not one of my problems!" Anna dropped onto the toilet seat and put her head in her hands. "He kicked me out. Claimed I was trespassing."

"Shit."

"I guess I've burned that bridge." Anna passed her hand over the candles burning next to the sink, the flames licking her fingers. "So, I say we go out tonight. We get shit-faced drunk, we pick up some guys—"

"Anna."

"Seriously, you can do better than him," Anna jerked a thumb over her shoulder. "We could go into Toronto, find some better bars, with better guys. Maybe a dance club."

"No." Helen swished her hands underwater. "No way."

"Second option. We stay here, we get drunk, I find out what kind of car Olly drives and I get myself a base-ball bat."

"Stop."

"Honestly, fuck that guy. 'No one cares about you,' he says, like he's the fucking mayor of Guelph. Like I'm dogshit. Less than dogshit."

Anna stood up and moved to the sink. She sniffed Thom's deodorant, then opened the drawer and picked out a MAC eyeliner. She swiped at the mirror to clear the fog and crayoned black pigment across her lids, her eyes blooming like dark flowers on time-lapse video, the stars at her temple seeming to twinkle in the steamy air.

"Hey, is your birthmark getting darker?"

"It's the heat." Helen lifted her hand. "When my body gets warmer...don't stare at it."

"People stare at me all the time." Anna turned back to the mirror.

"Anna." Helen blew out an exasperated breath. "Do you even remember what tomorrow is?"

"Tomorrow?" Anna frowned.

"May nineteenth. My birthday." Helen said. "Yeah. And Carmen scheduled me for a six-hour shift tomor-row, and I've already worked all day today. I'm tired, and I was trying to have a bath and relax, and you come bursting in here, and you didn't even ask how I'm doing! And I know you're worked up, over Olly, but like, what about me?"

Anna stared at Helen.

"I'm sorry," she said. "I forgot."

"I know." Helen said. "It's okay. I get why you're here, why you stayed in Guelph. It's just, you reach this crazy pitch, sometimes. I can't keep up."

"I'm sorry," Anna said. "I'll go."

"Anna—"

"It's fine. I get it. It's all good. I'll leave you alone. Or…," she tilted her head. "d'you want me to tell Thom to come join you?"

Helen flicked water at her, and Anna laughed.

"I'll take you out tomorrow, for your birthday. Okay? It'll be your day. I promise."

*

Helen's mother called first thing the next morning.

"Twenty-six! I can't believe it," said Linda. "When I was twenty-six, I was already pregnant with Julia. You were two years old."

"Crazy," Helen said.

"Different times. She sent me pictures of her dress. I'll email them to you." Linda said. "It's beautiful. Old-fashioned lace with a ribbon trim."

"Great." Helen's fingers tightened around the receiver. "Is Gord there too? Can I talk to him?"

"He had to go in early for an emergency surgery. A beagle, I think? He sends his best wishes. What about Shane? Did you hear from him?"

"He sent a card."

Every year, her father mailed her a birthday card containing a five-hundred-dollar cheque. Every year, Helen tore it up. When the card came last week, Helen didn't even open it, just ripped the envelope into satisfying halves, quarters, eighths. She'd rained the paper squares into the blue box, watched them settle over the milk cartons and junk mail.

Helen hung up the phone feeling worse than before. She always felt shitty on her birthday, even without her mother's reminders that her life was stalled, off-track. Meanwhile, Julia was speeding ahead, hitting all the right milestones. Law school. Marriage. Little Miss Perfect, doing everything right.

Helen left the apartment an hour early so she had time for her annual tradition: a birthday shopping spree at Rexall, loading up on cheap and cheerful new cosmetics before her shift at work. L'Oréal mascaras, Maybelline lip gloss, Cover Girl pencils.

She stopped by the pharmacy to fill her birth control prescription, then wandered the aisles. At the L'Oréal display, she popped the lid off a tester lipstick. *Honey Glow* was a light smoky nude, slightly shimmery, not too pink or too brown. The back of her hand was already striped with eyeliner and lipstick, so she drew a creamy beige line down the inside of her wrist and peered at the colour, considering. The texture wasn't bad for drugstore lipstick, the colour lighter than her other nude lipsticks: more fawn than taupe. And the smell? Helen brought the tester up to her face and sniffed: a little perfumey but definitely wearable. She recapped the tester and dropped an unopened tube in her basket.

She ran her fingers along a rack of spring lip gloss colours, from palest pink to darkest burgundy. Usually, Helen went for the tamer colours, but this year she'd get something bolder, something she could wear out with Anna. Maybe they'd even go dancing tonight. Maybe this birthday wouldn't be as shitty as last year's, as all the shitty years before that.

Helen's last decent birthday had been when she turned thirteen. That was when her mother finally agreed to let her try laser treatment. After months of Helen pestering, pleading, promising, "I can handle the pain!" Linda had stroked her hair, cried with her, and finally relented, signing her up for a twenty-course treatment at Sick Kids. The night of her thirteenth birthday, Helen had leaned close to the bathroom mirror and covered the burgundy blotch with one hand, imagining both cheeks even and clear.

Every Wednesday for the next three months, Linda booked the afternoon off work and drove Helen into Toronto. The sessions were forty-five minutes of agony. The laser snapped at her skin like a burning elastic band, leaving her reddened and swollen for the rest of the week. Of course this meant piling on more concealer, looking even more freakish and disfigured. Three months into the treatment, the doctor took her mother aside, confirming what they'd already figured out: it wasn't working. Helen wasn't a good candidate. Something in her pigmentation, in the position of her tiny malformed blood vessels, made the lasers ineffective.

Helen picked up a tube of liquid eyeliner, painted a thick black stroke across her hand and tossed the package into her basket. Things would be different, now that Anna was back at her side.

"Helen Wright?"

She grabbed a cellophane pack of false lashes and made her way to the back of the store, where the elderly pharmacist beckoned her to the counter.

"You're Helen Wright?" Helen could see his brown scalp through his thinning white hair, scaly patches crying out for moisturizer. "Just one month of the Arlesse today?"

"Three months."

He tapped at his keyboard. "Still no private drug plan?"

Helen shook her head. Hourly workers didn't get benefits. She'd applied for a management position last year, but the interview had been a disaster. She'd frozen up, sweated through her blouse, going so blank that the HR woman's questions all sounded as garbled as the adults in a Charlie Brown cartoon: "Mwah-wah wah. Wah wah?" Her co-worker Melissa, on the other hand, aced her interview. After a couple of months as a counter manager in Guelph, she'd snagged a job in Montreal with a full-time salary, trips to seminars, and a full benefits package.

"You can take a seat," the pharmacist said, peering over his bifocals. "It'll be another couple of minutes."

Helen settled into a metal chair beside a mother and a baby. The woman looked up briefly, then went back to her paperback romance. Her baby's head was tufted with dark hair. Blinking solemn blue eyes, the baby brought a pudgy hand to its mouth and sucked on its fingers.

Helen looked away. It was three years since she'd had that scare. Almost four. Imagine how life would be different, if she were here with a little boy with Thom's honey-brown eyes. Or a girl, all pink cheeks and pigtails. Just think, if she had a baby, she'd leapfrog her sister once and for all.

She turned to the magazine shelf and picked up the latest *Marie Claire*, flipping to the back to read her birthday horoscope. Taurus, the year ahead: *Rise above small problems and discomforts and tune into the bigger picture.*

Late spring is an excellent time for partnership. She looked at the Scorpio predictions for Anna: *Awareness is always the first step to healing. Keep an open mind and you'll see the opportunity that something holds.*

"Helen Wright?"

Helen kept her eyes on the register as the pharmacist scanned each item, biting the inside of her cheek as the total jumped higher and higher. When it passed a hundred dollars, she held up her hand and pulled the false lashes out of the basket. If she'd kept her father's cheque… but no. It wasn't worth it. Helen picked the lip pencil out of the basket, then the tube of *Honey Glow.* She didn't really need another nude lipstick. But it was her birthday. She handed the lipstick to the waiting pharmacist.

"Go ahead," she told him. "Run it through."

*

Helen had just demonstrated the Scar Reduction line to a teenaged girl with deep dog-bite scars when Anna came by the Façade counter. The poor girl was so thrilled with the coverage that she actually teared up, smudging her thick green eyeliner. Helen dropped a couple of extra samples into the shopping bag before stapling it closed.

Helen smiled to herself as she recorded the sale, adding the numbers to her weekly tally sheet. *Screw you, Carmen.* If she kept up this pace, she'd be 20 percent above her sales goal for the week.

Meanwhile, Anna sat reading a glossy product brochure, swivelling back and forth on the stool. She looked up when the teenaged girl walked away.

"Happy birthday!"

"Thanks. I've still got another hour until Barb takes over."

"I'll wait. Today's all about you." She smiled, then tapped the brochure. "Have you seen this bullshit?" Anna put on a high-pitched voice: "'Magic Blending Cream. Now in eight more shades of beautiful.' What are they saying? 'Now we make makeup for black people'?"

Helen glanced at the photo, a multicultural group of girls with their heads thrown back in melodramatic laughter.

"It's a cheesy ad. But it's a good product."

Anna turned the page. "Shit, look at that scar."

"Yeah, but see how the Vanishing Cream covers it up?" Helen pointed. "If you ever want to cover your tattoos, that's what you need. It's one of our bestsellers."

"That's what you use?"

Anna reached for the display photo of Helen's face.

"Put that down." Helen tucked the frame away, behind the lipsticks. "No, Vanishing Cream is for the body, it's heavier than our face products. Here, give me your arm. I'll show you. Say you want to hide your tattoos for a few hours."

Anna set her palm on the counter but flinched when Helen touched her wrist.

"Relax." Helen patted Anna's hand and rolled up the sleeve of her plaid shirt. "First, you clean the skin. Then we dab some product here and blend it outwards, adding more as we go."

Touching Anna's arm made Helen remember sitting together in her parents' basement, comparing skin tones over a bowl of popcorn. They'd lined up their forearms, Helen's warm olive contrasting with Annie's freckled milky white. Now, with the Vanishing Cream, she had the strange feeling that she was peeling Anna's skin back instead of covering it up.

"What do you think?" Helen asked, after she'd dusted with powder to set the colour.

"It's trippy. You think I could go undercover, sneak back into Laurier?"

"You could try."

"Don't I look young and innocent?" Anna tilted her wrists back and forth, then unhooked her nose ring and batted her eyes.

"Well…"

"Right. We're not talking about that today." Anna bent her fingers and furrowed her nails down her arm, clawing parallel lines through the fresh makeup. "You'll get a commission if I buy this shit?"

"Yeah. But it's not cheap." Helen picked up the cream. "This one is sixty dollars."

"That's fine." Anna fit her nose ring back in place. "If she sees the bill, my mother will be happy I'm finally buying makeup."

"You want the whole set? Brushes, sponges, too?"

"Load me up."

Helen was piling up products, calculating prices and commission, when her boss approached the counter.

"Helen." Carmen gave her a pained smile. "You know our policy. Please ask your friend to wait for you elsewhere until your shift is over."

"Hang on," said Anna. "She's selling me this stuff."

"Oh!" Carmen's voice changed. "Of course. I wasn't aware you were making a purchase."

"Can you add a few more bottles, Helen?" Anna gave a bright smile. "And those lipsticks you mentioned. Throw them in, too."

When Helen saw the total, she whistled. "Let me give you my employee discount," she said, entering the code.

Half an hour later, she met Anna outside the break room.

"Thanks for waiting," she said. "Sorry about my boss."

"I'm sorry that you have to deal with her. Now, tell me." Anna swept out her arm in a gesture that encompassed the whole department. "If you could buy whatever fancy high-priced makeup you wanted, what would you get?"

"Oh, man. Anything?" Helen scanned the floor, then nodded at Guerlain's limited-edition Météorites, a round silver box holding a jumble of shimmering pearls. "These, probably. But they're eighty dollars."

"Perfect." Anna signalled to the woman behind the counter. "Can we get one gift-wrapped?" She turned back to Helen and grinned. "Happy birthday, girl."

CHAPTER 11

A few days later, a naked Anna stretched languorously and rolled onto her belly, watching Johnnie Campbell scramble back into his blue coveralls.

"We can't do this anymore," Johnnie said. He stood up and looked in the mirror, fixing his mussed brown hair.

"Okay." She smiled up at him, resting her chin on her palms. "Whatever you say."

He turned. "I mean it this time. It's not fair on Samantha."

Johnnie's gaze wavered, travelling along her naked body. Every time he stopped by, they went through this charade. *I was in the neighbourhood. No, I shouldn't come in.* Then, as Anna tugged him over the threshold, *This has to be the last time.* Who did he think he was fooling?

Invitingly, she rolled onto her side and trailed her hand along her hip.

"You sure you can't stay a little longer?"

Johnnie shook his head. "I have to drop off my truck." He pulled a couple of neatly rolled joints from his hip pocket and laid them on the edge of her desk.

"Thanks," she said. "What do I owe you?"

"Don't worry about it." His cheeks went pink. God, he was adorable.

"And when can I expect my next delivery?"

"Not until next week. After Geoff's party."

"A party?" She yawned. "Can I come?"

"I mean…if you want. You remember Geoff Fraser? He won all those snowboarding awards. Almost made it to the Olympics. He's got the best weed in the city."

"Geoff Fraser?"

Anna's skin prickled. She sat up, looking towards the yearbook buried under the board games on her desk. Geoff was in that photo; half-crushed by his drunken friends, laughing, inches away from her teenaged self in that lost green sweater. She'd run out of steam on her map, and she was still waiting to hear from Xuan, but Geoff Fraser might provide some answers.

Anna stood up. "I want to come to this party."

"Yeah?" Johnnie's grey eyes widened. "I don't know how many people you'll know there. He lives with his brother, hangs out with a younger crowd—"

"I don't care." Shivering, she looked around for her T-shirt. "Give me his address. I'll be there."

*

"Enough already," said Anna, as Helen frowned at herself in the mirror, adjusting her turquoise peasant blouse. "It doesn't matter what you wear."

"I'm just not sure about this shirt." Helen lifted the shirt's beaded tassels and let them fall. "Tell me again how you heard about this party?"

"Johnnie mentioned it."

"Who?"

"Johnnie Campbell. You know him, he was at Laurier."

"When did you see him?"

Anna sighed. "We've hooked up a few times."

"A few times?" Helen turned her back and lifted the blouse over her head, thick beige bra corseting the soft skin of her torso. "I'm trying a different top. Really? Johnnie Campbell?"

"I thought we had a 'don't ask, don't tell' policy about who we're fucking. You don't want to talk about Thom—"

"I definitely don't." Helen turned her head, inspecting her black halter top. "What do you think of this one?"

"It's fine."

"I'm not sure." Helen fiddled with the strap behind her neck. "So, the party's at Geoff Fraser's? And you're going to talk to him?"

"Talk, or…whatever."

"Really?" Helen dropped her hands and looked at her. "Johnnie won't care?"

"What is this, the fifties? I'm a free agent." Anna drummed her fingers on the metal bed frame. "Everyone keeps talking about what happened *after* the party. But Geoff was there that night. I want his version of what happened. If he needs some convincing, I can handle that."

"And I'll be there for backup."

"Only if you hurry up." Anna flopped back on Helen's bed, gazing up at the exposed lightbulbs of the ceiling lamp until she blinked bright spots against her eyelids.

"Seriously, though. This top or that one? What do you think?"

"I think the party's going to be over by the time you're ready."

*

It was easy to find Geoff's party; they followed the deep thump of Eminem past rows of brick townhouses, past porches painted alternating shades of blue and brown. There was a huddle of people on his front steps, the red ember of a joint floating from one hand to the next.

Anna squinted through the warm darkness as Johnnie came running down the steps.

"You made it!" He handed the joint to Anna. "I wasn't sure you were coming."

"Wouldn't miss it." She inhaled and passed the joint to Helen, feeling the fragrant smoke glow deep inside her. "Johnnie, Helen. You remember each other?"

"I need to talk to you," Johnnie's bloodshot eyes were wide and intent. "I broke up with my girlfriend."

She nodded, looking away from Helen's I-told-you-so look.

"Good for you."

"I thought we could hang out, maybe? You and me. I could take you up in my uncle's balloon, if you wanted. They've got afternoon flights as well as early mornings. Maybe after dinner some night?"

"Sure. Maybe." Anna moved past him, through the front door. "Now, where's Geoff?"

Inside the crowded townhouse, a group of girls who looked like teenagers were dancing near the stairs, tossing their hair and swaying to 50 Cent rapping about being a P.I.M.P. Someone touched Anna's shoulder and she turned to see Johnnie's earnest face leaning over her.

"What?" Anna gestured at her ear.

"I said, can I get you a drink?"

"Just point me towards the bar!"

She turned away and bobbed to the music, lifting her arms, the air cooling her belly where her shirt rode up over her jeans. Her eyes flicked from one stranger's face to the next. As the music shifted, she glanced at Helen.

"Do you mind if we split up?"

"I'll go upstairs." Helen touched her face. "I need the bathroom."

Anna circled the living room, ignoring the whispers. She found Geoff Fraser sitting on the counter beside the kitchen sink, surrounded by buddies, a bottle of Labatt's between his meaty thighs. Her eyes locked on Geoff's and her brain performed its layering trick, fitting these chubby features over his high school face, lengthening this shaggy crop into the long ponytail he used to wear. He'd probably owned that shirt since high school, a black tee with the Thrasher logo stretched across his torso.

For a moment, Anna felt spotlit, uncertain. Then Geoff lifted his beer.

"Uh oh," he drawled. "We're in trouble now."

Anna straightened her shoulders.

"Funny," she said, as the guys around him laughed.

She squeezed past his friends, banging her hip against a folding table piled with crates of Molson, Labatt's, and Coors. Marching over to stand between his knees, she took the bottle from his hand and tilted her head to drink.

The other guys whooped in delight.

"Oh shit, Geoff!"

"Better not let Nicole see this!"

Ignoring them, Anna laid a hand on Geoff's thigh.

"You remember me?"

"You bet I do. Pete, another beer?" The muscles in Geoff's legs contracted, pulling her closer. "Everyone, this is Annie. Check out her tats." Or did he say *tits*? Geoff flicked his beer cap across the room. "I heard you were back. I didn't realize how much you'd changed."

"People change." Anna showed her teeth. "At least I didn't get fat like you."

The room erupted again. Anna ran her fingers up Geoff's leg.

"I'd love to catch up," she leaned in, whispering in his ear. "Come find me when you're ready to talk."

As she stepped back, a taller, slimmer version of Geoff—his younger brother?—held out a bottle of rum and poured her a shot. She threw it back and fished two beers out of a crate.

"I'll be waiting, Geoffrey," Anna called over her shoulder as she left the kitchen, to more jeers.

Back in the living room, Helen was over by the banister, swaying to the music.

"Success!" Anna yelled into her ear. "He was in the kitchen. Now I just need to get him alone."

Helen didn't answer, just kept her gaze fixed over Anna's shoulder. When Anna turned, she saw a handsome South Asian guy high-fiving the guys by the door.

"He's here," Helen breathed. "Dave Patel."

Anna started to laugh, then stopped as Geoff emerged from the kitchen. He bro-hugged Dave, pounding a fist against his back.

"Okay," she said. "You talk to Dave. I'll get Geoff upstairs."

"He's not going to remember me!"

"So what? It's a party. Introduce yourself."

Anna raised her eyebrows at Geoff, feeling the electricity arc between them. The crowd seemed to fall away as Geoff crossed the room and she reached out, taking his hand, completing the circuit. Then she pirouetted to lead him upstairs. His fingers were warm and loose in hers as they wove past the line for the bathroom, all the way to an empty bedroom at the end of the hall.

As soon as she kicked the door closed, Geoff was on her, hands thrusting under her T-shirt, hot mouth on hers tasting of beer and Doritos. Anna pushed against him, kissing him back, losing herself in the heat and the thrill, before a cold voice in her brain reminded her: *Slow down*. This was not about fun. This was about information.

"Whoa, tiger," said Anna, twisting out of his grasp. "There's no rush."

Geoff grunted and moved closer, plunging a hand down the back of her jeans.

"I can't be gone too long."

"Hey, I'm in charge here." She touched him lightly under the chin, rubbing the tender skin of his throat. "Let's play a game. Truth or dare?"

"I dare you to get naked," Geoff said, reaching out again.

"Fine. I'll start with this." Anna pulled her T-shirt over her head and dangled it towards him, then put a hand on his chest, keeping him at bay. "Now, my turn. Truth. Is this the first time we've hooked up?"

"You don't remember?" He made a little lunge forward. "That time we skipped class and drove to Riverside Park?"

Riverside Park. The memory circled under the surface.

"Just you and me?"

Geoff leered.

"You and me and Nate Gibson."

It came back then: Nate's sedan parked under the willows, the sound of seagulls through the open front window as they took turns with her in the back seat. Anna grimaced.

"What about before that? Weren't you at that party at Olly Sutton's? The one with the photos?"

Geoff's eyes lit up.

"Phil's Polaroids?"

"Phil McKinley?" Phil the rock star. He was in the yearbook picture too, grinning like a fool under his wild curly hair. Anna sat down on the king-sized bed. "Phil took those Polaroids?"

"Of course! He always had that camera. One night he scored with three different girls, boom boom boom, and he got pictures of all three." Geoff ran his fingers up Anna's gooseflesched arm. "He was a legend, man. Still is. I saw him last summer, when his band came through Toronto. Chicks everywhere." He dipped his head, licking at her skin. "You know, I've got a camera somewhere, if you want to recreate—"

"No." She jerked back in revulsion. "Hang on. I was pretty drunk that night. Phil took the Polaroids. Are you in them too? Or…"

Geoff pulled back and looked at her. "Me? Nah. I was only at that party for a bit. I caught a ride up to Collingwood to get to my ski club before midnight."

Anna's mind was on overdrive.

"But you're still friends with him? With Phil?"

"Yeah, I see him whenever he's in town. He lives in Vancouver. But you know, he'll be here this summer, for Hillside."

"Hillside?"

"In July. His band's headlining. You should come!"

Hillside. Anna let out a long breath. "Maybe I will." She reached for the button of his jeans.

"God, this is hot," Geoff said, as he fumbled his way inside her. "I can't believe we're doing this again. You won't tell anyone, right?"

After the first minute, Anna rolled him over so she was on top, grinding hard to drown out the echo of his voice in her head: *Phil McKinley. Hillside.* Afterwards, she pulled off and wiped herself down with his bedsheets. Then she got dressed and looked down at Geoff's heavy body sprawled on the bed, his stubby penis flaccid and lolling to one side. Impulsively, she bent and grabbed his jeans and his Thrasher shirt, bundling them in her arms.

"Stay," she said. "Good boy."

The bathroom was empty now. Anna slid the shower curtain aside, dumped Geoff's clothes into the bathtub and turned on the cold water. She sat on the toilet and pissed, smelling Geoff on her, watching his clothes darken as they absorbed water. How long would it take him to realize she wasn't coming back?

Phil McKinley. Hillside. Leaving the tap running in the bath, she pulled the door closed and went downstairs to find Helen.

CHAPTER 12

Helen leaned over her cookbook and paused with her finger on a carrot cake recipe, distracted by the swelling music from the living room. Thom was rewatching his *Gladiator* DVD. The orchestral soundtrack reverberated up through her feet, throbbing deep into her belly, a vibration that was intimate, almost sexual. She shifted, thinking about Dave Patel.

Helen couldn't get him out of her head. That smooth skin, that shiny dark hair. At Geoff's party, she'd trailed him from room to room, hanging back just out of earshot. Watching him helplessly, lit up by his deep chuckling laugh, the curve of his mouth when he smiled, the bob of his Adam's apple when he drank from his beer. At one point, he'd brushed past her and she'd breathed in his woodsy cologne, deeper and warmer than the bright citrus CK One he'd worn in high school.

Back at Laurier, he'd never noticed her either, even when he sat next to her in class, even when she'd twinned their names across the back of her binders: *Dave Patel, Mr. and Mrs. David Patel. Helen Patel.* The carefully inked names like a spell, a prayer, an invocation. Dave Patel had borrowed pencils and sheets of lined paper without ever registering her presence, without picking up on the adolescent longing that radiated out from her whole body. Anna used to shake her head at the way Helen cherished a pencil after he'd used it to graph functions in math class, the way her eyes followed him as he carried a tray across the cafeteria.

Since Geoff's party, she'd been studying Dave's photos in her yearbooks, touching his image like a scratch-and-sniff sticker from one of her childhood albums. If only she'd had the courage to approach him. If only she were another type of girl entirely.

Look at Anna. When she wanted something, she went for it. She had come tearing downstairs at Geoff's party, grabbing Helen's arm and hauling her out the front door, talking so fast Helen could barely keep up.

"Phil fucking McKinley, that's who took those Polaroids. And Geoff says he'll be here for Hillside! You know, the music festival, out at Guelph Lake? I'll get us tickets, we'll camp out for the weekend. There's no way he can avoid me there. Is that perfect, or what?"

"Camping isn't really my thing." Helen trailed her down the sidewalk. "Outdoor concerts, either."

Anna spun round. "Dave Patel might be there too. Unless you got his number already?"

The phone rang on the table behind Helen, making her jump. *Dave!* The thought flashed and was gone, leaving shame burning in its wake. Obviously, it wasn't him. It was her mother.

"Sweetheart, is everything okay?"

"I just thought you were someone else."

"I sent you an email about bridesmaid dresses. Julia's looking at navy blue and strapless. There's a sale this week at this place in Toronto, if you can come out for a fitting." Helen assembled her cooking supplies, alternating "Uh huh" with "Really?" every time her mother paused. "It's something to consider," Linda said, as Helen was weighing a foil-wrapped piece of butter in her palm. "Will you talk to him?"

Helen shut the fridge. "Talk to who?"

"The photographer."

"I thought he was already booked?"

"Helen! You aren't listening."

"Sorry. Tell me again."

"You remember my friend Mary, from work? Her son just got married in Cancun. They held a candlelight ceremony on the beach, but the photographer didn't adjust for the lighting. When the pictures came back, everyone looked awful, washed out and dirty. Mary is devastated."

"Devastated?"

"She's taking them to an expert to fix the colours, but there's no guarantee."

"Okay." Helen transferred the phone to her other shoulder and rapped an egg on the side of the bowl. "What does this have to do with Julia?"

"Not Julia." Linda hesitated. "You, sweetheart. Can you go see the photographer ahead of time, get some advice? Do some test shots? Make sure your concealer looks natural under the lights. You know?"

"You know it's my actual job to make people look good in makeup. The photos will be fine."

"It wouldn't hurt to make sure. You wouldn't want to look back and be embarrassed."

Once her mother was off the phone, Helen dumped grated carrot into the mixing bowl and pushed the spoon through the thick dough, ruminating. She wished she could pick up the phone, vent to Anna about her mother's ridiculous plans, but there were many reasons why that was a bad idea. For one, Anna's mother was way worse than Helen's. For another, Helen still hadn't told Anna who Julia was marrying.

Last week, in Anna's room, Helen had been looking through the stacks of board games while Anna twisted up her dreads into two Baby Spice pigtails.

"You want to play something?" Anna asked. "Anything except Monopoly. And I should warn you, most of these games are only fun if you cheat."

"Yeah, I used to play this with my sister. She always won," said Helen, easing the Game of Life's candy-coloured box out from the middle of the stack. "She had some trick with the spinner. And then my mom was always on her side: *She's younger than you. Let her win if she needs to, Helen. It's only a game.*"

"I'm so glad I never had siblings."

"Yeah." Helen examined the box. "I do like the little pegs you put in the cars."

"The children that you sell for cash at the end?"

Helen laughed. "I forgot about that."

"I always thought you should be able to sell your husband. And how dumb is it that it makes you get married?" Anna unfolded the game board with its blank cardboard spaces for mountains and buildings. "What's her boyfriend like, anyway?"

"He's fine."

"Just fine? You don't get along?"

"No, he's okay." Helen worked to keep her voice steady. "He's going to be a lawyer."

"Sounds charming." Anna tapped the pathways on the board. "I always chose the business track, but it doesn't make much difference, in the end. It looks like you have so many options, but you have to follow the map."

When Thom came up beside her, Helen jumped at his touch.

"Was that your friend on the phone?"

"My mom. Keeping me up to date on all the wedding plans." A lock of hair came loose from her ponytail, and

Helen twisted her head against her shoulder to get it out of her face. "Your movie's done?"

"I paused the movie." Thom reached out to tuck the errant lock behind her ear and then trailed his fingers down her arm. "Did you want to come take a break?"

"I'm not really in the mood."

"I'll make it worth your while."

He dropped his hand to her ass, pinching. Her irritation flared into anger.

"I said no!"

"Why not?" Thom asked. "It's not that time of the month, is it?"

Helen sucked in her breath.

"You know what?" she said. "I'm done."

"What do you mean?"

"This is getting too complicated. Whatever this is." She dropped the spoon in the mixing bowl and sketched a jagged line in the air between them.

"Complicated?" Thom laughed.

"I want to go back to just being roommates."

"Fine." He shrugged. "You're the one who's kept this going for so long, anyway. As long as you won't come knocking at my door when you get lonely—"

"Fuck off." She shook her head. "That's over. We're over."

"Whatever," Thom said. "You know, you've changed since you've been hanging out with that friend of yours."

"Anna. Her name is Anna."

"I know her fucking name," he said. "Things used to be fine, between us. You used to be..." He trailed off, leaving Helen to fill in the blank.

"Go on."

"It doesn't matter. Message received."

A minute later, his movie came on again, the volume louder than before.

"Great," said Helen, to the empty kitchen.

She turned back to the counter and dropped lumps of dough into the cake pan. Had she changed? Really? She shoved the pan into the oven and washed the dishes, running hot water over the bowls in the sink, scrubbing away the oily film of butter. Once everything was laid out in the drying rack, she wiped down the counter, the stovetop, and the fronts of the cabinets. She yanked the tea towel off the front of the oven and dried the dishes, one by one. When she opened the cupboard to put away the plates, she saw the bottle on the top shelf, Thom's fancy amber rum with the pirate on its label. What would Anna do, if she were here? Helen hesitated, then reached for the bottle.

Fuck you, Thom, she thought, as she poured a shot into her favourite flowered mug. The rum burned going down, like hot butterscotch. She smacked her lips and raised the cup in a toast to herself, to Anna, to not settling anymore.

"You've changed. Cheers to that," she whispered, pouring herself another drink.

CHAPTER 13

"And that's another thing," yelled Helen, above the Trasheteria's music. "Sometimes he wouldn't even use a condom! He was all, I want to feel closer to you, don't you trust me? And then I'd spend the next few weeks worrying that I was pregnant." She swayed to Soft Cell's "Tainted Love," swigging from her beer.

"I get it, Thom's a dick." Anna took the bottle out of Helen's hand and drained it. "Let's get you another drink."

She left Helen complaining to the empty air and threaded through the crowd, deploying her elbows to clear the path to the bar.

Anna wedged herself between a couple of baby punks, pressing forward to reach the sticky countertop. A tall kid with spiked green hair turned and glared down at her but Anna narrowed her eyes and glared right back, lifting herself up onto the toes of her boots to meet his pock-marked face. *Fuck you*, she put into her eyes, until he blinked and looked away.

She turned to the bartender, looking past the bottles of beer that clearly weren't potent enough. Helen needed to get fucked up tonight—or fucked—ideally both. Too bad that she was relying on alcohol, that she wouldn't take Anna's pills. Not quite as effective.

What should she order? Helen's voice still echoed in her ear: *Thom, Thom, Thom.*

"Two Tom Collins." Anna fished out a twenty. "Make them doubles."

When she handed over the pale green concoction, Helen made a face.

"What's this?"

"Something stronger," said Anna, bumping her own flimsy plastic glass against Helen's. The bright tang of gin shone through the sweet mix and this fourth drink finally did the trick. Helen stopped talking and concentrated on dancing. Beside her, Anna relaxed into the music, swinging her dreads and chanting along to the Ramones. This was what they needed, both of them. The pure adrenaline of a crowded dance floor. As the song ended with a crash of cymbals, Anna lifted a long sweaty curl out of Helen's face.

"You should cut off your hair!" She mimed a pair of scissors snipping. "Change things up!"

"Maybe I will!"

Helen slicked a hand through her damp hair and tilted her head back, grinning up at the giant papier-mâché lizard that crawled across the Trash's ceiling. Sweat had smeared the makeup at her temples but Helen was breathless and radiant as she sang along to a medley of Madonna tracks. On their left, Anna saw a stocky redhead watching them, his eyes fixed on Helen.

"Hey!" Anna nudged her, pointing at the guy with her chin. "What do you think? Ready for a little rebound action?"

Helen glanced at the guy and made a face. "No way," she yelled, above the music. "I could never. And he's so short!"

Anna looked back at the redhead, shuffling in place beside them.

"He's into you." Anna grabbed Helen's hand and twirled her around to face the guy, who took his cue and danced closer. "It doesn't have to mean anything."

"You take him! I have to pee." Helen broke away from her, giggling, and wove off through the crowd towards the bathrooms.

"Bring me back another drink!" Anna called.

She turned back to the redhead. It was true, he was on the short side, with a thick layer of freckles dusted across his snub nose. Not unattractive. A Jane's Addiction song came on and Anna met his watery blue eyes, holding out her hands as he approached. Why not? She stepped into a kiss, opening her mouth against his thick lips, pushing her tongue between his teeth. She swayed with him there in the middle of the dance floor, losing herself in the voluptuous trance of the pounding music, the warm anonymous body pressing up against her.

A pinch on her arm made her surface blearily to Helen's stare.

"What?" Anna wiped at her mouth, unsteady. "You said you didn't want him." She took the bottle from Helen's hand and tilted it up, funnelling beer down her throat.

Helen said something she couldn't hear and Anna bent closer, the soles of her boots catching on the dirty floor.

"Sean Wu," yelled Helen. She gestured over her shoulder, towards the back hall. "Here tonight!"

Anna stood on her toes to see over the crowd. "Where?"

She went where Helen pointed, ducking past the pogoing dancers and coming up next to the bar as the opening chords of "Smells Like Teen Spirit" crunched through the sound system and the crowd surged forward.

"Give me a shot," she called to the stone-faced bartender, digging for another bill in her jeans pocket. "Another one."

When Anna turned away, she had to clutch the edge of the bar to stop the spinning. But it was fine: there was Xuan, leaning against the black-painted wall, a good-looking taller guy at his side. His boyfriend? She lurched towards him, calling his name. "Xuan! Hey!"

Xuan broke off whatever he'd been saying and looked at her, raising his thick eyebrows. "Annie. Helen said you were here."

He glanced up at the guy next to him. "She's the one I told you about."

"I figured," said the tall one, his voice a deep baritone. "Hi, I'm Ryan."

Anna blinked. Her vision was splitting so she saw two Xuans, two boyfriends. She was supposed to ask him something. What was it? Wasn't he looking for something? She reached out to steady herself against his arm.

"You find it?" she said, or tried to say. The words were like pebbles in her mouth.

Xuan pushed her hand away.

"The photos? I looked through…boxes and found… from the party, plus…Phil McKinley. I think they're… night…Are you okay?"

Anna had been staring at the floor, but she pulled her head back, looking into Xuan's frowning face.

"I'm fine." She shook her head. "Phil's the Polaroid guy."

"What?" Xuan exchanged a look with his boyfriend. "Say that again? I didn't catch it."

Was he smiling? Was he laughing at her? Fuck him, then. She didn't need his condescension. The back of Anna's throat burned as she swallowed. What was she saying? What was…someone touched her back and she flared up, turned, but there was nobody there. Just Helen, rubbing her shoulder.

"She's wasted," Xuan was saying, above her head. "Did she take something?"

"She might have," came Helen's voice from far away. "Anna? Are you okay?"

Anna closed her eyes, focusing on not puking. Her Docs were hot and loose over her bare sweaty feet. When she opened her eyes, Helen stood in front of her. But Anna had been talking to someone else. Who was it? Where did they go? Her heartbeat sloshed in her ears, a sped-up tide that threatened to knock her off her feet.

"Should I call a cab?" Helen asked, her face too close. "If you need to throw up, just tell me."

Anna tried to laugh, to shake her head, but instead she lurched, clutching at the wall. There was a long sliding moment and then everything went black.

*

The next morning, Anna woke up stiff and sore, with Helen beside her in the queen-sized bed. Helen was frowning in her sleep, long hair tangled on the pillowcase. Without makeup, her birthmark was vivid red against the pale skin of her face, its edges raised and precise as the international borders on a map.

Anna had always woken up first when they'd slept over at each other's houses. This setting was new—the generic, inoffensive earth tones of her parents' spare room—but she'd spent many an early morning watching Helen asleep on the floor of her bedroom, tucked into a pink satin Barbie sleeping bag. Or the two of them under mismatched floral sheets on the pull-out sofa in

Helen's living room, with the smell of Gord's pancakes drifting in from the kitchen.

What time was it? Anna shifted her head to squint at the clock radio. 9:53. She swallowed past her scratchy throat, reconstituting the diced-up memories of last night. They'd gone to the Trasheteria. They'd been dancing. There'd been a red-haired guy—maybe also Xuan Wu?—but most of the night was missing, swallowed up by the void. Ah, well. The price of a night out.

She slipped out of bed. The AC had chilled the air in the room so she pulled on last night's T-shirt, which still smelled of sweat and cigarettes. A bolt of nausea sent her hustling to the bathroom, but she felt better once she'd thrown up, clearer. She splashed cold water on her face and smoothed back her dreads. What she needed was coffee. Even better would be a quick jump in the pool to get her blood flowing, but she'd have to get the maintenance people back first.

Her mother had called a few days ago to ask about the state of the backyard.

"We've received the most upsetting email from Maria Vetrone," Joyce had said, through a phone line buzzing with static. "Apparently our garden looks like a wasteland, with nothing planted for summer. What's happening? Where's Javier?"

"I told him to stop coming in." Anna kicked her heel against the wainscotting. She could picture Joyce adjusting her necklace in an elegant stateroom. Ocean waves shimmering out the porthole, impossibly blue. Behind her, a tiny closet packed with brightly-coloured dresses to compete with the plumage of the other passengers on the cruise. "He was showing up too early, waking me up—"

"You fired Javier?" Joyce's voice jumped.

"I didn't fire him! I asked him to take some time off."

"Well, Maria says our yard looks absolutely derelict. You call him today and get him back."

"Fine. I'll call him." Anna took a deep breath, counting to three. "How's the cruise?"

"Don't change the subject. Maria also says you've got people coming in and out, visiting the house at all hours. Is this true?"

A hysterical giggle built up in her throat. "You've got her spying on me?"

Her father took the phone. "Annie. Why didn't you pick up earlier?"

"I was out."

"Maria Vetrone is chair of the neighbourhood association. Her opinion carries a lot of weight."

"Dad—"

"Your mother takes this very seriously. I don't like to see her upset."

"I get it," she said. "Don't worry about a thing. Those flowerbeds are going to be so beautiful—"

"Don't take that tone with me."

"Come on, Dad. I said I'd call. You know I appreciate you letting me stay here."

"I would hope so." Joyce's voice sounded in the background. "Your mother is asking about your meetings. Have you been to the outpatient clinic?"

"Of course," Anna lied.

"Remember what the doctor said. You can't do this alone."

When Anna went back to the guest room, Helen was up, standing by the window.

"How are you feeling?" Helen asked, looking apprehensive. "How's your shoulder?"

"My shoulder?" Anna rotated her arms and felt a deep soreness on her right side. She touched her shoulder, feeling for damage.

"The bouncer grabbed you pretty hard," said Helen. "You're okay? You're not mad?"

"I'm fine. Well, a little hungover," Anna said, slouching against the doorframe. "Why would I be mad? Did we get kicked out?"

"You don't remember? There was that whole scene with Olly, at the bar."

"Olly? At the Trash?" Anna said. "What happened?"

"You went for him. You were screaming, then you tried to hit him. The bouncers made you stop. They were...I was scared one of them would break your arm." Helen hugged herself, staring at Anna. "You really don't remember?"

"No. Shit."

Anna spit out a painful laugh, retched and turned blindly into the hall. Back in the bathroom, she dropped to her knees in front of the toilet. Her mind filled with static as she hunched forward, heaving, until nothing came up but stringy bile. At last, she put an unsteady hand on the edge of the toilet.

"Olly was there."

"Yeah." Hovering behind her, Helen flushed the puke away and wiped Anna's face with a damp Kleenex. She rubbed Anna's back, making little circles across her spine. "You were a bit out of control."

"You're saying I made an ass of myself. It wouldn't be the first time." Coughing, Anna climbed to her feet. She moved to the sink, washed her hands, splashed more water on her face and met Helen's eyes in the mirror. "I didn't go anywhere alone with him?"

"No." Helen said. "He was with someone, anyway. Some girl. No, he came up to you and said something. I couldn't hear what. Then you just went for him."

"Fuck. I don't even want to know."

Anna closed her eyes. She could smell herself, the stink of fear and sweat and vomit. A swim wouldn't be enough. Helen backed out of the bathroom as Anna stripped off her T-shirt and underwear, stepped into the pink tub and turned on the water as hot as it would go. Ridiculous. She was ridiculous. This was like a real-life game of Snakes and Ladders. Why was she such a fuck-up?

She scalded herself clean, scrubbed off the top layer of skin. When the steamy air made Anna's head swim, she steadied herself against the wall and turned the dial the other way, forcing herself to stand under the ice-cold stream.

She shut off the water and towelled off, staring at herself in the full-length mirror. The sparrow on her arm for the birds she'd fed from her boarding-school window. The stick-and-poke motorcycle on her wrist after that accident in Honduras, when she'd flown off the back of the bike and rolled through the undergrowth, somehow missing every tree. The dragon on her torso from that summer in Thailand, a sinuous shape traced and filled in by that charming junkie. What was his name? She'd stayed with him for nearly two weeks, sleeping on his dirty rolled-out futon until the day he disappeared. She'd had to get the tail finished by one of his friends, the one with the mismatched eyes. Had she slept with him too? She couldn't remember.

Anna wiped the steam off the bathroom mirror and shook her head. No more booze, no more meds. No more missed opportunities. She marched down the hall to her old bedroom, where plastic bottles of pills were scattered across the desk, beside the board games. She gathered up the rattling plastic bottles and carried them to the bathroom. One by one, she popped off the lids and dumped out their contents, blue and yellow and white tablets collecting in the curve of the toilet bowl like coins in a fountain. She flushed them all away, then went looking for more: the first-aid kit in her enamel pillbox, even the expired Xanax at the back of the kitchen cabinet.

"I couldn't find the coffee," Helen said, when Anna made it back down to the kitchen. "And your fridge is nearly empty."

"Check the cupboards. Beside the cereal."

Anna went to the liquor cabinet and pulled out the bottles that remained. She yanked out the cork from a bottle of single malt and poured the fragrant whisky down the kitchen sink.

"I need to stop fucking around," she said. "Hillside is only two weeks away."

"Maybe it's not a good idea," Helen said. Her birthmark looked huge, a dull blotch dominating her pale face. "Hillside. I mean, how likely is it that you'll even see Phil? Much less talk to him?"

"I've already bought the tickets." Anna set the empty bottle on the edge of the counter. "I need to know what happened. Maybe Phil's still got the Polaroids! Did you think of that? I can't just let this go, not now, not when I'm getting so close!"

"I know." Helen looked uncertain. "I was going to say, *you'll get hurt.* But that's already happening."

"You don't have to come."

"I'm coming," Helen said. "I said I'd come."

"Don't worry, I can handle myself." Anna rubbed at her face, feeling the ache in her bruised shoulder. "And I'm going off the booze, okay? For real. Now, I thought there was a bottle of vodka somewhere. Would you check the freezer?"

Helen knelt down. "Here," she said, pulling a bottle of Grey Goose out of the freezer drawer. "It was next to the ice-cube tray."

"Pour it out."

"It's good stuff, though. Expensive." Helen was looking at the label. "I could take it home if you don't want it."

"Pour it out." Anna gripped the countertop. "I want to watch you do it."

Helen's eyebrows went up but she obeyed. Anna took a deep breath, inhaling the clean scent of vodka as the last of the alcohol swirled down the drain.

CHAPTER 14

The city bus was stifling, even with Helen standing in the middle of the aisle so she wouldn't sweat through her outfit, her arms and legs spread wide to catch what little breeze seeped through the dusty bus windows. She was grateful to enter the air-conditioned mall, to feel the cool artificial breeze of the Bay's cosmetics department.

"We finally got the summer promotion materials," said Barb, elbow-deep in packing peanuts. "But I don't know what they're thinking at head office. These colours are giving me flashbacks to the '80s." She unfolded a long banner in shades of peach and taupe. "It's no wonder we're struggling with market share. Can you give me a hand with the inventory sheets?"

"They're not that bad," said Helen. "I like that pink."

She took the clipboard out of Barb's hands and sat on the stool behind the counter, pulling the cotton folds of her skirt away from her damp skin.

"Where did you hear that we're struggling?"

"You didn't see the memo last week? About restructuring the department?" Barb looked at her, then went back to stacking small boxes along the countertop. "I'm not surprised. I think most people just go to Toronto for specialty products. Or else order them from the Internet."

Helen scoffed. "But then you have to pay shipping. And how can you colour-match from a website?"

"That's what I thought. Then last week, I was in Nashville to see my daughter. The American websites are offering free shipping and free returns. We can't compete with that." Barb pulled her leather purse out from under the counter. She unscrewed the lid of a sleek black jar and showed Helen the creamy beige foundation. "I've been using this all week. It's a liquid-to-powder finish, better than anything we've got here."

Helen looked around. "Put it away."

"You should be thinking long-term," said Barb, shrugging and tucking her purse back under the counter. "What if they close this counter?"

"They won't," Helen said. But she was suddenly conscious of how much she was sweating, of her shoes sliding as she shifted her feet. She shivered and rubbed her palms against the gooseflesh of her arms. When she looked down at her lap, there were two distinct handprints on the front of her cotton skirt.

*

Later that afternoon, after Barb had gone, Helen was standing on a chair to set up the summer promotion display when she saw Laura Sanders. Laura was wearing a white sundress, pushing a stroller in front of her huge belly. Striding beside her was a girl in jean shorts and a crop top. With a sick feeling, Helen recognized Jennifer Nicholson.

There'd been at least five Jennifers in their grade at Laurier, but the only one who counted was Jennifer Nicholson. Jennifer's raucous laugh was so loud it reverberated down the school hallways, making Helen do a U-turn whenever she heard it. When she absolutely had to walk past her and Laura and the rest of their group, Helen kept her head down and her shoulders hunched, praying she wouldn't attract their attention.

Laura and Jennifer still looked terrifyingly confident, sleek as well-fed lionesses, as if they owned the mall the way they'd owned the cafeteria at Laurier. As they approached the Façade counter, Jennifer lifted her head and stared directly at Helen.

Helen stared back, pinned by that predatory gaze. Then she set the last samples on the display pyramid and climbed down the ladder, praying she hadn't smudged her makeup.

"Helen!" said Laura in a high-pitched voice, parking the stroller in front of the counter. "I'm so glad you're working today!"

Helen forced a smile. She was acutely aware of the framed photograph standing by her elbow, the one with her port wine stain spattered across her naked face. *Ask me about my personal experience with Façade cosmetics!*

"Laura. Jennifer," she said. "How are you doing?"

"We're great, thanks. This is my daughter, Madison," said Laura, touching her toddler's blonde curls. "Look, Maddy, this nice lady works at the makeup counter! And she went to school with Mommy and Auntie Jen. Can you say hello?"

The little girl pushed her face into the side of the stroller and Laura stroked her hair, the light strands slipping through her fingers. "Madison turns three next week."

"And soon she'll be a big sister!" said Jennifer. She pulled at a long strand of her own hair, chestnut brown highlighted with blond streaks. "Man, I can't wait to have kids."

"But first comes marriage," said Laura. "Right, Maddy? Aren't we excited for Auntie Jen's wedding this summer?"

"Want to see my ring?"

Jennifer held out her hand to show Helen a sparkling square-cut emerald.

"Beautiful," said Helen. Her smile was starting to feel stretched and painful.

"Thank you! Mohamed—that's my fiancé—picked it up in Paris. He had it custom made. And what about you?" She gestured down at Helen's hand. "Come on, I showed you mine."

"Yeah, Helen, don't you have news to share?"

Helen looked from one expectant face to the other. "Me?"

"I saw you," said Jennifer. She put both hands on the glass counter. "At the wedding expo, in the Eaton Centre? Last week."

"Oh no. I mean yes, I was there, but it's my sister getting married. I'm just helping to plan her wedding."

Jennifer's laugh pealed across the cosmetics department, making Carmen and the other counter workers turn their heads.

"I told you, Laura. Her sister and Glenn Starkey are getting married!"

"I can't believe he'll be your brother-in-law!" Laura said. "You know, I went out with him in grade seven."

"I remember that!" Jennifer cackled. "I was sleeping over at your place when he called to ask you out. You guys were so cute together."

"God, I would hate it if my little sister got married before me. But don't worry, Helen, I'm sure your time will come."

"How long have they been dating, anyway?"

Helen's head felt thick, her thoughts slow and muddled. "A long time. Eight years." She cleared her throat and pulled herself up tall. "Can I help you find something today?"

"Oh yes," Laura said. "But first, I want to thank you for telling me about that clinic at Sick Kids. My nephew's starting treatment in a few weeks. They said his birthmark could be almost gone by the time he starts school. Isn't that great?"

"So great."

"I was hoping you could help me with this." Laura laid her fingers along her ruddy cheek. For a terrible moment, Helen thought she was mocking her birthmark. But no, Laura was tilting her face, touching a pink patch of skin. "See how red my cheeks are? Maybe it's the pregnancy, but I don't know. My skin was fine last time."

Helen let out her breath. "That looks like melasma."

"What's that?" Laura asked. "Will it go away?"

"It's a minor skin condition. Lots of women get it when they're pregnant. Don't worry, we can cover it up. I'll show you."

Soon, Helen was stippling beige dots across the tops of Laura's cheeks, while Jennifer crouched beside Madison's stroller, pointing at farm animals in a cardboard book.

"By the way," said Laura, meeting Helen's eyes in the stand mirror. "Are you still friends with Annie Leverett?"

Helen's hands went still.

"I can't believe she came back to Guelph," Jennifer said. "Is it true she's been working as a prostitute?"

"What? No!"

"I'm just repeating what I've heard." Jennifer lifted her hands in faux innocence. "We all know what she's like. Remember that time when Tracy Cho went for tutoring and walked in on her giving a…" She looked at little Madison. "You know, caught her with the chemistry teacher?"

Helen's sponge trembled as she blended the foundation into Laura's freckled skin.

"I don't feel comfortable talking about her like this."

"I get it, you were friends. It's sweet that you're defending her." Laura ran a hand through her shining red hair, splaying the ends into a sharp-edged fan. "But she seems like she's out of control."

"Don't you worry about that?" Jennifer said. "Especially with her moving back to Guelph. Laura, didn't Mike show her some condos in the South End?"

"Condos?" Helen stared at her.

"Yeah, last week. I told him, go ahead, help her out, but don't get sucked in."

Helen shivered. Mike Whitburg? Anna wouldn't, would she?

"Honestly, I feel bad for her," said Jennifer. "Look what she's done to herself! That's not normal, is it?"

"You don't know what she's been through," Helen said.

"Like what?"

"We won't tell anyone. Why don't you fill us in?"

Helen looked back and forth between them.

"It's private," Helen said at last, in a voice that meant *It's none of your fucking business.* She put down the sponge. "See how well this evens out your colour, Laura? But it's still light enough to let your skin breathe. And it's hypoallergenic so it won't cause any more irritation."

There was a moment of silence. Jennifer and Laura looked at each other.

"What size did you want to purchase?" Helen asked. "I can wrap it up for you, if you want. And then I need to get back to work."

*

That evening, after her shift, Helen caught a glimpse of her reflection in a shoe-repair window. She stopped and lifted a hand to her hair. She'd added too much product to combat the humidity, and now her hair looked lank and shapeless, frizzy and dull.

She turned around, heading for the salon beside the Orange Julius.

"Are you still open?" Helen asked the six-foot-tall glamazon sweeping the floor. She was broad-shouldered, more heavily made up than Helen herself. "I'm sorry, I don't have an appointment."

"Sure, honey. I'm Dominique. What are we doing today?"

"Something different." Helen said. "A whole new look."

Dominique nodded thoughtfully, running big hands through Helen's hair as she settled into the salon chair. She folded Helen's wavy hair underneath itself, demonstrating different lengths. To the shoulder? Above the chin? All the way up to her ears?

They settled on eight inches off, with blunt-cut bangs that grazed Helen's eyebrows. Dominique gathered a long ponytail, her scissors juddering as she sawed through the thick strands of hair. Helen held her breath, counting one-two-three-four-five slices, mesmerized by the sight of the hair dropping away until that final snip cut her free. Afterwards, her head was so light it floated off her shoulders.

*

The next day, Helen walked from her apartment over to Anna's house, her hair feeling strange and unfinished when she ran her fingers through it. She couldn't stop touching her bangs, adjusting the heavy strands so they lay smooth against her forehead, moving them again so they weren't too perfectly straight.

"Nice hair!" Anna beamed a huge smile at Helen when she met her at the side of her house. She unlatched the tall wooden gate and beckoned her past the lilac hedges.

"Thanks," said Helen. "I needed a change."

She stopped. Anna's backyard had been transformed. The stone paths were swept clean, and the tidy flowerbeds were filled with a profusion of newly planted greenery.

"Ta da! My parents' gardener came by yesterday."

"It's like a private oasis!"

"Not that private. My mother's got the neighbours watching." Anna gestured at the tall wooden fence, then pulled her T-shirt over her head and stepped out of her jean shorts. "I hope they're enjoying the show."

"Keep your clothes on!" Helen put up a hand to shield her view. "I can't talk to you when you're naked."

"You're such a prude." Anna stretched up, fingers brushing the leaves of the lilacs at the edge of the patio. A strange tattoo covered her torso. Half-squid, half-tree, its twisted tentacles and roots wormed along her right thigh, wrapped the pale nest of her pubic hair and curled up over her breasts.

Anna caught Helen's eye and did a little pirouette on the paving stones. "You'll have to get used to this. I plan on being out here every day this summer."

She ran a few steps and leapt into the pool. Helen walked to the edge as Anna swam from one end to the other, diving deep and shooting up to the surface in a cloud of bubbles.

"Jump in!" Anna said, treading water. "You can borrow a bathing suit, if you want."

"I'd look like I was melting." Helen sat on the edge, tucked her skirt under her thighs and dangled her legs in the cool water. "If you knew how much time I put into my makeup, you wouldn't even suggest it."

Anna snorted and splashed water towards Helen.

"Next time you stay over, then. We can swim first thing in the morning, before you get all spackled up."

"Spackled?" Helen put a hand to her chest, pretending offence. She stirred the water with her feet. "I just don't swim."

"Don't or can't?" Anna sank down under the surface and swam underwater to Helen's feet, then grabbed an ankle as she burst out of the water. "What if I pulled you in?"

"That would make you a shitty friend."

Helen smiled at her, reached for one of Anna's long wet dreadlocks and wrapped it around her wrist like the friendship bracelets they used to make for each other. Anna tilted her head, pulling at Helen's arm with her hair, as if she might drag her into the pool. She rested her arms against the grey slate edge and closed her eyes, basking in the sun. She had shadows under her eyes, dark as bruises.

Helen leaned back as well, the sunlight shining hot and red through her closed eyelids. After a few wordless peaceful moments, the sun went behind a cloud.

"Laura Sanders came to see me at work, yesterday," Helen said, unwinding the bracelet of hair. "With Jennifer Nicholson."

"Really?"

"They had Laura's little girl with them. Who was pretty cute, actually."

"What did they want?"

"Laura's got some skin issues with her pregnancy. I showed her how to cover them up. And they asked about you." She stirred the water with her foot. "Jennifer made some crack about you being a prostitute."

"What a bitch." Anna said. "Anything else?"

Helen hesitated.

"Just that Laura's nephew is starting treatment at Sick Kids. But how are you doing? You look…," she reached out and touched the constellation pulsing against the translucent skin of Anna's temple, searching for a nice way to say *terrible*, "tired."

Anna pushed off the wall, splashing backward into a star float. Her breasts rose out of the water, the silver loop of her nipple piercing glinting in the sun.

"I'm fine," she said to the sky. "I'm doing great."

She broke into a raspy cough, flipped over and kicked her way back to the edge of the pool, where she hawked a glob of phlegm out into the perfect green grass.

Helen pulled her feet out of the pool. "Gross."

"Sorry." Anna rested her chin on her crossed arms. "Have you ever been to Greece?"

"Greece?"

"What do you think about meeting out there, this fall? I'm thinking Mykonos. They have the best beaches there."

"I can't go to Greece!"

"Why not?" Anna coughed and spat again.

"Because I don't have thousands of dollars lying around for a vacation?"

"You could pay me back."

"With what?" Helen laughed. "I've still got student loan payments and I didn't even finish that degree."

"Can't your dad help with that?"

"That's not an option." Helen looked around at the manicured lawns, the flowers, the pool. Her chest suddenly felt tight. "So, you're definitely leaving again?"

"Of course. You know that. I want to be gone before my parents get back, in September."

"I forgot." Helen looked down at her toes, at the chipping pink polish. She scrambled to her feet and retreated to the shade of the fabric umbrella. "But what if your Hillside plan doesn't work out? What if you don't see Phil? If he's not there, or he won't talk to you, or if he doesn't know anything—"

Anna gave her a look. "He knows. He took those Polaroids."

"If you can't talk to him then, for whatever reason. You'll still leave?"

"There's nothing for me here. You know that," said Anna.

She hauled herself out of the pool.

"That's why you should come travel with me. Take some time off. Or quit your job. I know, you think it's so perfect, but it's just a job. You deserve to have some fun. And travelling isn't as expensive as you think. We'll get cheap plane tickets, stay in hostels, work a little under the table. All you need is a backpack and a passport."

"I don't have a passport."

"What?" Anna laughed. "Yes, you do. You said you've gone outlet shopping, in Buffalo."

"I just show my birth certificate when I cross the border."

"What about when you get on a plane?"

"I've never been on a plane."

"Get out of here!"

"We always drive down East, to see my family. The one time I went out West, to visit, I took the train. I think it took four days to get to Calgary. So yeah." Helen gave a sick little laugh. "I'm definitely not going to Greece."

CHAPTER 15

The moment Anna stepped off the Hillside shuttle bus, she knew this was going to be a good time. Intermingled drumbeats from the different stages, generations of hippies following paths through the forest, warm air scented with pine trees and porta potties. She felt high on sunshine, on optimism, on second-hand weed.

"It's a good thing I stayed," she told Helen. "I needed to get this place out of my system."

"Uh huh."

"Phil's band isn't on until tonight," Anna said, holding up her copy of the festival schedule. "Is there anyone else you want to see?"

"Gordon Lightfoot, but that's not until tomorrow. My stepdad's got all his albums and I promised I'd see him perform." Helen took the schedule and turned it over. "He's playing the Island Stage tomorrow at three o'clock."

Anna laughed. "You make it sound like homework."

"I'm not really into music."

They were standing in line for falafels when Anna looked across the field and spotted Dave Patel. He was wearing a green trucker hat and a faded Tragically Hip T-shirt.

She nudged Helen. "Look who's here!"

Helen lifted her eyes, but her expression didn't change. "He's with a girl."

"So?" Anna stepped forward with the line, bouncing to the music from the main stage. "Maybe she's his sister."

"He doesn't have a sister."

"I can't believe you know that." The girl was darker-skinned than Dave, her black hair caught in a shiny braid down her back. They stood close together, bent over a copy of the festival schedule. "You should go shoot your shot. It's not like guys are into monogamy."

"I don't even know what I'd say."

"Just say hello. I'll distract the girl while you work your magic on Dave." She looked at the menu board. "Fine. Do you want a falafel? I'm getting two. I'm starving."

The falafels were delicious. Oil and garlic and cumin, the spices cut with pickles and cool frilly lettuce. Anna relished each bite as they wandered through the central clearing, past the food vendors and over to the booths selling hammered silver jewellery and tie-dyed clothing. At a tattoos and piercings station, they stopped to watch a teenager getting her nose pierced. The girl sat on a metal folding chair, holding hands with an older version of herself who had to be her mother, with the same olive skin and thick eyebrows.

Helen looked away, but Anna crumpled her waxed paper wrapping and watched the tattoo artist press a needle through the girl's nostril. The girl squeaked, bringing up Anna's own memory of that quick stab of pain, the urge to sneeze. Then it was done, and the man slipped a silver hoop through the newly made hole, standing back so the grey-haired mother could hug her daughter. The artist stripped off his disposable gloves and caught Anna's eye, nodded to show his appreciation of the work she'd had done. Just like that, the old itch welled up under Anna's skin and she stepped forward.

"You do walk-ins?"

"Piercing? Or ink?" His voice was higher-pitched than she expected.

"Tattoos." Anna leaned in to study the flash posted on the wooden wall of his stand. "What do you say, Helen? Matching tattoos, to mark the occasion?"

"Tattoos?"

"Maybe the Hillside symbol?" The little stick figure was everywhere, from their festival wristbands to the giant billboard by the main stage. Its head was a sunny yellow circle, its arms and body a flying blue seagull, its legs a stripe of green hill.

"That's crazy. No way."

"Then I'll get something for both of us." Anna pointed at a sheet of retro beauty-themed designs. A tube of lipstick, a silver compact, a sultry kohl-lined eye, all circling a pouting Betty Boop. "Which one do you like?"

"Anna!"

"What about the mirror with the lipstick?" Anna touched a stylized hand mirror displaying a message scrawled in red: *you are beautiful*. She beckoned the artist over. "Can we change this? Lose the inspirational quote, do a pair of lips, instead? Model them on hers?"

"Anna." Helen sounded breathless. "Are you sure?"

"Totally. Then I can take you with me when I leave."

While the artist sketched out the transfer, Anna tugged off her tank top and found a spot near her hip between two tentacles, just above the stick-and-poke mermaid. Helen backed away, but Anna watched for the first few minutes as the artist did the linework, then closed her eyes and went into her pain trance, dark colours pulsing behind her eyelids to the rhythm of the tattoo gun. It was strange to be sober while she got inked, but the electric vibration of the needle kept her emphatically centred: in this booth, in this field, on this island, at this moment in time. As the endorphins kicked in, she felt like she was walking on clouds.

When it was done, the artist had her pose for a picture. Then he wiped the tattoo with rubbing alcohol and swathed it with Saran wrap. Anna pulled on her shirt and pressed her hand against the dressing, relishing the burn. She felt galvanized, vibrantly present, strong and confident and powerful. She wanted to skip through this crowd of concert-goers and whirl to a stop in front of Phil McKinley, who would cower before her.

"Come on!" She grabbed Helen's hand. "Let's go dance!"

They followed the crowd to the Main Stage, where Anna spun in energetic circles until Helen was dancing along, both of them laughing and making up steps. As the music changed from wailing ska to electric folk, Anna shook back her damp dreads and grinned at Helen.

"This is fun, right?"

"Yeah, but it's too hot! I need a drink."

They lined up at the water station on the side of the field and Anna scanned the crowd for Phil McKinley. Could that be him, by the stage, under the blue cowboy hat? She squinted until the man turned around, revealed a long grey moustache.

"Next up is the Blue Mountain Band. With special guests, it says." Helen fanned herself with the festival schedule, its paper creases dark with sweat. "And we should decide which bus we're taking home tonight. The ones after eleven will be super crowded."

"I'm not going home tonight."

"But we didn't bring camping stuff."

"I'll crash in someone's tent," Anna said. "Maybe Phil's, if I'm lucky."

They were almost at the water station, the line winding past a face-painted toddler who was stamping in the mud puddle. Behind them, the noise of the crowd suddenly leapt and a group of musicians walked out on stage, three of them in matching black cowboy hats. They waved and adjusted their instruments, then one of them stepped up to the mike and broke into a twangy bluegrass song. Anna looked closer at the guitar player with the curly mop of brown hair, his eyes shielded with aviators. *With special guests,* Helen had said, and there he was. Phil McKinley, live on stage.

Helen was saying something else but Anna's senses were recalibrating, refocusing. She flapped her hand at Helen and stalked through the crowd, treading on cotton blankets and swerving around dancers until she reached the base of the stage. When she reached the front, she threw her arms up in the air.

"Phil!" she called, over the music. "Phil!" His name ripped at her throat.

When the first song crashed to an end she screamed it one more time, and this time her voice broke through so that he looked up, searching. Anna waved her hands and leapt, catching his attention and pulling it down to where she stood below him, just a few feet away. Phil's eyebrows went up, his face changing with recognition as his fist came down on the chords for the next song.

*

Sometime after midnight, long after Helen had left on the shuttle bus, Anna sat with her legs stretched out to Phil's campfire. A score of people milled around, drinking and chatting and staring into the flames. Half of them were strangers, but some were faces from Laurier; a trio of girls who kept whispering her name but wouldn't meet her eyes, a couple of guys eyeing her openly in hopes of an easy score. Dave Patel was there, sitting with the same girl they'd seen earlier. So was Mike Whitburg, drunk and rambling through a long, disjointed football story. Even Johnnie Campbell dropped by for half an hour, reeking of pot, sulking when Anna wouldn't go for a walk with him. All of them distractions, bit players, eclipsed by Phil McKinley sitting across the fire with a guitar on his lap. She'd been circling him for hours, bumming a cigarette, sharing a joint, dipping close and then backing off. They'd exchanged small talk, of the *wow, you've changed* and *how's life treated you?* variety, but she was still waiting for her chance to get him alone.

Then a long-haired guy got to his feet, tossing an empty beer can into the fire.

"Who's up for a swim in the lake?"

"I need to finish my beer," said Mike.

"We didn't bring suits," said someone else.

Now, thought Anna. She stood up, batting away the smoke in her face.

"You guys are all pussies." She reached out towards the curly-haired silhouette that was Phil in the firelight. "But what about you, Mr. Rock Star?"

The beach was three feet of rock and gravel, the lake water black under the cloudy sky. The group fanned out along the shore, kicking off shoes, nudging each other ankle- and then knee-deep. Anna didn't hesitate. She strode forward, flicking her cigarette in a red arc to hiss against the water, stripping off her clothes and tossing them behind her on the rocky beach. Her arm brushed the plastic wrap as she pulled off her sports bra, then she was plunging forward into the lake, diving under the cold dark water, dragging her fingers through the slimy trailing weeds. When she surfaced, she swirled fluidly around to look back to where the others stood silent by the edge of the water. Their watching faces glowed in the moonlight.

"What's wrong with you?" she yelled, and then everyone was moving, stripping off shirts and shorts, splashing as they dashed or fell into the lake.

Anna treaded water and laughed, a wild glee rising up as Phil swam towards her. She kicked forward, put her hands out to meet him. She had planned on drawing this out, but here was his body warm against hers, his mouth open and his breath hot and spicy, tasting of Ketchup chips.

There was no need to talk as they emerged from the lake, as they pulled clothes over their wet skin and headed for the mustard-yellow dome of his tent. They tumbled onto his sleeping bag and Anna shivered as Phil ran his hands down her side, brushing the wet plastic wrap. Her body was on autopilot but her brain whirred and spun, picking out details as if Phil's touch might trip an internal alarm, resurrect her buried teenaged memories. She ramped up her movements, biting and pulling at his chest, his arms, his neck, but instead of matching her aggression, Phil slowed down, elongating the strokes of his fingers, dragging his tongue across her skin. Anna's breath came faster as she abandoned herself to this moment. No more thoughts, now. No more questions.

Afterwards they lay together, spooning on the bunched-up sleeping bag. Phil's breathing was slow against the back of her neck as Anna stared at the golden wall of the tent, at the shadows moving on the translucent nylon.

"Phil," she whispered, finally. "Don't go to sleep."

"Hmmm? Round two already?"

"Not yet." She took a deep breath. "Do you remember our first time?"

"First time at what?" Phil pulled her closer, spooning against her.

"Fucking, obviously."

She turned, squinting to see his shadowed face.

"We've never done this before." He propped himself up on one elbow and smoothed the dreads away from her face. "Although I remember some spectacular blow jobs in the back of my van."

He dipped to kiss her, but she shifted out of the way.

"Really. You don't have to lie." Her heart was so loud it seemed to echo off the dome of the tent. "I'm talking about that party. At Olly's place."

"Oh, that." He laughed. "I was just the cameraman. Remember?"

"I wish I could. I was blacked out."

"That was a wild night."

"Walk me through it."

"Come on."

"I keep hearing about your Polaroids." Anna sat up, tugging the satin fabric of the sleeping bag up over her waist. "It's not fair that everyone knows what happened except me."

"Well, you were pretty out of it. I remember you tripped coming up the stairs and you wanted to stay there on the ground. We had to convince you to get up again."

"Convince me?"

"Well, Olly helped you up. But you took off your own clothes."

"Like a striptease?"

"Not exactly." Now Phil's laugh was uncomfortable. "We'd been out in the hot tub, so you only had a towel over your underwear. Geoff pulled it off as you came in the kitchen and made a joke: 'Let's get you out of those wet clothes,' you know."

"A joke?" She shook her head. "It can't have been Geoff. I was at his house, and he said—"

"Yeah, it was him. You stepped out of your panties and stood there, naked. It was crazy. You didn't even care."

"I didn't care? I was just this sad drunk girl who took off her clothes? So fucked up that I fell down the stairs?" A cold, sick feeling was growing in her stomach. She pulled the sleeping bag up over her shoulders. "Were my eyes even open?"

"Hold on. Wait a second."

"I'm trying to understand. How aware was I? What happened? What did you do?"

Phil hesitated, eyes glinting at her from the shadows.

"It was Olly's idea."

"Of course." The breath whooshed out of her Anna bent forward. "Of course it was."

"It started off as just pictures. We led you over to his bed and set you up, naked. I had my camera. We were all laughing, and Olly sat beside you with his hands on your tits, you know. Posing. Then he took off his pants and things just…went from there. We were drunk, we got caught up in the moment. And you were so out of it, you didn't seem to care. We weren't trying to hurt you." He was quiet for a minute. "I'm sorry now."

"You're sorry now." Anna pulled the sleeping bag tighter over her shoulders. "Olly fucked me."

"Olly went first."

She winced. "And then? Who was next? Was it you?"

"No! I told you, I just took pictures. No, I…tried, after he was done. I was too drunk."

"You tried." Anna squeezed her eyes shut. "Really. Fuck you for trying."

"Sure. I know. Then…Starkey. He went next."

"Glenn Starkey?" She could picture him in that group photo, perched on the couch with his mussed blond hair, his gap-toothed smile. "After Olly?"

"It wasn't as funny that time. I think he was nervous. He took forever, even with us, uh, cheering him on."

"Glenn Starkey. Olly Sutton. And then? After those two?"

"I don't know. There were a bunch of us in the room. Me, Geoff, Olly's older brother, his brother's friend. There were guys there I didn't even know. Anyway, after I ran out of film, Olly and I went downstairs to show off the Polaroids." Phil put his head in his hands. "I swear, we weren't trying to hurt you."

"You weren't trying to hurt me." Anna repeated his words, but they still didn't make sense. "I was passed out, but you weren't trying to hurt me."

"We were young. And stupid." Phil stopped. After a minute, he went on in a different tone. "You know, I have this friend, a singer, and she was…assaulted, a couple of years ago, on tour. It took her a long time to work through it. She ended up finding a great therapist, though. That really helped. Have you done that? Talked to someone?"

"No."

Assaulted. That girl from the photo, sprawled naked on a bed, a faceless boy moving on top of her. More guys around him, waiting their turn. *Assaulted.* And what did that make her? Not a party girl, not a slut or a whore. A victim. Somehow, that label was worse than all the others.

"So, what then?" Anna asked. "After you went back downstairs and showed everyone the Polaroids? After you left me upstairs. Passed out. How many other guys…"

"I told you, I don't know."

"Everyone called me a slut." Anna said. "And you got to be, what, studs? Heroes?"

"Annie—"

"You think this is a joke?"

"You were just laughing!"

"I didn't know it happened like that! *Assaulted,*" Anna closed her eyes. "Where are they now? The Polaroids?"

"I don't know."

"I want to see them. You owe me that much."

"Honestly, I don't know who's got them now. They floated around the school for a few weeks, then they disappeared." Phil reached out, covered her hand with his. "But listen, tonight. This didn't, like, retraumatize you?"

A strange mirth bubbled up inside her. "With sex? No. You were sweet." She reached out, fumbling in the dark, and grabbed his face by the chin, navigating closer to kiss him. His lips were dry and closed, then he opened them and leaned in towards her. Anna felt something twist, deep inside her. Like an elastic band giving way with a snap.

Later, after Phil had fallen asleep, Anna lay staring up at the roof of the tent. Her new tattoo was burning under the damp Saran wrap. She picked at the tape and peeled back the plastic, fanning at the skin to cool it down.

Suddenly she needed to be outside. Anna sat up and felt around for her clothes, pulled on the clammy tank top and jean shorts. She unzipped the door and shoved through the tent flap to stand upright, gulping deep breaths of the cold night air. Above her, beyond the tree-tops, a white spray of stars prickled against the charcoal sky. She stepped out of the tent, zipped it up behind her. A quick piss in the grass, then Anna picked her way barefoot towards the hunched figures by the fire, rubbing at her bare arms to warm her skin.

"Annie?" A guy by the fire turned a pale face in her direction.

"Who wants to know?"

A cigarette floated to his mouth. In the brief flare of his inhale, she recognized Johnnie Campbell.

"You again." Her shoulders dropped. Feeling dull, unreal, Anna stepped forward to the log where he sat by the fire. "Can I get a drag off that?"

"I was looking for you." Johnnie was staring into the low blue flames. "Someone said you went off with Phil McKinley."

"Yeah? So?"

"So, I thought we had something going, me and you."

"You thought what?" Anna tried to laugh but it came out hard and bitter. "Come on. What are you, jealous?"

"Yeah, I'm fucking jealous. We've been hanging out, right? Then you go and bone Phil McKinley—"

"Bone him? What are we, back in grade six? Listen. I'll bone who I want, when I want. You and me, we're not together, okay? I don't do *together*."

"Fine," Johnnie said. "I get it. Thanks for clearing that up."

"Why would you even want that?" Anna cleared her throat and spat into the fire. The glob of mucus sizzled against the hot coals. "Can't you see what a fucking mess I am?"

"It's fine." Johnnie stood up and held out his cigarette. "Here, it's all yours." He dusted his palms on his jeans and walked away into the darkness.

*

Anna didn't get any sleep that night. She turned her back on the campsites and walked down to the lake, crouching on the stones and staring out over the water. She didn't know what was worse, the idea of the crowd of teenaged boys using that girl's body, Anna's body, *this* body, or the fact that they'd all lied about it, afterwards.

She kneeled on the beach and dragged her fingers through the cold pebbles, the grit catching under her bitten-off nails. Then she climbed to her feet and stepped out of her still-damp clothes. Naked, shivering, Anna waded out into the lake until the water was up to her knees, her hips, her waist. She spread her arms, leaned forward and let herself fall into the dark water.

*

The next morning, Anna paced by the side of the road, waiting as the shuttle bus emptied itself of bright-eyed families and old folks. Helen was one of the last to emerge. She looked clean and fresh in a flowered cotton dress, her bobbed chestnut hair shining in the sunshine.

"I forgot my hat," said Helen, lifting her hand to shield her face from the sun. "I'm so dumb, it's sitting on the table by the door. I'll end up with a burn—"

"Never mind." Anna's empty stomach felt tight. She grabbed Helen's arm and pulled her away from the bus. "I talked to Phil, last night."

"He talked to you?"

"He told me everything."

Helen's sandals skidded on the gravel as Anna tugged her towards the entry gate, holding out her wrist so the volunteer could check her bracelet.

"You were right," Anna said grimly, once they were through. "It was all bullshit. Not just Olly's story. Everyone's."

"Everyone's?"

"Geoff Fraser, for one. That fucker. You remember when we talked about the difference between blacked out and passed out?"

"Yeah?"

"According to Phil, I was so drunk I barely made it up the stairs. According to him…" She swallowed. "I passed out pretty quick. But that didn't stop anybody."

"No." Helen looked stricken. "No, but…Phil was there, then, in the room? Did he…"

"*He* said he only took pictures. That he didn't actually fuck me. He admitted that he tried, but apparently he was too wasted to get it up." Anna laughed mirthlessly. "He actually apologized, would you believe it? Asked if I've seen a shrink."

"So, but…Anna." Helen stopped, planting her feet in the middle of the path. Her voice dropped to a whisper. "Anna, that's…they had sex with you? While you were… isn't that rape?"

"I hate that word," she said, steering Helen towards a cluster of birch trees by a row of blue porta potties. "But yeah. Apparently so."

"But," Helen said, as they ducked under the over-hanging birch branches. She looked on the verge of tears. "Anna, that's awful. That's so awful. Did he say who did it? Who raped you?"

"He told me the first two. I don't know if…Olly went first. He's such a—" Anna spat on the ground, wiped her mouth. "Then one of his friends. Starkey."

"Glenn Starkey?"

"Yeah, he was part of their whole jock crowd. Olly Sutton and Glenn Starkey."

Saying their names made Anna feel as if the ground was tilting under her feet. She reached out and gripped one of the birch trees, its papery bark flaking off against her palm. Helen started to speak but Anna overrode her.

"For ten years, I've believed this bullshit. Ha ha, Annie got wasted, let loose, showed her true colours. But now? Now that I know what they did?" She shook her head. "I'm going to blow up their fucking lives."

"Wait." Helen ran her fingers through her hair. "Hold on. Sure, I believe that Olly lied. But how do you know that Phil's telling the truth?"

"About Glenn? There's that yearbook picture. He's right there on the couch."

"Still. I don't know."

"Why not?"

Helen shook her head and looked away.

"Why can't it be him?" Anna's skin tightened. "What aren't you telling me?"

Helen swallowed.

"Look, I should have told you. But you were so different when you first showed up. So angry. I didn't know what you'd say." Her wide brown eyes flicked up at Anna, then back to the dirt at her feet. She kicked at the twisted roots of the birch trees. "I thought I could tell you later on. I thought he was at the bottom of your list."

"My list?"

"Glenn Starkey." Helen dropped her voice. "He's the one marrying my sister."

Anna's head filled with white noise.

"No," she said. She reeled, backed away and tripped, banging her head against a tree trunk behind her. "No."

"Oh my God," said Helen. "Anna!"

Dazed, Anna touched the back of her skull, feeling for blood. Helen reached out but Anna batted her away.

"What the fuck, Helen? Your sister?"

"I'm sorry," Helen pulled her hands back, hugging herself. "They've been together for years. They're in the same law program, in Ottawa. They just—"

"Your sister."

"Anna. I didn't—"

"Stop. Stop talking."

Still sitting on the ground, Anna fumbled at her pocket, pulled out a bent cigarette and stuck it between her lips. Her hands shook so hard that she could hardly work the lighter, just flicked and flicked until she burned her thumb. Finally, the flame caught and she sucked in a desperate lungful of smoke.

"All this time," Anna said. "You've been lying. Protecting him."

"It's not like that!"

"You picked your sister's boyfriend, your sister who you don't even like, over me."

Helen shook her head. "No, that's not…it's not like that. Honestly, I don't believe it, that he would ever… He's such a good guy."

Anna reached back, clutched the tree and hauled herself upright.

"Have you seen him?"

"What?"

"Since I've been back. Does Glenn Starkey know I'm back in Guelph?"

Helen nodded miserably.

"But Olly told him, not me. They're still friends—"

"They're still *friends*?"

"He's in the wedding party."

"Oh my God." Anna felt giddy. "Fuck, Helen. I told you everything. Trusted you. 'We'll find out together,' that's what you said. I thought you were on my side."

"I am!" Helen sobbed. She wiped at her face, smearing her makeup across her cheeks. "I am on your side. I'm so sorry. You can still trust me. A hundred percent, from here on out. You can trust me."

"Then prove it," Anna said. "I want to see him, face to face. I want to look Glenn Starkey in the eye and make him admit what he did."

"I can't!" Helen said. "I can't, Anna. I'm sorry. I should have told you. But this is my family. It's not just him, it's my sister, my mom. I can't get involved."

"So, what are you going to do? Walk away?" Anna glared at her. "Again?"

"You don't understand!"

"All this time, it's been his fucking wedding you're planning." Anna. said. "You're the one who doesn't understand. You have to make a choice. If you're on my side, choose me."

CHAPTER 16

Helen spent the next week wrestling with Anna's ultimatum. *Choose me,* she'd insisted—but how far did that go? Would it really be enough to get her face-to-face with Glenn? Helen wasn't convinced by Phil McKinley's story. Why couldn't Anna see that he was deflecting all the blame? Probably Glenn hadn't even been involved. Probably he'd be appalled by Anna's accusations.

Standing at her parents' kitchen counter, Helen closed her eyes, picturing the stunned look on Glenn's face. *You think I did what?* She'd known Glenn since he was five years old. She remembered him shaking his head when the mean girls made fun of her birthmark, refusing to run when they tagged him with Helen's "cooties." Glenn was one of the good guys.

She sighed and looked over her cake recipe, running her finger down the list of ingredients. Sugar, flour, pistachios. She had them all. Helen double-checked the baking time and glanced at the clock on the wall. Nearly eleven. As long as her mother got home from the market soon with the blueberries and the eggs, the layers would have plenty of time to cool.

In the next room, Gord was playing guitar, picking out chords and singing "Landslide" in his soothing baritone. Helen hummed along as she pulled the ancient food processor out of the cupboard, set it on the counter beside his jar of sourdough starter, and looked back at the clock. Julia and Glenn were supposed to arrive by five. After dinner, Helen had agreed to take Glenn out for a walk. Anna would be waiting outside in the park across the street.

"Any time after seven," Anna had said. "Just get him outside. I'll take it from there."

Helen didn't have to make this a big production. The two of them could probably slip outside without anyone noticing they were gone.

"Tell him there's an old friend who wants to see him," Anna had suggested. She could do that. Or she could make up something else. Something about the wedding, maybe. And once she got Glenn outside, once she'd kept that promise to Anna, she could walk away.

Or she could forget this whole plan. Enjoy a quiet evening with her family without disrupting Gord's birthday celebration. Make up some excuse for Anna: *Sorry, Glenn refused to come outside.* Or *He wasn't feeling well. There was nothing I could do.* Let Anna track him down on her own. Staring up at the hands of the kitchen clock, Helen shivered. Eleven o'clock. Julia and Glenn would just be hitting the road. Soon they'd be barrelling down the 401, then walking through the door. Then she'd have to make her decision.

"Helen? Everything okay?" Gord stood in the archway between the kitchen and the living room. "You need any help?"

Helen looked up, attempting a smile. "You can't help with your own birthday cake!"

Gord scratched at his beard and ambled over to stand beside her. "Can I get a hint of what you're making? I know it involves blueberries."

"You know the rules." She put a hand over the recipe.

"Pistachios?" He fished a nut out of the plastic bag on the counter. "What else?"

"Stop! I only have enough for the cake!"

Gord laughed, scooped the cat into his arms and retreated to the kitchen table, where he leaned over his latest *Canadian Vet* magazine. Helen was sifting the first cup of flour into the mixing bowl when her mother bustled into the condo, cloth bags hanging from each arm.

Linda's batik dress flared as she set her bags on the counter.

"You'll never guess who I saw at the market: Marlene Simmons! She was in line for the bakery." She lifted out a pint of blueberries. "Will these work, Helen? I got the wild ones from Quebec."

"They're perfect. Thanks again for picking them up."

"Do you have enough pistachios?"

"I think we're okay. I managed to guard most of them from Gord."

Linda laughed and smoothed back her grey curls as she pulled the large Bialetti out of the cupboard. "Do you want coffee?"

"Always," said Gord. "Who's Marlene Simmons?"

"Claire Simmons's mother." Linda unhooked three cups from the wooden mug tree by the window and set them on the counter. "Helen, you remember Claire? She went through a trial at the Children's with you."

"Sure," said Helen. Claire's port wine stain had been even bigger than hers, a dense mulberry mass that extended from her hairline to her neck. Even her eye had been affected, the lid puffy and discoloured. "That poor girl," Linda always whispered when they saw her. Claire herself had been matter-of-fact about the birthmark. Helen remembered sharing Crayola markers with her in the hospital waiting room, watching aghast as she scribbled purple down the face of her self-portrait.

"I guess Claire's in med school now," Linda said. "But Marlene said she had a new laser treatment last year and it made a huge difference. Her birthmark's practically gone! She gave me a brochure, it's here in one of these bags."

"We've been through this, Mom. The lasers don't work for me."

"Marlene says this is a whole new process. Very state-of-the-art. She says it's a cold laser. There's less risk and the recovery's faster."

Helen cracked an egg against the counter and balanced it over a little ceramic bowl, letting the white drip away as she juggled the yolk back and forth between the two halves of the shell.

"It's a private clinic up in Forest Hill." Linda poured coffee. "I'm sure it's not cheap, but your father did offer to pay for any future—"

"Mom!" The shell of the next egg crunched and bright yolk spilled into the bowl of egg whites. "Shit!"

"We can talk about this later," Gord said.

"Or not at all," Helen said. "You know I'm not touching his money. And I don't need more lasers. Makeup is fine."

She pulled out a clean bowl.

"You do a wonderful job with your makeup," said Linda, watching Helen crack another egg. "You do. But think how much time and money you could save. Marlene said they guarantee a fifty percent reduction in pigmentation. And the whole process only takes three months. You could be done by Julia's wedding—"

"I should have guessed." Helen turned the mixer on high. "That's the real issue, isn't it? Everything's got to be perfect for Julia's wedding."

"Honey, no!" Linda pushed back her chair and moved to stand beside her. "I'm thinking about you. Here, come sit. Take a break."

Helen had her eyes squeezed shut, but she heard the mixer turn off, felt her mother's cool hands steering her over to the kitchen table.

"I'm sorry," Linda said. "Helen. Sweetheart. You know I just want to make things easier for you."

"I know." Helen blew her nose. "I know you do."

"What's this really about? You've been on edge since you got here. Hasn't she, Gord?"

"It's nothing." Helen looked down at the table, then up at the clock on the wall. Glenn and Julia would be out of Ottawa by now, driving down that first stretch of highway at a hundred kilometers an hour. For a moment, she wanted to blurt it all out, tell her parents everything: all about Anna, and the rape, and Olly and Phil and Glenn and this terrible place where Helen was trapped between them all.

"Is this about work?" Linda asked, stroking her arm. "Those rumours about restructuring? Is that why you're so worked up?"

"No." Helen let out her breath. "I mean, yes, maybe."

It wasn't a lie. Ever since Barb's warnings, Helen spent her shifts on edge, wiping down the counter every ten minutes, dawdling over makeovers. Then, when she got home, she was faced with Thom's closed bedroom door, the scribbled notes he'd taken to leaving around the apartment: *Rinse containers before recycling! Clean up after your friend comes over! Don't touch my mayo OR my ketchup!*

"Why don't you see if other places are hiring?" Linda said. "You've got so much experience. Anyone would be lucky to have you."

"On the other hand," said Gord. "You could think long-term. Maybe go back to school."

"I don't think so."

Helen started to stand but her mother tightened her grip, holding her in place.

"Listen to Gord," Linda said. "School's a great idea. You don't have to go back to university, but what about college? You could take classes in cosmology. Get some certification."

"You mean cosmetology."

"Right. Take time off your job. You could even move in here for a few months. Make a fresh start."

"I couldn't." Helen pulled free. "But you know I appreciate the offer."

"We've got space," Linda said. "You could work part-time while you take classes. Gord still needs a receptionist!"

For a moment, Helen let herself imagine the look on Carmen's face when she said she was quitting. The shock on Thom's when she said *I'm moving out.* Life would be so much simpler if she packed up and moved into her parents' spare room. She could take classes in skin care and esthetics, even branch out into stage makeup or special effects.

"We could definitely use the help," Gord said. "But look at university, not just college. How long would it take to finish your degree, a semester or two? And of course you have other talents." He nodded at the mixing bowls on the counter.

"I can't. I'm just going through a rough patch. It'll all work out."

Linda's smile dropped. "You know best." She carried her mug to the sink, turned on the water and started to rattle dishes around.

Helen met Gord's eyes. She stood up and crossed the cork floor to stand behind her mother.

"Mom. I'm going to be okay."

Linda turned, twisting a tea towel printed with the Nova Scotia flag.

"I just want you to know. You can always come home."

"I know, Mom." Helen put her arms around Linda's soft waist and hugged her tight. "I know."

*

Julia and Glenn arrived while Helen was decorating the cake. Her stomach fluttered at the sound of their voices, but she took deep breaths to stay calm, staring down at the cake as she dropped blueberries into the violet swirls of buttercream icing. She placed the berries one by one, playing her own version of he loves me, he loves me not: *Take Glenn outside. Don't say anything. Get him outside. Don't say anything.*

"Gord, happy birthday," Julia was saying in the hall. "Sorry we're late, traffic was awful. There were roadworks through Kingston, then an accident near the Peterborough turnoff."

"Don't worry about it. We'll order dinner now. Glenn, can I take that?"

"It's not that heavy, I've got it."

Helen's heart kicked in her chest at the sound of Glenn's voice. *Don't say anything.* That was definitely the easiest option.

Julia walked into the kitchen, cuddling Dusty against her white ribbed tank top. She looked pale and tired, with dark circles under her deep-set brown eyes.

"Hey," she said. "You changed your hair." She released the cat onto the floor, where she twined around her ankles. "What kind of cake are we having?"

Helen sprinkled the last pistachios around the edge of the cake.

"Mom picked up the blueberries at the market—"

"Are those pistachios?"

"It's a blueberry pistachio sponge cake. From *Bon Appetit*."

"Glenn's allergic. He can't have nuts. Mom didn't tell you?"

"Obviously not." A spasm twinged in Helen's right temple. She pressed on the spot with her thumb. "Fine, he won't have cake. There's still ice cream."

"That sucks, though." Julia leaned down to stroke the cat. "Hear that, Dusty? We drive five hours and poor Glenn doesn't even get cake."

"Oh my God."

Helen sucked her breath through her teeth as Glenn himself appeared in the doorway.

"Good to see you, Helen." Glenn pushed his blond hair back from his forehead, yellow rubber Livestrong wristband hugging his wrist. She felt a pinch in her gut as he smiled that familiar gap-toothed smile. *Get him outside.* Could she really go through with this? "Wow, that cake looks beautiful. Except—"

"I already told her," said Julia. "Don't worry, babe. I'll run out and get something else. There's a bakery on Jarvis that's probably still open."

"Sure," said Helen, her voice rising. "Should I toss this one? What do you think, Glenn, should I throw it out, all fifteen dollars' worth of organic pistachios that I specially bought, because, you know, they're Gord's favourite and it's *his* birthday? Or could you maybe survive without a slice of cake, just for this one day?"

"It's fine," Glenn said. "I don't need cake."

"What's happening in here?"

Gord's voice made Helen swing round.

"It's Julia. She thinks I'm poisoning Glenn."

"I just said he's allergic! I don't know why she's freaking out, she takes everything so personally—"

"Stop." Helen's head was pounding. "Just stop! This one thing I can do, this one good thing, and you have to ruin this too?" She ground her knuckle into her temple. "The cake is done. I'm going to go lie down. Someone can come get me when it's time for dinner."

In her parents' spare room, Helen collapsed onto the daybed, staring up at the craters of the popcorn ceiling.

What if he did it? A small voice asked in the back of her mind. Tall, athletic Glenn Starkey, so polite and easygoing. How well did Helen know him, really? *He's a good guy,* she'd said to Anna. That was true, of course, but what about behind closed doors? What about drunk sixteen-year-old Glenn in the middle of the night at a house party, surrounded by teenage buddies cheering him on? Was he a good guy then?

What if Anna had it right this time? What if Phil was telling the truth?

Helen sat up, hugging her knees. *What if he did it?* She stared out the window, a rectangle framing the peachy sunset sky. It was almost seven o'clock. Anna was probably already out there, waiting in the park across the street. Helen thought of that drive over to Olly's party, she and Anna giggling in the backseat of her father's car, giddy on adrenaline and stolen shots of vodka. Their first real New Year's party, the one Helen insisted they attend.

Fast forward a few hours, and Helen was calling her mother from the phone in the kitchen. "Can you come get me? I think Annie already left." And all that time, upstairs... *What if he did it?*

Outside, the sky was bleeding orange, streaked with pink. She got to her feet, pacing across the carpet between the window and the door. Eight steps one way, pivoting on bare feet, eight steps back. She thought of Anna slouching down the Laurier hallway in a stained black sweatshirt, greasy blond hair covering her empty face. She thought of Anna under the trees at Hillside, advancing on Helen, her dark eyes fierce and intent. All Anna wanted was the truth. Wasn't that what Helen wanted, too? *We can find out.* That's what Helen had promised. Didn't she owe it to Anna to help her now?

Helen was over by the window when the knock came on the door.

"It's just me," said Glenn. A narrow lozenge of light fell across the carpet as he pushed open the door. "Dinner should be here in a couple minutes. And you know, the cake thing's not a big deal. Julia's just been stressed—"

Suddenly Helen couldn't wait any longer.

"Glenn," she said. "Can I ask you something?"

"About Julia?" He stepped into the room, blocking the light from the hallway.

"About Annie Leverett." Helen kept her eyes fixed on his face. "About that New Year's party, back in high school."

"I wasn't there," said Glenn. But he wouldn't meet her eyes.

"I know you were there. There are pictures in the yearbook," Helen said. "Anna blacked out that night. She doesn't remember anything. But last week, at Hillside, she talked to Phil McKinley..." Glenn's face was so white his freckles stood out against his cheeks. "It's true, isn't it? You and Olly and whoever else. You raped her."

"Don't call it that!" Glenn raised his hands to his face, speaking through the cage of his fingers. "It was a mistake!"

"A *mistake*? Are you serious?"

"We were drunk. All of us, Annie too—"

"No." Helen said. "Don't blame her for what you did." Her headache was back, sharp pain stretching down her neck, across her shoulders.

"None of us were thinking straight." Glenn dropped his hands and stared past Helen, towards the window. "Olly thought it was funny. Like a prank, or something. But I felt terrible." He shuddered. "There was one picture that showed my face. I ripped it up. Flushed it. Honestly, I try to forget it ever happened. It's the worst thing I've ever done."

"Forget what happened?" The door swung wide and there was Julia. "Dinner's here. What are you talking about? The worst thing you've ever done?"

"Will you tell her?" Helen said. "Or should I?"

"Tell me what?"

"Don't," said Glenn. "Please."

"You remember Annie Leverett?" Helen said. "How she fell apart, in high school? There were all those rumours, about how she was drinking at school, sleeping around—"

"Yeah?" Julia looked back and forth between Helen and Glenn. Her fingers were white where they clenched the doorframe. "So?"

"It all started with this New Year's party, where supposedly she slept with a bunch of guys. But Anna and

I just found out what actually happened. She had too much to drink, she passed out, so Glenn here and his friends—"

"It wasn't my idea!"

"What did they do?"

Helen looked her sister in the eye.

"They raped her."

Julia sucked in her breath. She looked at Helen, then at Glenn. Then she turned and was gone, her footsteps rapid on the wooden floor as she fled down the hallway and out the front door.

"Julia!" Glenn called after her, as the front door slammed. He looked at Helen, eyes wild. "I have to talk to her!"

"No." Helen reached out and gripped his wrist. "No, there's something else you have to do first."

*

Anna was waiting for them outside, leaning against the iron lamppost like a detective in an old film noir. Her blond dreadlocks shone in the lamplight, haloing her face.

"Glenn Starkey," Anna said, stepping forward. "Long time no see."

"I asked him already." Helen said. "He admitted what he did."

For a moment Anna looked uncertain.

"You asked him? Glenn, it's true?"

Shivering in the hot August night air, Helen watched them face off in the lamplight. This felt unreal. The bubble separating Helen's family and her daily life had popped, and she had done this, she had brought them together, she was the one who'd confronted Glenn and made him confess. Again, she heard that voice in the back of her mind: *What about Julia?* Again, she saw Julia's stricken face as Helen brought her sky crashing down. Julia didn't deserve this, not really. But shouldn't she know who she was marrying?

"I'm sorry," Glenn was saying. "I thought, I hoped, if we never talked about it, it would be like it hadn't happened."

"You thought I wouldn't find out," said Anna.

"I'm so sorry." Glenn rocked from foot to foot like a little boy who needed the bathroom. "I was so drunk, I barely knew what I was doing. You just lay there, like you didn't even notice, and I think...I'd never... It was my first time, and—"

"Mine too."

Helen had to look away. Across the park, a camper van drove slowly by, its roof scraped by the tree branches overhanging the road.

"I swear. I never meant to hurt you," Glenn said, voice breaking on the word *hurt*. "Olly... we all just egged each other on. We all wanted to prove that we weren't..."

"That you weren't pussies?" Anna said, her voice hard. "That your dicks worked? That you knew which end of a girl to fuck?"

"I wish I could take it back," Glenn said. "And, afterwards? I know you didn't remember, but you were okay, weren't you? Or—"

"I was pregnant."

Helen's heart plunged. Pregnant? Anna had been pregnant? Wandering through the hallways of the school, eyes downcast and hair unkempt and pregnant?

"Don't worry. I got rid of it." Anna's eyes burned into Glenn's face. "But I thought you should know."

"Oh God." Glenn swayed. "Pregnant?"

"Who knows," Anna said. "Maybe it was Olly's."

Hope brightened Glenn's face. In that moment, Helen wanted to punch him.

"I need you to come forward," Anna said. "I need your word against Olly's. Publicly. In Guelph, where it matters."

"Where it matters. Oh God. Julia." Glenn wrenched his arm out of Helen's grasp. "I have to go. I have to talk to her!"

Anna lunged but he was gone, running down the sidewalk.

"Glenn!" She shouted after him, as he disappeared around the corner of the building. "Glenn!" She turned to Helen, her face full of despair. "Fuck! Now what?"

But Helen's thoughts had locked up. Numbly, she forced out the words: "You were pregnant?"

"Yeah." Anna looked away. Under the frizz of her blond dreads, her face was shadowed, unreadable. "Yeah."

CHAPTER 17

The days after Hillside were bad.

The days after Toronto were worse.

Anna lay on her parents' white leather couch with one hand behind her head, staring up at the plaster medallion on the living room ceiling, scratching at the new tattoo. Nearly two weeks since Hillside and it was still red and itchy, taking its time healing. All that goose shit floating around Guelph Lake probably hadn't helped.

An hour ago, she'd surfaced with a gasp from a murky dream, faceless men holding her down in a tank of water. Now the blazing sun read mid-afternoon. Somehow, she'd forgotten how to sleep properly. If she could just close her eyes, get some rest, maybe she could think more clearly. She'd lost track of what day it was. But what did it matter? She hadn't left the house all week. Stopped answering the phone. She needed time alone to work this out.

Once, when she was young, she and her father had taken a taxi from a Caribbean airport to the resort where they were staying. They'd driven through a tropical downpour, the cab's windshield wipers whipping back and forth, the road blotted out by fog and rain. Her brain felt like that now, scudding on high speed through zero visibility.

Why had she thought it would help, knowing what happened? It didn't matter that Phil and Glenn had both expressed remorse: *We were drunk. We never meant to hurt you.* The facts of the matter were plain: a group of laughing boys, snapping photos while they took turns with her, a stupid drunk passed-out teenaged girl.

Anna wiped at the tears running down the sides of her face. She should never have told Helen about the abortion. After Glenn took off, Helen had steered her to a nearby Tim Hortons, looking at her with wide helpless eyes while Anna shivered in the powerful air conditioning. More useless *I'm sorrys*, sympathy ten years too late. Still, it was ridiculous, how much she cried these days. Like a leaking tap. She was crying too much, unable to sleep, not eating enough. But what did it matter? What did any of it matter?

The exhaustion, the tears, the lack of appetite: she'd been through this before, after Olly's party. For days, she'd lain in bed with her face to the wall, tracing the repeating pattern of the roses in her wallpaper: pink, pink, pink, cream. She couldn't sleep then either, no matter how long she lay with her eyes closed and her curtains drawn. Days and days of staring at the wall, her mind a howling blank as the tenderness dulled between her legs, the bruises on her thighs faded from blue to yellowish-green.

Her parents had been furious when she got home that morning after the party. Her father with shadows under his eyes from his own New Year's celebrations. Her mother sitting on the stairs, pressing manicured fingers to her temples.

"Where have you been?"

"We've been worried sick."

"Jesus, Annie. You smell like a distillery!"

"You're not still drunk, are you?"

"How could you do this to your mother?"

Their anger turned to worry when she stopped coming down to meals. "Come on, Annie, you need to eat." Her father at the end of her bed with a bowl of chicken soup. Her mother with a glass of water and a magic pill: "Do you want to try a Xanax? It'll calm you down, help you sleep."

It had been her mother's idea to take the pregnancy test. That was weeks after the party. Annie was back in school by then, stumbling through days in a tranquilized haze, crawling into bed as soon as she got home. Her missing appetite had curdled into nausea. One morning, the smell of coffee sent her rushing to the sink. When she straightened up, Joyce caught her eye.

"How long have you been feeling sick?"

"I'm fine." Wiping her mouth on her sleeve like a child.

"I don't think so." Her mother stepping closer. "I think you've got yourself into trouble. Go on, upstairs."

A trip to the drugstore, then Joyce was ripping open a pregnancy test, thrusting the smooth plastic wand at her.

Annie had peed on a stick once before, peeling back the plastic and holding the tester under her chubby five-year-old thighs, her mother laughing with tears in her eyes when she caught her. Joyce had seen lots of positive tests. *Getting* pregnant was never her problem.

"I want to watch you do it."

The dizziness of that moment.

Then: the look on Joyce's face as the double pink lines swam across the tiny window.

And then: her mother screaming so loudly it hurt her ears. Annie cowering by the toilet and screaming back, tasting blood. Malcolm rushing in to pull Joyce out of the bathroom.

The deadly silence of the next few days. Annie lay in bed, covers up to her neck, refusing to talk to either of her parents. Blocking it all out, staring at the roses on her wallpaper: pink, pink, pink, cream.

And then: Joyce's ultimatum.

Annie might have run away, if she'd had an ounce of energy left. Or any idea where to go. Her grandmother's condo? It was locked; she spent her winters in Mexico. A friend's house? There was only Helen, and they hadn't spoken in weeks.

Then: her father's unexpected appearance in her doorway.

"I've made you an appointment at a clinic in Kitchener." Her mattress creaking as he sat by her feet. "We don't have to tell your mother."

Pulling on her softest sweatshirt and her loosest jeans. Staring out the passenger window as he drove out of Guelph, up and down the snow-covered hills on the road to Kitchener. The yellow brick building housing the clinic. The lone protester in the parking lot, Malcolm's protective hand on the shoulder of Annie's oversized coat. The faded colours of the waiting room, wilted paper snowflakes dangling from the low ceiling. The carefully blank faces of the nurses. The ultrasound…

Anna sat up abruptly. Was that her mother's voice? Keys rattled in the lock, then the front door opened and her parents bustled across the threshold.

"You shouldn't have tipped him so much, Malcolm. That's not white-glove service, he just left the bags on the driveway…Oh." Joyce's fingers stopped unbuttoning her beige trench coat as she caught sight of Anna through the glass of the French doors. "Hello."

Her parents? Here, now? Surely they weren't supposed to be home yet. Surely their six-month cruise lasted until September.

Joyce sniffed the air. "You've been smoking inside? We'll have to get the carpets deep-cleaned." She undid her last button and fluffed out her ash blond hair. "Well, say something. What kind of welcome is this?"

Anna got to her feet and pushed open the French doors. Here was her father, his skin a deep bronze, his hair combed back from his forehead like an old-fashioned movie star. He lifted a suitcase over the threshold, glanced up with a tired smile. Joyce was hanging her coat in the hall closet. As she turned, the clove-and-citrus scent of her Opium perfume wafted over Anna and suddenly this was all real.

"You guys are back?"

Anna put a hand on the wall to steady herself.

"Us guys?" Anna caught a grimace on Joyce's face as she leaned in to kiss her cheek. "You can't even pretend to be happy to see us?"

Up close her mother looked exhausted, with new wrinkles around her eyes, her hairline ringed with white coming in under the blond.

"I thought you were in Dubai."

Their weekly phone calls had covered three topics: Was Anna staying "out of trouble"? How was everything in the house and the yard? Which country had Malcolm and Joyce just seen and where were they heading?

"We emailed," said Joyce. "And I called from Schiphol. Didn't you check the messages?"

"Your mother caught a bug in Madras. She couldn't face the Red Sea crossing, so we disembarked in Bombay." Malcolm shrugged out of his leather jacket and placed his hands against his lower back, wincing as he stretched. "I still can't believe we missed the pyramids."

"They claim the restaurants are vetted," Joyce said. "But God only knows what conditions they've got in those kitchens."

"I need a drink." Malcolm disappeared towards the kitchen, his thinning blond hair sticking up at the back of his head.

Anna couldn't speak. Her vision was constricting, narrowing so that all she could see was her mother as she leaned over the rolltop desk and rummaged through her handbag. Or was it Joyce who was getting bigger, expanding to take up all the space in the hall, all the oxygen in the house?

Then Malcolm was back, brushing past Anna, making her sway on her feet.

"Where's our duty-free?" He ripped open a plastic bag and pulled out a litre of Scotch, the amber liquid sloshing in the heavy bottle. "I was planning to save this. But since it appears someone has worked her way through my entire collection, I'll open it now."

"I didn't want to keep booze in the house."

"Twenty-five-year-old Macallan is not *booze*. It's an investment."

"I'm sorry," said Joyce. "I'm exhausted. I'm taking an Ambien and going to bed."

Anna stared after her mother as she climbed the stairs.

"She's no traveller," said Malcolm from the end of the hallway. "Not like you and me, Annie. You'll join me in a drink?"

"Not now," Anna said. "I'm not feeling great either."

"There's Dramamine in your mother's purse." Malcolm raised the tumbler of whisky in his tanned hand. "Now, if you'll excuse me." He disappeared into

his office, his leather chair giving a soft wheeze as he settled behind his desk.

Anna shivered. Alone in the hallway, she felt acutely
aware of her father on the other side of the wall; her mother
lying down upstairs. But she wouldn't let them chase her
away. Not this time. She wasn't finished here yet.

*

The next day, Anna forced herself out of bed before noon.
Before she did anything else, she opened a black garbage
bag and shoved in all her old board games. The cardboard buckled under her fists, spilling dice and tokens
and mismatched game pieces into the bottom of the bag.
She shoved in her map of Guelph, too, ripping the ink-
stained paper as she pushed it down to the bottom of the
bag. Then she tied it all off with a double knot and set the
garbage bag by her door.

She opened her window and perched on the sill,
where the arctic breeze of the AC met the sticky August
heat. Below, in the backyard, the kidney-shaped pool
glittered in the sunlight. She could see the top of her
father's Panama hat, his long legs crossed in the shaded
recliner as he flipped through the newspaper. She could
hear the hiss of her mother spraying sunscreen, the shrill
drone of cicadas.

She slid off the sill and padded down the hall to her
parents' bathroom, where she opened the mirrored medicine cabinet. It was filled with her mother's pills, lined
up neatly along the narrow glass shelf. Xanax, Codeine,
Ambien and all the rest of her old friends.

Looking up, Anna caught a glimpse of herself in the
mirror: sallow skin under the ink, her cheekbones more
prominent than usual, as if she was changing shape

under her skin. She scratched at her new tattoo and stared at the green triangular pills jumbled together in the orange plastic Xanax bottle. *Just one,* she told herself as she popped the lid and shook a tablet into her palm. Then she set the bottle back on its shelf, turning it carefully so the label faced forward to match the others.

After the calm spread through her, she picked up the phone.

*

She met Helen at the Bookshelf, just off the downtown square.

Helen was already there when Anna arrived, sitting at a table near the back, under a giant framed poster of Greta Garbo. She didn't smile when Anna arrived, didn't meet her eyes, just stared past her towards the string of fairy lights on the exposed brick wall.

"You're all right?" Anna asked, as she settled into the chair opposite.

"Why wouldn't I be?"

"That's why I'm asking." Helen was more dolled up than usual, her cheekbones shimmering under the restaurant's lights. Her manicured fingers were wrapped around a black paper shopping bag that took up half the little table. "What's in the bag?"

Helen tilted the bag forward so Anna could see inside.

"Some of the new fall lines came out today." She lifted a long black and white box. "Dior's new mascara. A couple of other things."

"Fancy." Anna glimpsed interlocking Cs on a black and gold package. "Is that Chanel?"

"I needed a pick-me-up." Helen folded the bag shut and tucked it under her chair.

Anna leaned across the table.

"Listen. I need your help."

"Again? I thought you got what you wanted. You talked to Glenn."

"You know I'm not done with those guys. And you said you'd help."

"That's all you want from me?"

"What?" Anna sat back. "What do you mean?"

"I mean I'm sick of being used." The nails of Helen's interlaced fingers dug into the backs of her hands. Her voice dropped, making Anna lean forward to catch her words. "We set off this nuclear bomb in my family, then you disappear. You only call when you want my help. This isn't how friends are supposed to treat each other."

Anna stared at her. "I thought you were on my side."

"What does that even mean to you? Don't I get a side?"

"Where's our waiter?" Anna signalled to a long-haired guy with a notepad, who weaved his way to their table. "Two vodka martinis. Lots of olives, easy on the ice."

"I thought you'd quit drinking," Helen said. "And I hate olives."

"Great, I'll take yours."

"I need the washroom."

And then Helen was up, walking away, following the waiter towards the back of the restaurant. *This isn't how friends are supposed to treat each other.* Anna's stomach twisted. What did Helen expect, gossip sessions and manicures?

She returned just as the server slid their drinks onto the table. Helen had applied some kind of glitter over her cheeks and her whole face shone like it was made of glass.

Anna took a deep breath.

"I'm sorry," she said. She picked up her drink and gulped at the vodka, clean and briny as the ocean. "For being a shitty friend. I'm not trying to use you, I'm just out of practice. And I do want to keep hanging out with you."

"Really?"

"Yes! And I don't want things to be heavy all the time. I know you've got your own shit going on, with family and work."

"And Thom."

"Uh huh. Sure."

"Anna!"

"Sorry. And Thom."

"It is heavy," Helen said. She trailed her finger down the condensation on her glass. "I appreciate the apology."

"Yeah." Anna bit an olive off her toothpick. "Look, my life has been fucked up for a long time. And it's actually been nice, these last few months, hanging out with you, thinking we could fix some of this, together. It's been huge for me. Whatever happens, I want us to stay friends. Can we do that?"

"Yes," Helen said. "But only if you promise not to disappear again."

"I needed time alone," Anna said. "But you're right. I should have told you."

Helen made a noise, something between a hum and a cough. She sipped at her martini and made a face. "This is really strong."

"That's the idea." Anna held out her drink. "To you and me."

Helen smiled, at last. "To us."

They clinked glasses.

"So." Anna said. "Big news. My parents are home. They abandoned ship in India after my mother got food poisoning."

"What? Is she okay?"

"Oh yeah. Knowing her, it was probably an excuse to bail on the cruise. They say they tried to call, but I wasn't answering. As you know."

"So, what did they say?"

"About…?"

"You know. Everything you found out. The party. Phil and Olly and Glenn. The photographs."

"I'm not telling them anything. I'm staying out of their way."

"You have to tell them."

"There's no point. I just want to get moving, with taking down Olly," Anna said. "I need Glenn Starkey to come clean. Can you give me his number?"

Helen was already shaking her head.

"I know you don't want to be involved—"

"It's not just that. He moved out. Julia made him leave."

"Really?" Anna felt a bitter surge of satisfaction. "Good for Julia."

"Yeah, I knew you'd be happy," Helen said. "Their wedding's off. Or postponed, officially. But I'll be shocked if it goes ahead."

"Amazing. How'd you like that, Starkey? How's it feel to have your life turned upside down?"

"My mom is freaking out. I'm trying to stay out of it. But Julia won't tell her what happened, so Mom keeps calling me, asking if I know what went wrong between them. She thinks Julia should give Glenn another chance, try and work things out."

"He's done some shitty things. He should pay for them."

"And Julia? And my mom? And Gord, even? It's not fair on them."

"Fair? None of this is fair!" Anna's laugh caught in her throat. "Fine. What about email? Or could we contact Starkey's parents?"

"No. I can't help, Anna. Not until things get worked out with him and Julia."

"And what if they don't?" Anna was appalled to feel tears welling up. "Jesus, Helen. If you won't help me, what am I supposed to do now?"

CHAPTER 18

Helen was at work when a woman in her fifties strolled up to the Façade counter. The woman was dressed in a linen sundress and heels, her silver hair a sleek bob. With rosacea-splotched cheeks and a Louis Vuitton handbag, she looked like the perfect client.

"Can I offer you a makeover?" Helen stepped out from behind the counter and gestured to the stool in front of the mirror. "Façade can help you put your best face forward. It'll only take ten minutes. And there's no obligation to buy anything."

Helen loved giving makeovers. Mixing shades to match each person's individual skin tone, erasing scars and birthmarks with cosmetic magic. Sometimes a client cried when they saw how good they looked. *It's gone!* they'd exclaim, a trembling hand hovering over their hidden imperfections. *You can't even see it anymore!* They'd look at Helen with awe, ready to buy every product she recommended.

Once she had the woman perched in front of the mirror, Helen dipped her brush in the green-tinted primer and drew it across the ruddy skin of her cheeks.

"See how we neutralized the redness? You'll want to go back and forth," she said. "Right-handed people usually spend more time on the left side, but we need to apply products evenly."

Helen stroked the brush along the skin and smiled at the woman, meeting her eyes in the mirror.

"Next, I'm choosing our Invisible Foundation cover stick. I'm using Neutral Three, to match the liquid version."

Helen could see herself in the mirror too, her face glowing silver and pink with her new MAC highlighter and Chanel gloss. She uncapped the tube and tapped it along the woman's jaw, blotting out the last few broken blood vessels with dabs of foundation.

"What do you think?"

The client peered at her reflection. "It's very shiny."

"It just needs to finish drying. But isn't the coverage fabulous?"

"You said this would only take a few minutes. Are you almost done?"

Helen was reaching for the setting powder when she noticed Carmen watching from the end of the counter. Flustered, she dropped the powder brush, snatched it off the floor and spritzed it with cleaning solution.

"The best thing about our Invisible Foundation Stick is that it comes with an SPF of fifty," she said, speaking faster now. "You'll conceal imperfections while protecting your epidermis from UV exposure damage. People with rosacea need to avoid the sun. And you want products with a lighter—"

Carmen made a noise and Helen's mind went briefly blank, forgetting the word for *coverage*. She stumbled through her patter, trying to cover her lapse.

"You want something that won't be...you know how some makeup is really heavy? This will hardly show, it just disappears into your skin. And it'll last all day."

Helen laid the brush on the counter as the woman peered into the mirror.

"You can see how we've restored the texture, giving you smooth, younger-looking skin as well as a perfect match to your natural colour." Helen paused, then went in for the kill. "If you're buying three products at full price, I can offer you a 25-percent discount on the fourth. Or would you be ready to invest in our full collection today?"

"I don't know," said the woman. "I'll think about it. It's very expensive, your line." She slid down and smoothed back her silver hair, handbag swinging from her wrist.

"No problem." Helen forced a smile. "My name's Helen, for when you come back."

As the woman strode away, Carmen slid up beside her.

"You've really got to work on those customer engagement skills. Remember, it's not just product expertise. You need to create a meaningful emotional connection."

Helen pressed her lips together to stop herself from answering. She sprayed each of the brushes with cleaning solution and set the testers back in the display cases. As she was wiping down the counter, she caught another glimpse of herself in the mirror, her face gleaming like an otherworldly mask. Sighing, Helen pulled a tissue from the box, rubbed at her cheeks and wiped off her sticky pink lip gloss.

*

When she got home from work, Helen found a basket of zucchini on the porch and a note in her landlady's handwriting. An hour later, she was flipping through a *Glamour* magazine when Thom stormed into the kitchen.

"God, Helen. Do you have to leave dishes everywhere?"

"I've got zucchini bread in the oven. I'd rather do all my dishes at once."

"So, my dinner has to wait?"

"I'll do them now. It's not a big deal."

"Whatever." Thom opened the fridge. "Where's my cheese?"

"I haven't touched it."

"Sure, it just walked away on its own." He turned around and leaned against the counter with the jar of mayonnaise. As she watched, he unscrewed the lid, stuck in a finger and licked it.

"Don't be gross." Helen shuddered.

"I'm gross? Me? You leave your mess everywhere. And what about your friend?" He never used Anna's name. "You let her smoke in the apartment now?"

"She only did that once." Helen closed her magazine and pushed back her chair. "Can you move? I need to check the oven."

She crouched down to peer at the zucchini bread, which hadn't yet risen past the top of the loaf pan. When she stood up, Thom was standing so close that she could see the stubble on his cheeks, smell his Old Spice deodorant.

"Can you give me some space?"

"All I do is give you space," he said. "Have you seen the bathroom? You've got so many bottles on the counter there's literally no room for my toothbrush."

"I've been organizing my products." Helen set a hand against his chest, pushing him back. "You don't have to be an asshole about it."

"*I'm* the asshole? Fuck you, Helen. You're the one who can't make normal conversation anymore." Thom sucked in a breath, staring down into her eyes. Then he grabbed her shoulders and kissed her.

For a moment, Helen was stunned. Then she raised her hands and wriggled free.

"Hey," she gasped. "What the fuck was that?"

He looked shaken.

"You kissed me back!"

"You can't do that." Helen backed away, banging her hip against the counter. "We're done with that."

"You can't turn things off and on between us—"

"It's off, keep it off!"

*

Helen hid in her room for the rest of that evening. The next day, she left early for work and didn't come home until mid-afternoon, after Thom had left for a weekend at his family cottage.

When she unwrapped the zucchini bread, she saw that Thom had removed a section from the middle and shoved the ends of the loaf back together, as if she might not notice how much he'd taken.

Helen cut herself a slice and ate over the sink, staring out the kitchen window at the yellowing leaves of the maple in the backyard. She brushed off her hands and took a beer out of the fridge, holding the cold bottle against her forehead while she searched for the opener. The phone rang as she was popping the lid.

"Hello?" She slid down the cupboards to sit on the mismatched linoleum, taking a long drink. "Hey, Mom."

"The wedding's back on!"

Helen choked. "What?"

"I just spoke to Julia! Glenn's moving back home. She still won't tell me what happened. Maybe he got cold feet? But they're working things out."

"Oh my God. Did she say anything else?"

"No, and I'm not asking. I'm just so happy for them. Gord is too. You know he couldn't sleep for worrying? He's been up making bread in the middle of the night.

He just worries so much about you both. And I hadn't said anything to the rest of the family, so this is really the best-case scenario."

Helen shivered. Best-case scenario? Part of her had wondered if she'd even see Glenn again, after their confrontation in the park. She'd been asleep when he and Julia got back to the condo, and the next morning he was gone by the time she woke up.

At first, Helen had been relieved. How was she supposed to sit across the table from him, eat breakfast and drink coffee and pretend she didn't know what he'd done? That morning, Julia's deep-set brown eyes were hollowed with fatigue, her dark Amélie hair dishevelled. Maybe Helen should have felt guilty, but it was strangely gratifying to see her sister suffer, to know she was facing her own setback, for once. *Not Little Miss Perfect anymore,* she'd thought, watching Julia push her scrambled eggs around her plate, lips tight, eyes downcast.

Helen's remorse only kicked in a few days later, when she found out Julia had cancelled the wedding. "Glenn's broken her heart," Linda had wailed into the phone. Helen had stood frozen in this very kitchen, holding the receiver to her ear. *I'm going to blow up their lives,* Anna had said, but it was Helen who'd pulled the pin on the grenade and tossed it in her sister's face. Standing there, listening to Linda weep into the phone, Helen wished she could take it all back.

Now she dug her fingernails under the label of the sweating beer bottle, peeling away the paper, rubbing her thumb against the sticky residue left behind. *Best-case scenario.* So why did Helen feel so bad?

*

An hour later, when Anna rang the doorbell, Helen had already finished a third bottle of beer. How could she tell Anna that the wedding was back on? But how could she not?

"God, it's hot out there," said Anna, puffing as she climbed the stairs and handed Helen a bag of ketchup chips. She wore a white tank top over cut-off jean shorts, along with her usual Doc Martens. "You don't have AC?"

"Sorry." Helen held out a beer. "I can offer you a cold drink and a shady balcony."

Outside, they settled on a dusty yoga mat and stretched their legs through the balcony's wooden railings.

"Peace at last," said Anna, leaning back against the warm brick wall and closing her eyes. "You don't know how lucky you are, having your own place."

"Am I?" Helen looked down at her beer. This time the label had come off in one piece. She pasted the damp paper against her bare thigh and ripped open the bag, scattering chips across the yoga mat. "Shit, sorry!"

"It's fine. Chill out."

"Sorry," Helen said again. "Work today was…not great. And the Thom situation's getting tense."

"I thought he was gone for the weekend?"

"Yeah." Helen took a handful of chips and stared out through the wooden railings to the empty street below. "We had a stupid argument yesterday. Then he kissed me."

"Really?" Anna said. "I'm glad one of us is getting some action. Did you fuck him again?"

"No! We're done with that. I've raised my standards." Helen thought again of Dave Patel, his brown skin shining in the sun. The white teeth of his easy smile.

"As you should." Anna held out her beer and clinked it against Helen's. She hiked up her tank top and pressed the bottle against a patch of reddened skin. "We'll find you someone better. Maybe tonight."

"What's that? Heat rash?"

"It's the tattoo I got at Hillside. The guy must have used cheap ink. But it's no big deal. You should see what happened here." She pointed out a distorted monkey on her left calf and mimed a mass the size of a cantaloupe. "I got bitten by a spider and the whole area got infected. I was staying on a beach in Vietnam. We poured vodka overtop to keep the swelling down."

She laughed at Helen's shudder and leaned back against the bricks, closing her eyes against the bright sun.

Helen nibbled at the chips, sneaking sidelong glances at Anna. Her knowledge about the wedding was floating between them like an invisible Mylar balloon. But wasn't there some way forward that didn't involve Glenn?

"What do you want to happen?" Helen asked, abruptly. "With Olly Sutton?"

"Murder is off the table?" Anna said. "I want to expose the truth. What he did, who he really is. Something permanent that he can't hide. How about a nice big tattoo across his forehead, in capital letters? *RAPIST*. You can hold him down, I'll do the work. Or how about branding? That would hurt more."

"Anna," Helen said. "We're talking real life, not comic books."

"That's not realistic? Okay, what about some old-fashioned 'wanted' posters? Olly's face, with a message underneath: 'Warning, rapist!' We could put them all over town."

Anna stabbed out her cigarette, leaving a black smudge on the paint. When she spoke again, her voice had changed.

"The problem is that people trust him. Can you believe that he works in a fucking high school, around teenagers? They should know he's a predator. That's why I need evidence."

"What about Phil McKinley? Couldn't he help?"

"Phil." Anna stared into the street, turning her head to watch an old brown Mercury cruise past Helen's building. "He gave me a phone number. I tried calling him, after we talked to Starkey. Disconnected."

"What if I came with you, if we talked to Olly together? I was there when Glenn told us what happened. I heard everything he said."

"Like a witness."

"Maybe Olly would come clean, if he knows Glenn already admitted everything. He might even apologize."

"Right," Anna snorted. "But you have his address?"

"I'm the one who sent out the save-the-date cards," Helen said. "Maybe if we talked to him, both of us together—"

"Okay." Anna dropped the cigarette butt into her beer bottle and climbed to her feet, brushing off her jean shorts. "Let's give it a try."

"What? Now?"

"No time like the present."

*

A dog barked as they approached the apartment, and a girl opened the door before they could knock. She was wearing a loose top over yoga pants, gripping the collar of a tall grey poodle. Her freckled face was bare, her chestnut hair in a high ponytail.

"You're not pizza," she said, readjusting her stance as the dog strained forward. Behind them was a bright, open living room, with plants lining a window that looked out over the limestone buildings of Guelph's downtown core. "Wait, aren't you the girl who freaked out at the Trash?"

Before Anna could answer, Olly walked into the room. "What the fuck is this?"

"Sorry, I buzzed them in." The girl was still wrestling the dog between her legs. "I thought it was the delivery guy."

The poodle barked again.

"Quiet, Max!" Olly wore a sleeveless grey T-shirt and his blond hair was wet, like he'd just come back from a run. His blue eyes were fixed on Anna. "Fiona, put Maximus in the bedroom. I'll deal with this."

"That's right," Anna said. "We need to talk."

Anna popped her knuckles and looked around like she was memorizing every detail; the widescreen TV, the leather couch, the bookshelf lined with athletic trophies, the bar stools tucked under the kitchen counter.

Olly watched her for a minute, then his eyes slid to Helen, his gaze lingering on the side of her face. Helen felt herself shrink. She fought the urge to lift her hand, to cover the cheek with the birthmark. Instead, she lifted her chin.

"We talked to Glenn," she said. "He told us what really happened, at your New Year's party."

Olly's expression changed.

"Why are you letting her drag you into this?"

"This was my idea," Helen said. "I thought the two of you should talk things out. Clear the air."

"Clear the air." Olly slicked back his hair and shook his hand, scattering drops of sweat across the white carpet. "Like you, with Starkey and your sister? Because that worked out *so* well, didn't it?"

"Starkey admitted everything," Anna said. "Same with Phil, at Hillside. Both of them had the balls to apologize."

"I heard about that. Your little sob story." Olly's voice rose. "*Poor me, I don't remember anything. Oh my God, I was pregnant.*"

"You think that's funny?" Anna said.

"I think it's bullshit." Olly's eyes were cold. "You fuck enough guys, you're going to get knocked up. And we all know you fucked enough guys."

"But not at the party," said Helen.

He turned on her. "What?"

"At your party. You made it sound like she wanted it."

"So?"

"So, you started that rumour." Helen swallowed, holding his gaze. She thought of Glenn, white-faced and agonized. *None of us were thinking straight.* "But that's not how it happened. It was rape."

"Rape?"

"You and Glenn, right? And who else?"

Olly stared at Helen, then shrugged. "Who cares?"

"But—"

"It's not going to work," Anna interrupted. "You see what he's like."

"What I'm like?" Olly said. "Nobody forced vodka down your throat, Annie. Nobody dragged you into the hot tub. You took off your own clothes, climbed into my bed. What did you think was going to happen?"

"She was drunk," said Helen. "Passed out."

"I don't know why you're getting involved." Olly rounded on Helen impatiently. "Why are you even here?"

"She's my friend."

"Yeah? You don't know the first thing about her. Did she tell you how many times she fucked me? Not at my party, I mean afterwards, at school, in the bathroom stalls. Me and every other guy at Laurier."

Helen looked at Anna. She was staring at Olly, her face full of loathing.

"Do you know what she's been doing since she flunked out of school? Did you know she's been arrested, multiple times? In and out of rehab? Our parents are friends. I hear all the dirt. She's a spoiled little rich girl. Always has been."

Helen put a hand on Anna's arm, felt her trembling beneath her fingers.

"Hold on," Helen said. "Let's stay calm."

"I've known her since we were toddlers. Right, Annie? Those Christmas parties at the club, when you wouldn't talk to anyone? You thought you were so much better than us. Little innocent Annie. I always knew that was an act."

Olly moved to the shelf by the TV and opened a carved wooden box, pulling out an envelope.

"Here. Look at these and tell me if you still think she's innocent."

He tossed the envelope towards Helen. It opened in the air and a dozen Polaroids rained down on the white carpet.

Anna stood frozen, looking past Olly at the darkening sky beyond the living room window. But Helen crouched down and gathered up the pictures. Pale bodies twisted on a rumpled bed. Annie's young face was blurry but recognizable, eyes open but empty. Hands shaking, Helen stacked the pictures into a pile.

"Why would you keep these?"

"They show everyone what a slut she was," Olly said. "But you can have them. Nobody cares anymore."

"You're such an asshole. You don't deserve any of this." Anna flicked her fingers to encompass the TV, the shelves, the hallway where his girlfriend had led the dog. "I'm going to make sure you lose it all."

"Is that a threat?"

Olly stepped forward, thick biceps flexing under his T-shirt. From behind the bedroom door, the dog barked again.

"We're leaving," said Helen. "We're going. We shouldn't have come."

Clutching the Polaroids, she pulled Anna backwards, out of the apartment and into the hallway. They were barely over the threshold before Olly slammed the door in their faces. Helen let out her breath, releasing her grip. She'd left marks on Anna's bare arm, red blotches against the tangled lines of her tattoos.

"What a psycho," said Helen. "I'm sorry. This was a terrible idea."

"Are you kidding?" Anna's dark eyes glittered with triumph. "I can't believe he gave us the Polaroids. What a fucking idiot he is, after all."

CHAPTER 19

"Do you want me to keep the pictures?" Helen asked, outside Olly's door.

"Nope." Anna grabbed the photos out of her hand. The old Polaroids were sticky, their corners cutting into her fingers. "I want them with me."

"What will you do with them?"

"I don't know yet." Anna stuffed them back into the envelope. "Make copies, maybe. Plaster them all over town. Or send them to everyone Olly knows; his parents, his boss, his girlfriend."

Her elation lasted until she got home, until she spread the square-cut photos across her bedroom carpet. Then Anna sat back on her heels, touching the shiny surfaces, staring down at this young girl with her face. The pink curve of someone's cock pressed against her slack cheek. The dark hair on the hand that spread open her thighs. Olly's smirk at the edge of the frame as he turned Annie's unseeing face towards the camera, his hands pressed against her throat. *That poor thing*, Anna thought, laying out the Polaroids, trying to put them into some kind of order. Whose hand was that, squeezing her breast? Whose hairy legs against her thighs? *That poor girl.* How could she show these to anyone?

In the end, she stashed them under the staircase in her old dollhouse. Nobody would find them there. Nobody but Anna, who couldn't stop thinking about them, couldn't stay away. There was something so intensely physical about the images, burned into chemical paper within seconds and inches of the events they captured, spat out of Phil's camera, passed among his friends like a dirty joke. These pictures were the closest Anna would ever get to her missing memories, to closing that loop between before and after. Of course she couldn't leave them alone, couldn't walk past the room without kneeling in front of that dollhouse, slipping the envelope out from its hiding place and dealing out the pictures, one by one.

*

The next day, Anna came downstairs to find her father taping up a cardboard box at the kitchen table.

"What's that?"

"This? It's a digital camera. Point-and-shoot, state-of-the-art. I picked it up before our cruise but I hardly touched it on the trip. I'm going to see if the store will take it back."

Malcolm paused and looked at Anna.

"Unless you want to try it out?"

Back upstairs, she took the sleek camera out of its box and weighed it in her hand. "It's got twelve shooting modes," Malcolm had told her. "Automatic focus, built-in zoom. The memory card will hold hundreds of pictures."

She could feel the Polaroids calling from their hiding space, but when Anna put the camera to her eye, everything went quiet. She walked downstairs, looking through the viewfinder at the framed prints on the wall, the grandfather clock at the base of the stairs, the gilt-framed mirror over the rolltop desk. There she stopped, studying her reflection through the lens. The camera covered most of her face but the tattoos on her forearms were sharp and clear, the long dreads fountaining out from her ponytail. Smiling, Anna moved closer, until she was nearly touching the glass, until all she could see was the camera reflecting itself.

Click.

"What are you doing?"

Her mother squinted at her from the other side of the French doors. Joyce's blond hair was mussed, her face pale over her green silk wrap.

Instantly, Anna's mood deflated.

"Nothing."

She snapped a shot of her mother. Joyce flinched, lifting her hand to her temple.

"I'm trying to take a nap and all I hear is you stomping around. Can't you go somewhere else?"

Out in the backyard, the thick August air pressed against Anna's skin, heavy and damp as a velvet curtain. She lit a cigarette and aimed her camera up at the sky, framing the wispy clouds overhead.

"Can I bum one of those?"

She turned to see Johnnie Campbell, his tanned forearms draped over the back fence. His face was shadowed under the brim of his Blue Jays cap.

Anna narrowed her eyes.

"You're stalking me now?"

"I was in the neighbourhood. I thought I'd stop by, see how you're doing." Johnnie took off his baseball cap. "Also, I wanted to apologize for acting like a dick, back at Hillside." He cleared his throat, smoothed back his sweaty hair and repositioned his hat. "Obviously you can do whatever you want."

"Obviously."

"I mean, you can bone whoever you want, whenever you want. I'm just hoping that sometimes, that might be me."

Anna let out a short laugh.

"So, what do you say? Can you spare a smoke?"

She picked her way down the path to stand across from him, the patio stones burning her bare feet.

"First, say cheese."

She snapped a shot, then examined it, using her hand to shield the digital screen from the bright sun.

"Your eyes were closed."

"Sorry," said Johnnie. "I'm not very photogenic."

When Anna passed him a cigarette, the tips of their fingers touched. The brief contact made her want to grab his hand, drag him upstairs and strip him naked on the spare room mattress. She hadn't had sex since Hillside, nearly a month ago. But she'd have to sneak him past her mother. And what would Johnnie think of the rash across her belly, pink lines and itchy pustules that stretched from one tattooed hip to the other?

They stood in companionable silence, their twin columns of white smoke rising from either side of the wooden fence.

"So, listen," Johnnie said. "That offer's still open, for a balloon ride, sometime. It doesn't have to be a date."

Behind Anna, the glass patio door squeaked open. Her mother emerged wearing a caftan and a broad straw hat.

"Annie?"

"Shit," said Anna. "You'd better take off."

"Would you put out that cigarette?" Joyce settled on the lounge chair, fanning at her face. "I can smell it from here."

Anna leaned against the fence and looked down at her camera, clicking through photos until she reached the one of her mother, formless and white as a ghost behind the French door. She pressed the button to zoom in, closer and closer, dissolving the face into bleached-out pixels. She couldn't think straight in Joyce's presence. It was no good hiding in the house; she couldn't think there either, not with those Polaroids humming away in their envelope.

She tossed the butt over the fence and walked the burning patio stones to the edge of the pool, where one yellow maple leaf floated on the rippling surface.

"Who were you talking to, back there? Be honest." Joyce pushed back her hat and slid on her sunglasses. "Was it your drug dealer?"

"It wasn't anybody."

"I can't stand this skulking around. You might have your father fooled, but not me."

Anna looked down at the swirling leaf and flexed her toes, skin rasping against the cement. Had Joyce noticed the pills missing from her medicine cabinet?

"When people ask me, *What's Anna doing these days?* I'm ashamed to say I have no idea." Joyce plucked at the fabric of her caftan. "Maria Vetrone just got back from a mother-daughter trip to New York City, just the two of them. She's starting med school this fall."

"Maria or her daughter?"

"Everything's a joke to you. But my friends are so close with their daughters. Some of them talk every day," said Joyce. "You were so attached to me when you were a little girl. When we left you with a sitter, you used to cry and cry. Malcolm would say, 'It doesn't matter if we can't have more children. We've got Annie. What else could anyone want?'"

Sweat trickled beneath Anna's dreads, down her neck. She was conscious of her own breathing, loud gulps of humid air.

"You think your life will go a certain way." Joyce shook her head. "Didn't we give you everything? I don't understand where things went wrong."

Anna stared down into the pool. One step and she'd plunge under the surface, sink down into the depths. She wavered, leaned forward, and the digital camera swung from its shoulder strap. She caught herself just in time.

"Tell me, what are we supposed to do? You can't stay here much longer," Joyce said. "Help you find a job? God knows who would hire you, looking like you do."

Anna winced, screwing up her eyes against the sun. Maybe she should give up. Leave. But no matter where she went, she'd never unsee those Polaroids, unhear all those words. *Olly sat beside you with his hands on your tits. Glenn took forever, even with us cheering him on.* Was she really going to let Starkey off with that half-assed apology? Leave Olly to his smug successful life? She wasn't like Helen, who wanted to keep smoothing things over, hunkering down in her crappy apartment.

Suddenly, there it was, the path forward.

"You're right," Anna said, turning to stare into the opaque lenses of Joyce's sunglasses. "I'm too old to be living at home. Why don't you rent me a place of my own? Lots of Dad's buddies are into real estate. Maybe someone's got space in one of their buildings?"

Her mother stared back at her, thin face shadowed by her straw hat. Anna held her breath as a neighbour's lawnmower droned in the silence between them.

Finally, Joyce exhaled. "It's a thought."

CHAPTER 20

Helen stepped off her bus into the heavy rain and humid air of a late-August thunderstorm. She ducked her head and wrestled with her umbrella, pushing at the flimsy nylon until one of the metal struts broke and scratched her hand.

"Ow! Fuck!"

Helen was coming from work, meeting Anna downtown to see her potential new apartment. God, she wished she was going home instead. She wanted to take off her makeup, slather on a honey-and-oatmeal face mask, read a magazine from cover to cover and take a long cool shower. Even if Thom was home, she'd turn up her stereo and blast a Norah Jones CD until she felt better.

"Helen!" Anna darted into her peripheral vision, wearing a bright yellow raincoat. "I thought you might bail because of the weather."

"I almost did." Helen shifted the broken umbrella over her head and examined the cut on her hand. "I had to work through lunch to stock our fall displays. We're not going far, are we?"

"This way. Around this corner." Anna turned onto Carden Street. "Apparently it's next to a music shop."

They stopped in front of a small restaurant with a red and yellow sign.

"Wok's Taste!" Helen said, squinting up through the rain. "I know this place!"

She remembered standing out here with Gord, her small mittened hand enclosed in his. Then lining up at the counter, inhaling the warm, steamy fragrance of sesame oil, gazing up at the jar of plastic-wrapped fortune cookies.

"Gord used to bring us here for Chinese takeout. The best hot-and-sour soup in Guelph, he always said."

"I'll have to try it," said Anna. She checked a paper, then knocked on an unmarked door, which opened to reveal a man with a grey beard and an enormous potbelly. When he saw Anna and Helen, he broke into a big smile.

"Annie Leverett?"

"Hi, Mr. Bergman."

"Call me Ragnar, okay? Your dad says you're looking for an apartment." His growling voice reverberated as he climbed the narrow staircase. "I told him you're in luck. I just finished renovations on this place."

Anna took the stairs two at a time. Helen followed more slowly. When he reached the landing, Ragnar pulled out a set of keys.

"I was supposed to have a student from Nigeria moving in September first, but his visa fell through." He waved them into a white-painted loft with plain Ikea couches, a boxy TV, wooden floors. "Fully furnished. If you want it, it's yours."

Anna stepped into the middle of the room and spun around, her dreads fanning out over her yellow coat like the chairs in a swing carousel.

"This is what I'm talking about! Helen, what do you think?"

Helen shook out her umbrella. The floorboards creaked under her feet as she crossed the room and flicked the kitchen lights on and off, admiring the long row of cupboards, the stainless-steel fridge.

"It's nice," she said, running her hand along the gleaming glass cooktop. "Really nice."

"Look," Anna called. "This bedroom has a fireplace!"

Helen turned the corner and found Anna in an empty bedroom beside a tall wood-framed window, looking out at the rain. In the pale filtered light, Anna looked like a girl in a Vermeer painting, if seventeenth-century Dutch girls had septum rings and tattoos.

"How much is the rent?"

"I don't know, exactly. I think Ragnar's giving my parents a deal," Anna said. "But my mother and I are driving each other crazy. They'd probably pay whatever he asks."

"Lucky you."

She looked up at the plaster medallion in the centre of the ceiling, thinking of her father. Shane paid for Julia's rent, her tuition, and now apparently her wedding, too. Would he buy her and Glenn a house next?

Anna tapped on the large window, opened it and stuck her head out into the rain. "Check out the fire escape."

"So, you can get away faster when you burn the place down?"

"Jesus, Wright," Anna said. "The stairs go down to that parking lot."

"Is it safe? Couldn't someone come in that way?"

"Maybe if I invite them." Anna pulled her head back into the room and closed the window. She lifted a silver camera to her face and pointed it at Helen. "So, what do you say?"

"What do you mean?"

"Do you want to move in with me?" The shutter clicked and Anna lowered the camera. "You keep complaining about your place, about Thom. Come live here instead."

"Are you serious?"

"We always talked about moving in together after high school. And okay, full disclosure," Anna said. "My parents will only pay the rent if you're here too. You'd be like my chaperone. What do you say? We can sign the lease today, right now."

"Hang on. Give me a minute," Helen said. "Let me use the bathroom."

Behind the latched door, she sat on the closed toilet, catching her breath. This would be her bathroom, if she moved in. She'd be taking bubble baths in this claw-foot tub, doing her laundry in that stacked washer and dryer.

Helen got to her feet and looked into the beveled mirror of the medicine cabinet. Her foundation had held up in the rain, but her eye makeup had melted, tracing gritty lines of pigment down her cheeks. She ran her thumbs under her eyes, then stopped. The dark smudges under her eyes made her look badass, like a rockstar, a rebel. Less like Helen, more like Anna. She stared at this new version of herself, watching the corners of her mouth turn up. *Fuck it*, Helen thought. *Why not?*

*

Helen put off telling Thom for nearly a week. She did most of her packing in the early mornings, before he got up. Stuffing her clothes into suitcases and recycling bags. Crouching on the cracked tiles of the bathroom, sorting through her collection of foundations: checking expiration dates, tossing the bottles that had separated into chalky layers or darkened to a sickly taupe. She was hauling a stack of flattened cardboard boxes up the stairs when Thom stepped out of the kitchen.

"That's a lot of boxes." Thom said. "What are they for?"

Helen stopped. For a moment, she wanted to lie. *I'm giving some things to Goodwill.* Then she took a breath. "I'm moving out."

"You're what?"

"Anna found us a place downtown." The cardboard was slipping from under Helen's arm. She readjusted, avoiding Thom's eyes. "I was going to tell you."

"You're leaving?" He sagged against the doorframe. "When?"

"Soon. Okay, this weekend. But I'll keep paying rent for the next couple of months, or until you find someone else. Maybe one of your friends? They could sublet until you get them on the lease, like you did when Crystal left." Helen looked away from Thom's stricken face. "I thought you'd be happy to see me go."

"So that's it? We can't talk about this?"

"Things have been tense for weeks. Months, even," she said. "I thought this was what you wanted."

"I wanted things to go back to how they were before." Thom's last word reverberated plaintively through the stairwell, expanding to fill the air between them. Helen felt an unexpected swell of compassion. An impulse to climb the stairs and wrap her arms around him, bury her face in his cotton hoodie, maybe even kiss that stubbly neck, take his hand and bring him back to her room. Just once more, for old times' sake, before she left him behind.

Helen shifted her arms, feeling the sharp edges of cardboard digging in.

"This is best for us both."

*

By Saturday night, Helen was officially moved in with Anna. Their fridge was still mostly empty, but the bathroom cupboards and her closet were full.

"Is it too early for bed?"

Helen collapsed onto the sofa.

"What? We're celebrating!" Anna hauled her up. "We need a night out. Let's go dancing!"

"I could maybe handle takeout and a movie."

"Go put on your sluttiest outfit. You'll feel better once you're dressed."

Anna was right, Helen did feel better after she pulled on low-rise jeans and a halter top, after she'd fixed her hair and swiped on red lipstick.

"Sexy lady!" Anna said, watching Helen line her eyes with black, flicking up the ends into dark wings. "You're going to pick up tonight!"

A couple of warm-up shots of tequila, then they headed down the block to the Palace.

"I'm too old for this place!" Helen called over the pulsing electronic music as they pushed onto a dance floor packed with baby-faced girls in skimpy tops, baseball-capped bros just out of their teens.

"Ignore them!" Anna caught Helen's hands and started singing along to Kylie Minogue: *"I just can't get you out of my head, boy, your loving's all I think about."*

Anna danced fluidly, naturally, while Helen felt like a wooden puppet, her feet stumbling against the rhythm.

"La la la-la-la," Anna sang, holding Helen's hands, turning her in circles. They spun until Helen was breathless and laughing, until she stopped caring how

she looked. Then trumpets blared the glorious opening to "Crazy in Love" and Helen finally caught the beat, forgetting to be tired as she rolled her hips and traced shapes in the air, lifting her voice with Beyonce's.

"Yes, girl!" Anna yelled, grinning wide. "Aren't you glad you came out tonight?"

Helen grinned back. She felt powerful, sexy, swept along by the music, by the energy and the movement of the crowd. Why didn't she come dancing more often? *My milkshake brings all the boys to the yard and, damn right, it's better than yours.*

The song changed again and Anna was swinging her ass, looking over her own shoulder with an exaggerated come-hither pout. Beside them, a guy in a Maple Leafs jersey imitated her move, batting his eyelashes until Helen laughed out loud. He smiled down at her and turned, moving closer until he was dancing with her. With her, Helen Wright! Anna's words rang in her head: *You're going to pick up tonight!*

Helen smiled up at the guy, into his deep-set eyes under a backwards ball cap. He was heavyset but cute, a shitty but enthusiastic dancer, his sturdy shoulders filling out his blue hockey jersey. Thom had a Maple Leafs jersey just like that, but Helen didn't want to think about Thom tonight. She didn't want to think about anything. She was here to dance.

Anna caught her attention and gave a thumbs-up that shifted into a gesture towards the bar. "Have fun," she mouthed.

Helen nodded as the beat geared down into the sinuous thump of Nine Inch Nails. "*Help me,*" Trent Reznor moaned. The crowd tightened, roaring its approval, and Leafs guy moved closer, grinding against Helen. There was someone behind her now too, pressing his body against hers so she was sandwiched between two men. One of them had his hands on Helen's hips, peeling up the hem of her top.

"*I want to fuck you like an animal,*" one of the guys crooned along with the song, right into her ear, and Helen felt a hot lump pushing against her back.

"Let go!" Helen squirmed, trying to free herself. "Stop!"

But the guy in the Leafs jersey bent down and put his lips on hers. A thick sour tongue filled Helen's mouth. She couldn't talk, couldn't breathe, felt increasingly panicked as she pounded at his arm with her fists. Then, all at once, he pulled back.

"Fuck off!" Anna yelled, as Helen staggered free. "Both of you, fuck off! Leave her alone!"

Anna led her out of the crowd, which instantly closed behind them. Helen leaned against a concrete pillar in the corner, feeling shaken and nauseous.

"You're okay." Anna put a hand on her arm. "Jesus, what a creep. You want me to go back and kick his ass?"

"No," Helen said. "Let's just go home."

"It's still early! Don't let a couple of assholes ruin your night. Here." Anna opened her hand to show a pillbox filled with little blue tablets. "Magic pills. Take one, feel better."

Helen stared down into the enamel box.

"What are they?"

"Just Valium." Anna pinched one and held it out. "It'll help. I promise."

Helen hesitated for a moment, then swallowed the pill, tasting a faint bitterness.

"Good girl." Anna hooked Helen's elbow. "Now, let's find somewhere more your speed. How about the Albion?"

Gradually, Helen's shallow breathing deepened as Anna tugged her through the exit, onto the street and up the hill.

The Albion was definitely an older crowd. Helen saw men with trim goatees, women with chunky highlights in their layered hair, and there, over by the bar... Dave Patel. The collar was popped on his Ed Hardy shirt and he had a leather coat slung over his arm. As Helen watched, he handed a pint glass of beer to the girl beside him; the same girl they'd seen at Hillside. Then the two of them turned towards the stairs.

"Anna!" Helen clutched her friend's arm. "You saw that? You saw him? We have to go downstairs!"

"Yes, okay." Anna peeled Helen's fingers off her arm. "Let me get drinks first."

A line of red felt pool tables crowded the bar's dimly lit, low-ceilinged basement. Dave Patel and the girl were at the farthest pool table, by the dartboard.

Anna didn't hesitate.

"Hey," she called. "It's Dave, right? Mind if we join you?"

Helen's feet moved her forward until she was face to face with Dave Patel. Mechanically, awkwardly, she stuck out her hand.

"Hi."

Dave's perfect eyebrows went up, almost touching the shining wave of his hair.

"Hi yourself. It's Helen, isn't it?"

Dave Patel knew her name? The room tilted as Helen shook his hand.

"This is my cousin, Sarita." He nodded at the girl across the table. "She just moved here for school."

His cousin! Helen glowed with happiness. When Dave turned back to the pool table, the afterimage of his smile burned into Helen's retinas. She watched Sarita lean down to take a shot. Yes, Helen could see the family resemblance; the cousins had the same thick eyebrows, the same aristocratic tilt of the head. Neatly, Sarita potted the eight ball.

"That's game," Sarita said, straightening.

"Nice!" Anna said. "I'll be on your team. Helen, you be with Dave."

They played. With every shot, Helen felt more alive to Dave's nearness, to his tall body next to hers. When she fumbled, he was there, wrapping his hand around hers to guide the cue, making her breathing catch and her heart beat fast. Really, she thought, this was another kind of dance, the way they moved together and apart, hands lingering on the wooden cue as it passed between them.

"Can I get you another drink?" Dave asked, at some point.

His touch made the hair stand up on Helen's arms.

"I'm not thirsty," she whispered as she looked up, into his eyes.

Then it was happening, Dave Patel was lowering his head, his stubble rasping her cheek. Helen pushed her tongue into his mouth and they kissed until her head swam, until Dave Patel took her hand and led her stumbling to the bathroom at the back of the room.

The stall door didn't lock so Dave Patel leaned back against it, bracing it closed as his zipper caught and then slid downwards. The bathroom floor was cold and sticky, hard on her knees, but it didn't matter, nothing mattered anymore except her vision pulsing in flashes, except Dave Patel's long fingers warm against the back of her skull.

CHAPTER 21

"My cousin is quite the ladies' man."

Anna turned to see Sarita tossing the eight ball from one hand to the other. Her long dark hair was tucked behind her ears, revealing the shaved sections at her temples that gleamed in the overhead lights.

"Everywhere we go, he meets another girl. He's irresistible."

"I don't know," said Anna, as the look between them pulled tighter. "Some of us can resist him."

All night, with every word, they'd been asking and answering the same question. Now, Anna widened her smile and stepped forward. *Yes*, she said with her eyes. *Our turn now.* Sarita's smile deepened, revealing dimples. Delicately, she set the eight ball onto the felt and leaned into the kiss they'd both been waiting for.

Anna closed her eyes, giving herself up to the softness of Sarita's lips, the clean scent of her shampoo. It had been too long since she'd been with a girl, too long since anyone had touched her at all. She looped a finger into Sarita's gold hoop earring as Sarita's hands circled Anna's waist, stroking the bare skin above her jeans.

"Careful," Anna said, twisting back.

"What?"

"You scratched me."

"With what?" Sarita held up her hands, showing smooth filed-down nails. She touched Anna's hip, lifted the hem of her shirt and sucked in her breath. "What the hell is this?"

"A scrape?" Anna craned her neck.

"Worse than that. Your back's a mess."

"It's nothing."

Sarita wiped her hand on her jeans. "Is it contagious?"

"Of course not."

Anna tried to catch her eye, but Sarita's expression had gone distant, impersonal. She shook her head and moved to the other side of the pool table, putting the crimson expanse of felt between them.

"Sarita," Anna said. "Don't be like that."

The bathroom door opened and out swaggered Dave, making a show of adjusting his belt. Helen was a step behind him. Her wavy hair was mussed, her careful lipstick smeared.

"Hey," Dave said. "You started another game?"

"No." Sarita wouldn't look at Anna. "We're all done. You ready to take off?"

"Sure. We'll do this again sometime, eh?"

Helen nodded up at him, starry-eyed. As Dave and Sarita headed for the stairs, she tugged on Anna's arm like a little girl.

"Anna. Anna," she whispered. "Guess what just happened?"

"First, look at this." Anna hiked up her T-shirt, turning around. "Does this look bad to you?"

"Jesus." Helen's voice changed. "What happened?"

"It's that rash from my Hillside tattoo. It's spreading everywhere."

Anna rolled back her sleeves to expose the oozing tattoos on her arms, the faint red lines stretching up her wrists. She lifted her arm and sniffed a fungal reek like wet socks.

"Should we go to Emerg? That looks bad."

"Nah," Anna hissed as Helen touched the raw skin. "I'll find a walk-in tomorrow. They'll give me some cream or something."

"I'll come with you. I can book off work."

"It's fine, I'll figure it out. Now, your turn. You want to tell me about fucking Dave Patel in the bathroom?"

"Anna!" Helen's neck flushed. "I didn't actually fuck him."

*

The next day, Anna suffered through a lecture from a white-coated doctor who looked like a seventeen-year-old surfer. She stared at the cracks in the clinic wall as he scraped pus from her shoulder into a vial for testing, ran warm hands under her chin where her lymph nodes were swollen and sore.

"You should have come in weeks ago." He tossed shaggy hair away from his eyes. "This is the worst systemic skin infection I've ever seen. You're lucky you don't have blood poisoning or necrosis."

Lucky. "I need antibiotics?"

"Among other things. Any drug allergies? Then I'm giving you two weeks of doxycycline." He scrawled on his prescription pad. "An extra-strength antibiotic ointment, a topical corticosteroid and Betadine for wound disinfection."

Anna wrinkled her nose at the word *wound*.

"How about something for the pain? It's keeping me up at night." Hating herself a little, she put on a pitiful expression. "Nothing over-the-counter is helping."

The surfer doctor sighed and clicked his pen.

"There's controlled-release oxycodone. It won't interfere with the antibiotics, but it's an opiate. Do you have any experience with this class of drugs?"

"Don't worry." Anna looked down. "I'll be careful."

"Make sure the pharmacist goes over all the contraindications," he said, tearing papers off his pad. "Antibiotics don't mix with alcohol."

*

Three weeks later, Anna crouched by the window in her new bedroom, pushing the pink oxys from one side of her palm to the other. She'd lucked out with these, for sure. *No refills*, the pharmacist had said, but Anna had sweet-talked him into one extra bottle of pink floaty relief. The rest of her meds were awful; a crinkled tube of hospital-smelling ointment, thick as greasy toothpaste. Turquoise antibiotic capsules that stuck in her throat and ran through her like a muddy tide, leaving her numb and exhausted.

Anna tipped her last seven oxys back into their plastic bottle on the windowsill, scratching at her arm where layers of skin were peeling off. Outside the window, a pigeon fluttered down to squat on the fire-escape railing, its grey feathers puffy in the chill autumn wind.

She was spending these days moving from bed to sofa, napping and watching 90s reruns: *X-Files*, *Law and Order*, *Jerry Springer*. Sometimes she muted the TV and drifted through elaborate revenge fantasies: kidnapping Olly's big grey poodle, say, or even his girlfriend. Sabotaging Olly's car, booby-trapping his classroom, breaking into his apartment and poisoning the food.

Outside, the air was getting thinner and colder. Anna had to keep her bedroom window closed, which made her feel like she was cutting off her escape. The nights were getting longer, until the trees Anna could see from her window were tinged with orange and yellow and red, until Helen was leaving for work in the dark.

Anna could hear Helen now in the other room, talking to her mother on the phone about the takeout salad she'd eaten for lunch: "Tuna and chickpeas, yes, and tomatoes!"

How did Helen stand those vapid conversations with her mother, day after day? And how could she spend so many hours in the bathroom? Truth be told, Helen was driving her crazy. Baking cookies that Anna didn't want to eat, bringing mugs of tea she left to cool on the floor beside her bed. "How are you feeling?" Helen asked, a hundred times a day. "Do you want me to put more cream on your back? Run you another bath?" She wouldn't leave Anna alone.

"That won't work," Helen said now, through the wall. "I don't know if I'm coming for Thanksgiving. No, the week after." Her voice dropped, murmuring something about a shower.

Anna lifted her arm and sniffed. She couldn't remember the last time she'd bathed. Two days ago? Three? She wiped at her running nose, shivering as she watched the pigeon hunch and peck at its feet. Really, she wanted another oxy. But she had to make them last.

Helen's voice rose. "I don't care, I'm not sending the invitations."

Anna was up on her feet before she knew what she was doing. She nearly tripped over the coffee table as she rounded the corner into the living room.

"The wedding's back on?"

"What?" Helen looked up.

"Your sister and Starkey?" Glenn Starkey standing at the altar in a black suit. Olly beside him, polished and smirking. What did the minister say in the movies? *If anyone here objects to this union, speak now or forever hold your peace.* "I'm crashing their wedding, then! It's perfect. I'll have them both together, Olly and Starkey, in public, with no way out—"

"He's not coming." Helen held her palm over the receiver. "Olly's out of the wedding."

"Well, shit." Anna's energy drained away. "But why didn't you tell me it was happening?"

"Mom, one sec," Helen said into the phone. She gazed up at Anna, chewing on her lip. "I didn't want to bother you."

"Bullshit!" Anna kicked the side of the couch with her bare foot. The pain was instant, intense, clarifying. "So what, Starkey and your sister get to live happily ever after?" She kicked again, shoving the couch back against the wall.

"Hey! They're seeing a counsellor twice a week. It's not exactly a fairy tale." Helen twisted to look behind the couch, then lifted the phone. "Mom? I'll call you back. Anna, stop! You made a mark on the wall!"

"As if I fucking care." Anna was trembling now. She put on a high-pitched voice. "*I can't help you, Anna. Glenn moved out, Anna.*"

"He did! And he already apologized. Isn't that what you want? Isn't it Olly you're after now?"

"Don't fucking tell me what I want!" Anna kicked the couch again. Something cracked in her foot as the wooden frame rocked into the wall. "Fuck!"

"You have those Polaroids—"

"I can't use them." Anna slumped onto the carpet, rubbing at her foot. The envelope of Polaroids was tucked up inside the old brick fireplace in her bedroom.

They hummed at her from their hiding place whenever she looked across her room. "I can't let anyone else see them."

"Well," Helen hugged a cushion to her chest. "Maybe you need another approach."

"You think I should give up?"

Part of Anna relaxed as she said the words. Give up, go back to her room, take more pills, drift away. Wouldn't that be nice?

"No," Helen said. "I think it's time for you to get serious."

"You think I'm not?"

"I think you should talk to a lawyer."

"A lawyer?" She snorted. "Like Starkey?"

"Someone who's not involved. You need information. Like, what's the statute of limitations on rape?"

"I have no idea."

Anna's foot throbbed. The tiredness was back, sucking her down until she was lying on the carpet, the cheap wool scratching the skin of her arms, her bare legs.

"Maybe you could press charges. And I still think you should talk to your parents."

"My parents?" Anna said, to the ceiling. She closed her eyes.

"Tell them what happened. Be honest. Maybe they'll surprise you."

*

"Come for dinner," Anna's father said, when she called. "We want to hear how you've settled in to the apartment."

Two days later, Anna stood in the darkness in her parents' backyard. A full moon hung in the sky like pale fruit. She crouched down by the covered pool and dabbled her fingers in the water. Part of her wanted to peel back the cover, take a quick dip in the moonlight. Or step forward and let the black tarp twist around her like a shroud.

"Annie?" The back door slid open and the outside lights flicked on. There was Joyce, holding her long cardigan closed with one hand. "How did you get back here? I thought we'd locked that side gate."

Anna didn't answer, just tugged the pool cover back into place and stood up. She'd perfected this route years ago; one foot on the garden gnome's head, the other on the lilac's cropped branch, then the top of the fence was an easy hop. Well, less easy than she remembered; tonight, her jeans had caught, nearly toppling her onto the paving stones.

Inside the kitchen, a half-empty bottle of red wine stood beside her mother's glass. The room filled with a savoury aroma as Joyce pulled a roasted chicken out of the oven. As she transferred the chicken to a platter, she looked relaxed, almost serene.

This is how she looks without you around, thought Anna.

"I hope you're hungry," Joyce said. "Can you set the table?"

"Sure. After I use the bathroom."

Anna slipped upstairs to her parents' bathroom, skimmed a few pills out of each bottle and slid the mirrored medicine cabinet closed. For a moment, she stood looking at her reflection. She'd showered before she came, scrubbed away the shreds of peeling skin. She looked clean but tired, her skin pale as milk.

The dining room table was strewn with catalogues and samples of animal-print wallpaper. Anna smoothed a tablecloth over the wooden dining table, laid out three placemats and three sets of silver cutlery. She paused at the sideboard, looking at the family photos. Here was her grandparents' black and white wedding photo; him dapper in his army uniform, her upright and smiling primly under the lace veil, both squinting in the spring sunshine. Her parents' wedding picture was here too; Joyce's creamy gown high-necked and edged with ribbons, Malcolm sporting sideburns and a pale-blue jacket.

Anna bent down to examine a photo of herself as a toddler in a purple bathing suit, perched at the top of a playground slide. Anna could still remember the heat from the shining metal slide, the way it burned the backs of her bare legs. Standing beside the slide, holding on with protective hands, stood her mother in a green bikini. There was a distinct curve to Joyce's tanned stomach.

The most recent photo of Anna was from her middle school graduation. She picked it up, grimacing at the puff of carefully curled bangs, the close-mouthed smile hiding her braces. Little blond preteen Annie, starched and wholesome as a collectible doll, with no hint of the disaster to come.

Back in the kitchen, her mother had set the roasting pan on the stove and leaned over the pan, stirring. What would happen if she went over and touched her mother's arm? Put her arms around that waist, rested her head on that shoulder, breathed in the scent of Opium perfume?

Anna cleared her throat. "You should teach me how to do that."

"Teach you what? To make gravy?"

"Sure. Yeah."

"Well, all right. You can start by stirring."

Joyce held out the wooden spoon. Anna hesitated, then took it.

"For how long?"

"Until it thickens." Joyce stood back and watched. "I used to help my mother in the kitchen. She had that bad leg, from polio. She couldn't stand for very long. She used to have me prep the vegetables, do the dishes. You know, I thought I'd have daughters to cook with me. A big family to cook for."

Anna stirred. Tiny bubbles rose through the thin brown liquid.

"Am I doing this right?"

"Slower. Like this." Joyce put her hand over Anna's. "I can't believe you don't know how to cook. When I was your age, we were hosting dinner parties for twelve."

After another minute, Joyce stepped back, picked up a knife and sliced into the roast chicken.

"Doesn't Dad usually carve?" Anna asked. "Where is he, anyway?"

"He won't be joining us." With a twist of her knife, Joyce split a leg into two parts. "I asked him to bring the Range Rover in for service. The front axle's making a noise when we turn."

"He had to do that tonight?" Anna stopped stirring. "I wanted to see him. I haven't seen you guys in a month."

"I thought the two of us should talk. About you and your so-called plans. Watch that gravy!" Joyce darted forward to push the pan off the flame. "I told you to stir!"

"My so-called plans?" Anna asked, as her mother wiped off the stove.

"Let's sit down."

Joyce heaped two plates with chicken and vegetables. Anna wasn't hungry anymore, but she carried her plate into the dining room and slid onto her chair.

"How is it?" Joyce asked, after a few minutes. She'd folded her chicken skin into a little packet, diced her meat into little cubes. "Aren't you eating?"

Anna took a bite and swallowed past her dry throat. "It's great."

"Thank you." Joyce took a sip of wine. "Now. What are you doing here?"

"Here?" Anna said. "You mean tonight? Or here, in Guelph?"

"We can start with tonight. Lord knows, we only hear from you when there's something you want."

"Okay. Well, I wanted to know: Do you have a lawyer?"

"What have you done this time?"

"Nothing. I'm just asking."

"Michael Sutton's handled our affairs for years." Joyce put down her fork. "You're sure you're not in trouble?"

"Michael Sutton? Olly Sutton's father?"

"That's right. We had dinner with him and Janice just last week. In fact, they asked about you. Did you go to their son's apartment?"

Anna went very still.

"And his work. Your old high school, Laurier? Did you go there, too?" Joyce narrowed her eyes. "Do you have some kind of grudge against that boy?"

"A grudge?" Anna gripped the edge of the table and took a deep breath. "You really want to know? Mother. He raped me."

Joyce held her eyes. For a second, something flickered there, in the blue depths. Then she looked away.

"That's a very serious allegation."

"Him and his friends," said Anna. "That New Year's party, when I was sixteen? When I stayed out all night? I passed out, I guess, and Olly…he and his friends had sex with me. Raped me. Another guy took pictures."

"*Rape*. How much did you have to drink that night?"

"It doesn't matter. It wasn't my fault."

"It's never your fault, is it? At school, in rehab, when the police call. It's always someone else's fault," Joyce said. "You can't wait ten years and then cry rape. Why wouldn't you say anything at the time?"

"I just found out." Anna's hands tightened on the edge of the table. "Me and Helen, we found out this summer. Some of the others admitted what they did. We've even got the photos, from the party. Now I want Olly to face what he did."

"What *he* did?" Joyce drained her glass. "That's convenient."

"It's not fucking *convenient*! Don't you believe me?"

"I believe you're out of control." Joyce leaned across the table and picked up Anna's nearly full plate. "I believe it was a mistake to let you stay here. That's what I've told your father. And I refuse to support this vendetta."

Joyce carried Anna's plate into the kitchen, stepped on the pedal to open the garbage and scraped the food into the bin.

"I want to press changes," Anna said, following her. "Take him to court."

"I suppose you want their money? Is that it?"

"I want him to admit what he did!"

"You're determined to hurt us, aren't you? Determined to make me suffer."

"This isn't about you!"

"You've never even apologized." Joyce put the plate in the dishwasher. "Never taken responsibility."

"I'm talking to Dad," said Anna. "I'll call him tomorrow. Maybe he'll listen."

"You leave him alone." Joyce lifted her hand to her forehead. "God, you're giving me a headache. Your father has done enough. And I tell you, if you go to him with this story, I will see you out on the street. I'll see you cut off without another penny. Now, go. It's time for you to leave."

CHAPTER 22

After her alarm went off, Helen lay in bed and stared at her ceiling for another ten minutes. *Get up,* she ordered herself. *Time to face another day.*

She took a deep breath before she climbed off the mattress. Every movement felt precarious these days. Moving in with Anna hadn't been a mistake, exactly, but Helen might have overreached, leapt onto a stepping stone that turned out to be unstable, with no space to turn around when the quiet river of her life became a fast-moving flood. The only way to stay upright was to move very, very carefully.

Ever since that night at the Albion, Helen's and Anna's lives had slipped out of alignment. That crazy night. Helen thought of Dave Patel, the musky smell of his body. She'd left a sultry voicemail, the morning after: "Hey, you. I had a great time last night. I can't wait to hang out again. Call me back. Let's make plans."

When she and Anna got back from the walk-in clinic, she tried again: "Dave? It's Helen Wright. Just checking you got my message. Here's my number again."

Helen spent the next week fussing over Anna, bullying her into regular meals and showers, scolding her into taking her antibiotics. Then, like a fool, Helen called one more time: "I hope this is the right number? This is Helen Wright, calling for Dave Patel. I'd really like to see you again. Please, could you call me back?"

Breakfast this morning was a piece of toast over the sink, contemplating Anna's dirty Docs by the front door. At least that meant she'd come home last night.

Sometimes Anna's coat and boots were still missing when Helen left for work in the morning.

Helen was trying not to take it personally. *My life has been fucked up for a long time,* Anna had said. And that was before the skin infection, before she'd gone begging to her parents and come home mute and furious, slamming doors and kicking walls, disappearing into her room without a word. When Helen checked on her, she found Anna's bedroom empty, the window by the fire escape propped open with a plastic bottle of pills. Anna hadn't come home for two days after that. That was weeks ago, and Helen still didn't know what had happened.

Helen swallowed her last bite of toast and brushed the crumbs off her hands. She was holding on to Anna's promise: *Whatever happens, I want us to stay friends.* Tugging her jacket over her shoulders, Helen left to catch her bus.

*

At work, Helen tossed old samples, spritzed displays with cleaning solution and wiped the dust off the framed photos. Then she picked up her box cutter and sliced open the flaps on a box of holiday merchandise.

She used to love the process of unpacking; the plastic scent of bubble wrap, the anticipation of each new product. Now she was moving mechanically, taking inventory of the holiday-themed mineralized powders, the winter lipsticks in shades from pomegranate to blackcurrant. When the box was empty, she punched through its bottom flaps, dropped it on the ground, stomped the cardboard flat under her heel.

"Working through something?" said a thick male voice.

Helen looked up to see Thom standing at her counter. His hair was buzzed short and he wore a winter coat with a long brown scarf wrapped around his neck.

"Hey," Thom sneezed. "Sorry. Do you have a Kleenex?"

Wordlessly, Helen held out the box of tissues. Thom coughed and blew his nose. What was he doing, visiting her at work, as if they were friends? She fought a sudden impulse to lean forward and touch his bristly hair. She picked up the box cutter and fiddled with the blade, pushing it in and out of the handle.

"You sound terrible," she said.

"I won't come close." Thom's forlorn brown eyes met hers and flicked away, as if remembering just how close they used to get. He dug in his coat pocket and pulled out a cream-coloured envelope. "I stopped by to give you this. Doesn't your sister know you moved?"

Helen took the envelope and turned it over to see her name inscribed in gold. A wedding invitation. She felt a pang of guilt, wondering who'd mailed these out. One of the bridesmaids? Julia herself?

"We're not talking much these days," she said.

Thom sneezed again. "How are you, anyway? Doing okay in your new place?"

"Fine." Helen felt the tightness of her smile. "Thanks."

"What about your friend?"

"Anna?" As if she had any other friends. Helen thought of Anna's closed door, the pills lining her windowsill. "She's fine too. Yeah, everything's great."

*

Anna's door was still closed when she got home. Helen flopped on the couch and considered her sister's wedding invitation. At the top, embossed gold confetti glittered around a clock with both hands pointing to twelve.

Mrs. Linda McArthur
Mr. Shane Wright
request the honour of your presence
at the marriage of their daughter
Julia Margaret Wright
to
Glenn Alexander Starkey
New Year's Eve
December 31st 2004
Half past four in the afternoon
St. George's Anglican Church, Guelph, Ontario

New Year's Eve was such a ridiculous date for a wedding. And how could Julia include Shane and not Gord? It was disloyal. Disrespectful. Helen held a thumb over the raised letters of her father's name, blotting it out. Had their mother seen this invitation? She must have. The wedding was the only thing Linda talked about these days. Every time she called, she added something to Helen's duties as maid of honour. This week alone, she wanted Helen to call the florist, drop off the caterer's cheque and meet with the wedding planner at the Marriott to go over table settings for the reception.

At least Helen could skip the bridal shower. That was this weekend, at a fancy spa near Ottawa. Linda had offered to drive but Helen had begged off, claiming she had to work. Anyway, Julia knew she'd never attend. Helen didn't do spas. Her makeup would crack in a sauna's heat, drip down her face in a steam room's humidity.

Helen reread the invitation, slicing the sharp edge of her fingernail through the embossed script. *Glenn Alexander Starkey*. How would Helen look him in the eye? And what if Olly Sutton was there too? She'd told Anna he wasn't coming to the wedding, but the truth was that she had no idea. She hadn't talked to Julia since that Sunday morning at their parents' condo.

Helen folded the invitation and tossed it to the back of her vanity. She pulled a plastic storage box filled with eyeshadows from under her bed and sat on the carpet, dividing the singles and quads into desultory piles: shimmery versus matte, cardboard versus plastic containers, light to dark gradations of colour. After thirty distracted minutes, she tipped them all back into the box.

She went to the kitchen, switched on the oven and assembled ingredients: flour, sugar, baking soda, chocolate chips. When she cracked the eggs, the shiny yolks stared up at her from the bottom of the bowl. She was prying the lid off a can of pumpkin puree when the front door opened with a bang and her hand slipped against the sharp metal. Bright blood splattered the contents of the bowl. She gasped and stuck her finger in her mouth, tasting copper, stars twinkling at the edges of her vision.

"Sit down," said Anna's voice, from far away. Her hand guided Helen to the floor, pushed her head between her knees. "That's right. Stay down. You're okay."

Helen sucked air, smelling cigarettes and floor cleaner. She blinked at her knees, focusing on the weave of her tights, black threads criss-crossing over her pale skin.

Anna crouched beside her, squeezing her injured hand against her sweatshirt.

"It's okay. It doesn't look too bad."

Helen darted a look and felt dizzy again.

"I'm bleeding all over your shirt."

"It's fine. Helen, hey. Don't look at that. Look at me."

She looked. Anna's thin body was hunched tight as a fist. This close, her skin looked papery and dry, as if she'd aged ten years in the past few weeks.

"You need to moisturize," Helen said.

Anna laughed. "Uh huh. What were you baking?"

"Muffins. Pumpkin chocolate chip. I just—" Helen blinked back tears as a siren whooped outside the window, the kitchen flashing blue and red. Her finger throbbed in Anna's fist. "I wanted something nice. For both of us."

Anna stripped off her sweatshirt and wound it around Helen's hand. "Hold that pressure. You want something to take the edge off?" She held out her enamel pillbox.

"No, thanks." Helen shivered as Anna swallowed a tablet. "Aren't you taking too many of those?"

Another police car sped past their window, its siren rising and falling in pitch.

"Fucking cops," said Anna.

"You never talked to them, did you? The cops?"

"What's the point?"

"They're not like lawyers." The cut on Helen's finger pulsed faster. "You wouldn't have to pay anyone."

Anna moved away from the window. "Cops are never on my side."

"You could tell them what happened," Helen said. "Maybe they'd bring Olly in for questioning. Imagine, there he is, teaching his grade ten history class or whatever, then the cops burst into the room and slap him in handcuffs."

"In front of his students?"

"Totally." Helen held out her non-injured hand and let Anna pull her to her feet. "Olly'd be yelling, freaking out as they dragged him down the hall, in front of all the other teachers. They'd haul him outside, stuff him in the back of the cop car."

"And I'd be there." Anna mimed holding a camera, snapping a picture. "Ready to capture the moment."

"Ultimate humiliation."

They grinned at each other, then Anna's smile faltered. She looked out the kitchen window again.

"You'll come with me?"

"Of course." Helen wanted to hug her, to hold on tight until Anna softened against her. Instead, she looked at her cut. It had stopped bleeding and looked old and white, as if her finger was made of wax. "Whenever you want. I'm sure it's just paperwork. Filling in forms, filing a report."

"Okay." Anna took a breath. "Let's go see what they can do."

*

A group of cops stood in front of the police station's entrance. They all wore the same black uniforms with red stripes down their pant legs. All held identical brown Tim Hortons cups. They turned in unison as Helen and Anna approached, their row of mirrored sunglasses reflecting the late-afternoon sky.

Anna slowed, but Helen took her arm and pulled her forward. As they got closer, the differences between the cops became more obvious. One was taller, one had a grey goatee. And one was Wayne Reilly, their old Laurier classmate.

"Hey," Helen called. She raised her hand. "Wayne!"

Wayne nodded at her. He said something to the other cops and they walked away towards the parking lot, leaving him alone in front of the station's glass doors.

Helen thought of Wayne's picture in the yearbook, his wavy blond hair hanging over a Tragically Hip T-shirt as he bent over his guitar, smiling. He wasn't smiling now. His face was impassive behind his Ray-Bans, his head shaved to the skin under his shiny black cap.

"Hey, Wayne," Helen said, as they reached him. "Remember Anna? She's here to report an assault. Something that happened in high school."

"At Laurier?" Wayne's eyebrows lifted over the metal frame of his sunglasses.

"Well, not at school, exactly. At a party. Could you tell us where to go?"

"Oh, I can tell you where to go."

"Great." Helen laughed uncertainly. "Where?"

"Do I need to spell this out?" His hand dropped to rest on his leather holster. "You can turn around and go home."

"What?" Helen said. "Why?"

"Let us through." Anna stepped up beside her. "Come on, Wayne. I never did anything to you."

"Oh, you did plenty. Remember, those carrels at the back of the library? And at least once in Tyler's car?"

"Fuck you," Anna said tiredly. "I told you, Helen. There's no point to this."

"That's right," Wayne said. "You're not filing any false claims on my watch. Olly told me you've been stalking him, making threats. Trying to rewrite history."

"You really think Olly's the victim here?" Helen said. "Wayne, come on. You can't stop us filing a report."

"You call me Officer Reilly, when I'm on duty," Wayne said. "Helen, I don't have anything against you, but you're wasting my time. We've got real crimes to worry about."

"Rape's a crime," Helen said. "We've got witnesses. Photographic evidence."

"The Polaroids?" Wayne laughed. "I'd love to see those again. I think my favourite's the one with her ass up in the air, with Olly's arm reaching under her legs, you know?"

He stepped closer, until he was right in Anna's face. "Everyone knows you were the class whore, trying to piss off your rich daddy. You don't get to start slandering my friends. Now, I'm giving you ten seconds to walk away, or I'm charging you with mischief. Obstruction of justice, too. Your choice. Ten—"

Anna raised her hands to his chest and shoved with all her strength. For a moment, Helen wanted to cheer, then Wayne caught hold of Anna's wrists.

"Police interference? Okay, that's a good one." Anna's face twisted as Wayne pressed his freckled nose against her hair. "And what's that I smell? A little weed, maybe? Why don't I strip you down, do a search for controlled substances?"

Wayne tightened his grip, smiling, until Anna cried out.

"Let her go!" Helen stepped forward and Wayne's head swivelled towards her, the movement so menacing that the hair stood up on her arms. "Please, Wayne. Officer Reilly. We'll leave. Let her go before you hurt her."

He held Anna for another few seconds, just to show that he could. Then he released his grip. Shaking his head, Wayne wiped his palms down the red stripes on his pants and turned away.

"Come on, Anna. Let's go home."

Helen put her arm around Anna's shoulders.

"I told you, all cops are assholes."

"Not all of them! Wayne won't always be on duty. We'll come back, some other time. We'll try again."

Anna shook her off and turned on her, dark eyes cold with anger.

"How much humiliation do you think I can take?"

CHAPTER 23

Anna shivered and tugged her black puffy jacket tighter around her body. She was sitting outside on her fire escape and the cold October wind came from all directions at once: into her face, down her neck, up the metal stairs to freeze her ass through her jeans.

She flipped through Helen's yearbook, looking at the glossy team photos. Here was Olly Sutton, over and over, in a Laurier burgundy football uniform, a basketball jersey, even a curling sweatshirt. Always with that cocky grin, with his arms slung over the shoulders of his friends.

Anna turned to the photo from the party. By now, she could probably draw this image from memory: the flushed and grinning boys on Olly's couch, Anna's pale teenage face above her green sweater. She counted them off: Olly, Phil, Starkey, Geoff, Mike, Xuan. Xuan had promised to help her, but what had he done? Combed through some boxes of yearbook crap. Confirmed what she already knew about Phil's Polaroids. Big fucking deal.

The next page showed Johnnie Campbell towering over the other nerds in the AV club. She studied his bad skin, his skater undercut. Was he already into weed back in high school? Too bad he wouldn't be hooking her up anymore. He'd made that clear when she saw him a few nights ago, sitting at the bar at Club Denim, watching a baseball game on their giant TV.

"Johnnie!" She'd leaned in, twined a hand through his short brown hair. "Where you been, guy? I haven't seen you in forever!"

Gently, he'd unlatched her fingers from around his neck.

"Anna. Might be time to slow down on the drinking, eh?"

"I'm fine." Anna reached a hand to the zipper of his jeans, felt him move under her fingers. "You know you've missed me."

"How about you give me a call when you're sober?"

So much for him. So much for all these assholes, she thought, flipping the pages, scratching at the back of her hand. Her skin was still itchy in places, tender and pink. Some of her tattoos had faded after the infection, their lines blurring, the colours smeared. She'd get them fixed, eventually. But Anna felt blurry herself these days.

Once, in her early teens, Malcolm took her to a museum in Toronto, to an exhibit of early photography. "The very first picture of a person," he'd said, pointing at an indistinct silhouette on an empty Paris street. "Back then, film exposures took so long that anything moving got erased. Probably this street was full of carriages, horses, people walking by. The camera only caught this man because he stopped to get his shoes shined."

Anna had leaned in, searching the scratched-up picture for other signs of life. Now, she knew it was better to blur. If she kept moving, she could disappear.

That's what everyone wanted, wasn't it? Olly, Starkey, Wayne. Even Anna's own mother: *You can't wait ten years and then cry rape.* Other than Helen, everyone wanted to keep Anna silent, to preserve their precious status quo.

Anna lifted her head, staring through the iron bars of the fire escape. Why was she making life easier for them?

She slammed the yearbook shut and climbed to her feet, feeling the metal platform sway beneath her.

Behind her, in their apartment, she heard the phone ring. Probably Helen's mom. Or Helen herself, calling from work, checking in. *Are you feeling any better today?* Naïve, innocent Helen, who still believed in the justice system, as if life was fair and bad guys got punished.

When the phone rang again, Anna slid the yearbook through her window and ran down the metal fire escape. She had to jump the last few feet, sprawling forward onto the gravel-covered asphalt. Then she was up, cursing, brushing her stinging palms against her thighs and limping across the back parking lot towards the newspaper office.

*

Hallowe'en was still two weeks away, but the Guelph Mercury had gone nuts with their decorations. Fake spiderwebs fringed the windows and a pyramid of jack-o'-lanterns was balanced on an actual bale of hay by the front desk. The receptionist even sported a yellow and orange candy-corn manicure.

"I need to talk to Xuan Wu. That's Shooo-ann." Anna leaned over the counter, overemphasizing his name. "Can you let him know Anna Leverett's here?"

When Xuan appeared, Anna let out a breath she hadn't realized she'd been holding. She motioned him over to the window, beside a plastic spider tangled in nylon.

"What's up?" Xuan adjusted his blazer over his grey dress shirt. "I'm on deadline."

"I want you to write up my story," Anna said. "Blow the whistle on Olly and his buddies. *Teenage Rapists,* we could call it. It could be huge."

Xuan was already shaking his head.

"You said you were on my side! Remember? You said *Olly Sutton is a homophobic asshole.* You said you'd help take him down."

"That was before."

"Before what?"

"I saw you go off on Olly, that night at the Trash. Annie, you're out of control. Maybe if you'd taken the high road, we could have talked to him—"

"I'm done talking." Anna grabbed Xuan's arm. "We need to write this up. Get the news out. What parent's going to want him teaching their teenage daughters, after what he did to me?"

"That's not how this works." Xuan tried to pull away, but she gripped tighter. "There are libel laws."

"Fuck the laws!" Anna's nails dug in.

"Shit!" Xuan jerked back. "What is wrong with you? You can't attack people! Someone's going to press charges!"

"I'm sorry. Did I break the skin?"

He popped the button on his cuff and rolled back the sleeve, rubbing his arm.

"Fuck, Anna. You need therapy." Xuan glared at her. "Bad things happened. I get it. You think I don't get that? That's part of why I left Toronto; my ex got jumped coming out of a bar in the Village. It took eight staples and thirty-odd stitches to close the cut in his head. He was off work for six months recovering from the concussion. I missed a whole semester at Ryerson, taking care of him. I know you're having a hard time. But come on, you make choices, too. Is this how you want to live?"

"No one wants to hear what I'm saying. But I've got the Polaroids," Anna said. She swayed towards him. "What if I let you print those too?"

"Are you drunk?" Xuan said. "It's not even noon! God, Annie. You're such a mess."

"Forget it." Ridiculously, Anna could feel tears rising. "I'm sorry to bother you. I'll let you get back to your deadline."

She turned away, blindly. At the end of the block, she deked into a parking lot and squatted between a pickup truck and a dented metal railing. She rested her head on her hands, squeezing the metal railing until the sharp edge cut into her fingers. Then she smudged away the tears, climbed to her feet and looked up at the faded slogan painted on the cement wall. *Vote for Nobody!* The mural proclaimed, beside a faceless man in a suit and tie. *Nobody will listen to your concerns. Nobody tells the truth. Nobody cares!*

*

Anna stumbled past the Albion, Jimmy Jazz, the Trasheteria, the Palace; all of them closed this early in the day. *You need therapy*. She'd tried that, of course. Rehab too. Twelve-steps, urban retreats, wilderness programs, as far from home as her parents could send her. Those places were all the same. They dried you out, threw you in with a bunch of other addicts who spent mornings proselytizing about the dangers of drugs, afternoons reminiscing about the fun they used to have and evenings whispering about where they could score.

When Anna reached the Via Rail station, she circled the squat brick building and looked down the tracks. Toronto was that way, wasn't it? The big city, connected to all the other big cities around the world. And the other direction—she turned unsteadily—Windsor. Detroit. The big old U S of A.

She stepped down onto the train tracks and wobbled along the metal rail, arms outstretched for balance. The tracks led her up a dusty gravel slope, past thin maples with fluttering orange leaves, towards the railway bridge over the river. Chain-link fences funnelled her forward until she was walking the tracks above a bustling intersection. Then she paused, watching a woman with a black Lab overtake a troupe of daycare kids, each of the toddlers reaching out to pet the dog as it went by.

Anna lifted her eyes and looked out over the city. From here, she could see how the smaller streets radiated out from the main roads, like spokes on a wheel, like fingers on a hand. Wasn't that how Guelph was laid out, back when the first rich white guy chopped down a tree and staked his claim? She lifted her own hand, squinting to match up the streets with her stretched-wide fingers. For a moment, she and the city fit together perfectly.

She walked along the rail until the ground fell away and she was on the bridge stepping from one oil-soaked railway tie to the next, breathing in the smoky smell of creosote. Halfway across, she stopped and lit a cigarette, shielding the flame from the wind. Anna looked down, between the ties to the smooth surface of the river, where ripples betrayed the current beneath. If a train came now, she'd have to jump.

Shivering, she raised her head and looked upstream, at the concrete footbridge that leapt from one bank to the other. That footbridge was only a block from her parents' house. After the party, when everything was falling apart, Anna had discovered the spot underneath that bridge.

Actually, no. It was after her mother came up with her plan.

"Here's what we'll say," Joyce had said. "You've got a bad case of mono. You're contagious, can't leave the house, so you'll finish the school year by correspondence. Meanwhile, I'm on bed rest with a difficult pregnancy—"

"No." Anna had pushed back her blankets, sat up in bed. "You can't make me do that."

"It's best for everyone, Annie." The eagerness in Joyce's voice, the hope on her face. "We'll give that baby a good life. And you should be grateful. Seven, eight months of vacation, then you're back on track to graduate with your friends."

It was after the abortion, then, that Anna found the spot under that bridge, where the concrete arch buried itself in the riverbank. Anything was better than going home, even sitting in the dirt beside broken bottles and half-drowned plastic bags, watching the trembling reflections of buildings in the slow-moving river. Sometimes alone, sometimes with a boy or two. Drunk, stoned, day after day, rereading the graffiti on the underside of the bridge: *Kristy loves anal* and *Jason is a fag* along with crooked swastikas and penises. Waiting for her own name to show up beside the other dirty words.

Part of Anna was still under there, a broken sixteen-year-old hiding from the world. She would always be there. That girl, her girlhood, had been left behind.

Olly and Glenn and their friends had gone on with their lives. They had jobs, partners, children, bright futures. They never had to think about that party again. Even if they came forward, if Olly and his buddies faced some form of justice, Anna had to live with this black hole in her memory. She had to live with this grief. She would always know too much and not enough.

She leaned out to watch the river, staring down into the whirlpool by the concrete abutment, the wind whistling past her ears. How cold was that water? How deep?

She leaned further, staring down into the shifting waters, the metal barrier creaking under her weight.

Who would miss her, if she fell? If she jumped?

Anna swayed another moment, teetering. Then, with a jolt, she caught the railing.

Helen would miss her. Helen kept trying to reach her, to take care of her, and Anna kept pushing her away. If anything happened, Helen would blame herself. Anna couldn't do that to her. Not again.

She stepped back, away from the edge. Whatever happened with Olly, with his asshole friends, with Anna's messed-up family, Helen kept proving that she'd be there. However long it took for Anna to work through her shit, Helen would be there, by her side.

Anna looked back upstream, towards the concrete footbridge. Maybe it was time to give up on these dreams of justice or revenge. Try to live in the present. Maybe even look for a job, break free from the golden handcuffs of her parents' credit cards.

Anna picked her way back across the bridge, feeling lighter as she skidded down the grassy embankment and headed for home.

She could hear Helen moving in her bedroom when she came in the door.

"Helen?" Anna called, as she unzipped her coat and stepped out of her boots. "Hey, I want to take you out for dinner. We can go anywhere you want, my treat."

She walked into Helen's room to find her stuffing clothes into a suitcase.

"What's going on?"

"I have to go," said Helen. "My mom called me at work. She said Gord's in the hospital. They think he had a heart attack."

CHAPTER 24

Helen took a deep breath before pushing open the door to Gord's hospital room. Nothing had changed: her stepfather was still asleep, his white-bearded face slack under the fluorescent lights. Linda sat beside him in the battered armchair, clutching the hand without the IV, her eyes locked on the thin tube that snaked up into Gord's nose.

Helen held out the paper bag.

"You wanted the chicken wrap?" Helen pulled out the plastic-wrapped sandwich and laid it on her mother's lap. "Mom. You need to eat."

Linda glanced up with empty eyes. She'd aged ten years since Tuesday, hadn't left Gord's bedside since he came out of the ICU after the double bypass. Helen had tried to convince her to go home, to catch up on sleep in her own bed, but even when she offered to take her place, Linda shook her head.

"I need to be here."

Helen was staying in their condo. She was taking care of the cat, watering the plants, bringing back clean clothes for Linda. That had been hardest on the first morning, when she'd opened the closet to the wall of Gord's fleece jackets and buried her face in the soft fabrics. What if he never came home? Gord was the keystone of their family, the one who held the rest of them together. He'd made Linda smile again, coached Julia's soccer teams, taste-tested every one of Helen's beginner recipe attempts. She closed her eyes and was there beside him at the kitchen counter, watching him lift the tea towel off the risen bread dough. "Punch it down," he'd say, and she'd plunge small fists into the elastic dough, the smell of yeast rising to envelop them both.

Sweet, steadfast Gord. What if he never baked another loaf of bread, never played another song on his guitar, never hugged her again? Helen leaned into the fleece sweatshirts and cried heedlessly, messily, smearing her makeup against the fabrics. Then she pulled herself together, assembled Linda's bag and walked back to St. Mike's.

Helen had only cried once in front of her mother, and that was during Gord's bypass operation. She'd taken the bus from Guelph, arriving in time to clasp Gord's hand as they wheeled him into surgery. When the doors swung shut behind his gurney, Helen collapsed against her mother. She'd wished for some of Anna's pills as they endured the endless five hours it took for the doctors to pry open Gord's chest, divert his blood flow, resect his arteries and sew him back together.

Finally, the surgeon found them in the waiting room. "The procedure went well," the doctor said, and that was it, Linda's cue to fall apart. Suddenly Helen was the adult in the room, her mother weeping as they listened to the surgeon's foreign language of stents and grafts and atherosclerosis. "You can see him as soon as he's out of recovery," the surgeon said, as Helen guided Linda into a hard plastic chair.

"Hear that, Mom? Don't cry. He's going to be okay."

Now, three days later, this hospital schedule had become routine. Meals at seven, twelve and five o'clock. Morning rounds at eight, the white-coated doctors murmuring in medical code. Shift change for the nurses at seven o'clock, morning and evening.

"Any change while I was downstairs?"

Helen glanced at Gord's pale sleeping face, then over at the monitors with their blinking red numbers. Linda shook her head.

"That's good, right?" Helen pulled up the other chair, the one with the big rip in the vinyl seat. "They said he needs sleep to get better."

"What do they know? These tests don't tell us anything. And I don't like this nurse. That monitor keeps beeping and all she does is reset it."

"I'm sure she's doing her job." Helen patted her mother's hand, feeling the tremor in her fingers. "Isn't the cardiologist coming by today? You can ask him."

Helen had met him yesterday, a tall, brown-skinned doctor rattling off recovery statistics and rehabilitation advice. He'd shot her a quick smile as he left the room, the white teeth in his dark face making her think of Dave Patel.

"I'll believe it when I see it," said Linda, in her new querulous voice. She draped a napkin over her untouched chicken wrap. "Is Julia coming today?"

"She says she'll try to make it tomorrow."

On Tuesday, Julia had promised to catch the Megabus from Ottawa right away, to come directly to the hospital after the surgery. Late that night, when Helen finally made it back to the condo, she'd found a message on the answering machine: Julia was sorry, but she had a term project to finish. She'd get there Wednesday, for sure. The next day brought another message: Julia hated to do this, she was so, so sorry, but she couldn't make it. Now she was supposed to drive down Friday, but Helen had heard the strain in Julia's voice, the way it cracked on every *sorry*. She fully expected to see the light flashing on the machine when she got back to the condo tonight.

Linda gripped her hand. "It's the end of the semester. She's got so much to do for school. And what about you, honey? When do you need to be back at work?"

"They're giving me time off."

That was true, sort of. Helen had called on Tuesday, once she knew Gord had made it through the operation.

"I can't come in for a few days," she'd told Carmen. "There's a family emergency."

"You've missed three shifts this month. I'm sorry. You'll have to come in."

"I can't." Helen looked down the hospital hallway to where her mother sat slumped in her plastic chair. "I'm staying in Toronto. My stepdad had a heart attack."

"Really?"

"Yes, really! God, why would I lie about that?"

There was a pause. When Carmen spoke again, she sounded younger, less certain.

"Sorry. I just thought; first Barb, now you?"

"What happened to Barb?"

"She's given her notice. Helen, please. If you don't come in, I'll have to take you off the schedule. You'll lose your seniority."

Helen was too tired to argue, too tired to care. "I get it."

"How about you take tomorrow and Thursday? I'll rearrange the schedule, put you in for double shifts for the weekend so you can make up the time—"

"No, thanks."

"I can't let you do this. You'll lose everything, you'll have to apply to be reinstated. It's store policy. I won't be able do anything for you."

Helen stared at her blurred reflection in the pay-phone's scratched metal faceplate. *Who cares,* she mouthed silently. *I quit.*

Out loud, into the phone, she said: "Do what you have to do."

"I'll try and cover for you, but I can't make any guarantees. Let me know when you're ready to come back. You can call me at home, day or night. And Helen?"

"Yeah?"

"I hope your stepdad's okay."

*

Back at the condo that evening, Helen set her takeout sushi on the kitchen table and looked at the answering machine. No blinking light. Maybe Julia was coming after all.

Helen fed the cat and sat down for dinner, flattening a new issue of *Allure* as she draped pickled ginger over a California roll. Angelina Jolie was on the cover, dark-eyed and sultry. Helen scanned the headlines: *Ten Biggest Beauty Mistakes. Perfect Skin. Sexy Smouldering Eyes.* She flipped past ads to the table of contents. *Update Your Look. Tone Your Problem Areas. Are You Having Too Much Sex?*

Helen chewed the sushi roll, thinking about Anna. Since coming to Toronto, she'd called home five times but Anna never picked up. Maybe she was out, or maybe she was on a massive bender, drinking, loading up on pills. Maybe she was fine, or maybe she was passed out on their kitchen floor, vomit puddled beneath her ashen face.

Helen laid down her chopsticks and reached for the phone. It rang four times before switching to the machine.

"Hey, Anna, it's me again. It's Thursday night. If you're there, could you call me back, let me know that everything's okay? Otherwise, I'll try again later. Take care."

She hung up and stared down at her food. The rice looked dull and swollen now, the sesame seeds gritty as dirt. She picked up the phone again. This time, it was answered after the second ring.

"Thom. Hi." Helen felt suddenly bashful. "How's it going?"

"Hey, Helen. I got promoted today! You're talking to a level three NetXperts support technician. How are you?"

"Not great." She pushed the tray of sushi away. "Gord had a heart attack on Monday."

"Oh my God. Jesus. He's not, is he—"

"They say he's going to be okay. They did an emergency double bypass. My mom still won't leave his side." Helen picked up a red pen and doodled circles on Angelina's face. "I'm staying here in Toronto, helping out."

"A heart attack? I thought he was in such good shape for his age."

"I know." She closed her eyes, listening to him breathing through the phone.

"How are you doing?" Thom said. "How are you dealing with it all?"

"Me? I'm…" Helen stopped, sinuses prickling. She put down the pen to pinch the bridge of her nose. "It's hard. I'm taking it day by day, trying to take care of my mom. I've never seen her like this."

"What about your sister? Is she there too?"

"She's still in Ottawa." Helen blew her nose and balled up the Kleenex. "Sorry, I don't mean to dump this on you."

"Can I do anything? I could drive in after work tomorrow," Thom said. "Or whatever you need. I know you've got Anna—"

"No, that's why I'm calling. She's not answering the phone. And she's been…sick. Having a bad time. Is there any way you could you go by our place, check that she's okay?"

As soon as she said the words, Helen wished she could take them back. Why hadn't she called Anna's parents? They had a key to the apartment. They were the ones paying the rent, the ones who'd appointed her Anna's chaperone.

"What's the address? I'll go over there now."

Helen let out a long breath. "Thank you."

"If she's there, I'll have her give you a call. Is that cool?"

"For sure. Thanks, Thom. You're the best. And congrats on the promotion. That's amazing."

"It means I don't have to stress about finding a new roommate. So, you know, your old room is still free."

"Oh. Right. Cool."

Helen looked down at the magazine cover, at the red birthmark she'd drawn over Angelina's cheek. A map of Switzerland.

"Give me your number there, so I can reach you," he said. "Then I'll go check on your friend."

*

The next day, Gord beckoned Helen to his bedside when Linda went to the bathroom.

"I'm worried about your mom," he said hoarsely. "She's going to have her own heart attack if she doesn't take some time for herself."

"I know. She's hardly eating. And she can't be getting much sleep in that recliner."

"Can you get her outside for a walk? They're taking me for more tests. I don't want her sitting here, worrying."

"I can try." Helen's throat made a clicking sound as she swallowed. "I keep trying."

"I know," Gord said. "And you? How are you holding up?"

Before she could answer, Julia swept into the room, holding a bouquet of carnations. She was more dressed up than usual in a denim skirt and a white button-down shirt, her pixie cut freshly trimmed. Glenn was a step behind her, more casual in jeans and a green Celtics sweatshirt.

"Sorry it took me so long to get here." Julia leaned over the bed to kiss Gord's bearded cheek. "It's been a crazy week."

"Julia! You made it!"

Linda appeared in the doorway, her face so bright with joy that Helen had to look away.

"It's too crowded in here," Helen said. "I'm going for a walk."

Helen had been doing this all week. Long aimless walks past the hushed urgency of the ER, the crying babies of the maternity ward, the closed curtains of palliative care. This time, when she reached the elevator, she punched the top button and rode up to the twelfth floor, staring at her reflection in the smeared glass of the mirror. Her makeup was minimal today, her birthmark barely covered with thin foundation. What did it matter, compared to the stitches and staples in Gord's chest, the new wrinkles in her mother's forehead?

She headed down the hallway, turning randomly left, then right, then left. She couldn't stop seeing her mother's face light up when Julia walked into the room. All week, she'd wanted her sister to arrive, but she'd forgotten how Julia sucked the air out of the room. And what was Glenn doing here, anyway?

She turned a corner and stopped, staring at a guy in his twenties with a purple birthmark across his forehead. He was sitting on a waiting room couch, under a hospital sign that said *Vascular Surgery*.

Helen raised a hand to the bumpy surface of her own port wine stain. *A vascular anomaly.* That's what the doctors called it. *Nevus flammeus.* She thought of Laura Sanders' baby nephew, Claire Simmons' puffy discoloured face. Helen was lucky, really. Lots of people had serious complications: Seizures, vision loss, brain damage. Her case was purely superficial. Easily covered with makeup.

Except that it wasn't really covered, today. Helen stared at the young man. He'd be good-looking if it weren't for his birthmark.

On Wednesday, she'd stopped by the Toronto Eaton Centre. She'd drifted from the MAC counter to Dior, from Stila to Urban Decay, unmoved by the expensive creams and powders. Somehow, the old spell was broken. Even when Helen tried a limited-edition Nars blush, she felt no thrill at seeing the gold flakes shimmer within the coral pink. It remained a plastic case of pigment, barely distinguishable from the other fifty blushes she'd collected over the years. She'd snapped the compact shut and walked away.

Helen nodded at the guy with the birthmark, then turned around. At a floor-to-ceiling window down the hall, she watched a crow circle and dip between power lines and buildings, past a deflated yellow balloon caught in the branches of a tree. She pressed her face against the window as the balloon strained against the wind. When the cold from the window seeped into her forehead, she pulled back and grimaced at her reflection, at the faint smear of colour across her cheek.

Back in Gord's hospital room, she found him asleep, her mother reading a detective novel in the bedside armchair. Julia's pink carnations stood beside the bed.

"Julia couldn't stay," Linda said, setting her thumb between the pages to mark her place. "She's got work to finish."

"She was only here for twenty minutes?"

"I told her to go. Gord needed a nap." Linda pushed up her glasses and squinted at Helen. "Give her a break, honey. They drove five hours to get here."

"Yeah." Helen pressed her lips together. "Julia's a saint."

*

By the time she got back to the condo, Helen was so angry she felt like she was giving off sparks. She tossed her keys on the kitchen table, shouting for her sister.

"Julia!"

When she saw the light flashing on the answering machine, she sucked in her breath. Had they left? Would they dare? Blood pounding in her ears, she stabbed the playback button.

"Helen, hi, it's me. I hope Gord's okay."

The raspy voice was so quiet that it took Helen a moment to recognize Anna.

"I'm sorry I haven't called you back. It's hard to get shit done, without you bossing me around. But you'll be proud of me, I went to an NA meeting, downtown. It was fucking awkward. Some old man read from his Bible. I stayed for the whole meeting, though."

The voice trailed off, but there was no beep to signal the end of the message. Helen stared into the grid of holes in the answering machine as if she might see Anna on the other side. After a long few seconds, there was a cough.

"Anyway. Your old roommate came by to check up on me. I told him to fuck off, but I figured I should give you a call."

"Was that Annie?"

Helen turned to see Glenn standing in the kitchen doorway. She'd always seen him as a grown-up version of the gap-toothed kid in her kindergarten class, but this Glenn was a stranger, unknown and unlikable.

She frowned at him. "Where's Julia?"

"At the gym."

"The gym?"

"You know, the fitness centre, over by the parking garage," Glenn said. "Your mom gave her a keycard."

"What's she doing there? If she's not at the hospital, what's the point?"

"This isn't easy for her. She's doing her best. You don't understand her at all."

"I really don't. Julia's a fucking mystery to me." Helen stared at Glenn until he looked away. For the first time, she noticed that his hairline was starting to creep back away from his temples. It made him look older, a tarnished version of the golden boy. "Aren't you going to ask about Anna?"

Glenn hesitated.

"She's staying in Guelph. We moved in together." Helen narrowed her eyes. "Or did you already know that?"

"No. I'm not really—"

"Olly has probably filled you in. We had a run-in with Wayne Reilly, outside the Guelph police station. Officer Reilly. You heard about that too?"

"I haven't talked to anyone. I want to put all that behind me. Our therapist says—"

"Your therapist."

"She says it's no good dwelling on the past, we have to focus on the future."

"The future." A wave of exhaustion washed through Helen, flattening the anger. "What about the present? What about Anna? She'd like to start over too, you know."

"I can't get involved. For Julia's sake—"

"For your sake."

"For the sake of our families, then. Look, I'm not trying to pretend it didn't happen. But I was sixteen. I'm not that same kid anymore."

"Sure." Helen closed her eyes, blocking out Glenn's face. "Yeah. You're great. A real stand-up guy."

*

Helen called Anna back as soon as Glenn left the room. The phone rang four times, then the machine clicked and she heard her own voice begin its *leave a message* spiel. She hung up and paced across the kitchen. Should she call Thom again, ask how Anna looked when she answered the door? Really, Helen ought to get back to Guelph and check on Anna herself, especially with Julia here to look after their mom.

In the meantime, she would do something useful. She hauled the mixer out from the cupboard, pulled out butter and sugar and started making cookies. When a high-pitched meow cut through the grinding sound of the motor, Helen swung around to see her sister crouched in the hallway, petting the cat.

Instantly, the anger roared back.

"How was the gym?"

"Don't start."

Julia didn't look up. She was wearing a loose T-shirt and black leggings that made her thighs look as spindly as sticks.

"No, I get it. You want to get in shape for the wedding."

Julia glared at her and stood up, joints popping like gunshots, as Glenn came into the kitchen.

"Hey, babe," he said, kissing Julia's cheek. He hiked the strap of his duffle bag across his shoulders. "I'm heading out. I'll be back tomorrow afternoon."

"You're leaving?" Helen asked.

"Glenn's going to Guelph to see his family. Not that it's any of your business. Hon, are you sure you don't want me to come?"

Helen turned away, willing the sound of the ancient motor to block out their conversation. When that wasn't enough, she switched on the electric kettle for more white noise. If Glenn were anyone else, Helen could have asked him to check on Anna. For that matter, he could have driven her back to the apartment.

After Glenn left, Julia stepped up to the sink and filled a glass of water.

Helen pressed her lips together, picked up the kettle and poured hot water into the teapot, dropping in a sachet of Gord's dried mint and chamomile.

"You were ready to go with him," she said. "Honestly, why did you come? Don't they have gyms in Ottawa?"

"Says the girl baking cookies."

"Mom needs to eat something."

"You're such a fucking martyr." Julia drained the glass, slammed it onto the counter and ran a hand through her sweaty curls. "I need to take a shower."

"You do that. Whatever you need."

Julia's thin body went rigid.

"What do you even want from me?!" She wheeled around, her eyes wide, her face filled with anger and bitterness—and fear, Helen suddenly saw, as the scene turned like a kaleidoscope. Julia was a stretched-out wire, ready to snap.

"I don't want to fight," Helen said, stepping back.

"Oh no? Since when?"

"I mean it." She picked up the teapot and poured two cups of tea. "Truce, okay? Can we take five minutes and talk this through?"

"You sound like Gord," snapped Julia, but she yanked out a wooden chair and slumped on its seat. "Five minutes."

Helen sat across from her, wrapping her hands around her mother's blue U of T mug. She'd given her sister Gord's favourite mug, an oversized cup with *Trust me, I'm a dogtor* over a cartoon puppy in a lab coat. Julia blew on the surface of her tea, dipped in a fingertip and stuck it in her mouth. The gesture was unexpectedly childlike.

"I need your help," said Helen.

Julia screwed her face into a scowl. "What? How?"

"You know Mom's not sleeping. She's barely eating. I swear, she's lost five pounds since the heart attack."

"What do you want me to do?"

"Could you take her out for dinner? Distract her with something positive, for once?"

"She doesn't listen to me." Julia looked down at her tea.

"Of course she does. She talks about you all the time. Julia this, Julia that. Your wedding, law school. You're her perfect daughter."

"Perfect..." Julia shook her head. "Did you know I used to be anorexic?"

"What?" Helen's stomach tightened. "No, you didn't."

"In high school. I was living off gum and celery sticks, I joined all sorts of clubs so I could skip meals. Then one day I was at my friend Denise's house and I fainted in the kitchen. Her mom's a nurse. She sat me down and made me admit what was going on."

"How come I never heard about this?"

"I made them promise they wouldn't tell Mom. I knew she couldn't handle another daughter with problems."

"Problems?" Helen recoiled.

"You know what I mean."

"Yeah, and that's messed up. Like I'm some kind of freak." She hesitated. "But I am sorry I made that crack about the gym. About getting in shape."

"You don't need me here. And I can't fuck up this semester."

"We do need you. Mom definitely needs you. Didn't you see her face when you walked in today?" She shook her head. "And who cares about your semester? Gord almost died!"

"They know how important this is to me. Mom and Gord, Dad and Karen, the whole family. I'd be letting them down, too. They know I've got papers due, exams coming up, internship applications—"

"Hey." Helen put out a hand to stop her. "I'm not asking you to stay."

"You're not?"

"I took time off work. I'll stick around as long as Mom needs me. Anyway, things in Guelph have been messy, lately."

"Yeah. I bet." Julia's eyes flicked up and back, making Helen clench her teeth. "You just don't know what it's like for me. I'm not like you, Helen. I'm not allowed to make mistakes."

"Allowed?" Helen flared. "Everyone makes mistakes."

"He feels terrible, you know."

"Gord?" Something wrenched in her chest. "Glenn. He feels terrible?"

"He says you won't even look at him anymore. He's terrified you're going to tell Mom and Gord."

"I wouldn't do that." Helen said. "But how am I supposed to look at him? He raped my best friend."

"And he apologized. He'd take it back, if he could. They were all drunk, he says. He didn't even want to do it, but there were all these guys, all this pressure. He says it happened fast. And it's not like it was violent—"

"How do you know?"

"I know Glenn."

"Do you?"

They stared at each other. A memory jumped into Helen's mind: Julia crouched over the dented coffee table in their old Guelph house, spinning the rainbow wheel in the Game of Life and directing her plastic minivan ahead of Helen's on the red and yellow track.

"I know Glenn," Julia said again. "I know you think I'm crazy for sticking with him, after finding out—"

"I didn't say that."

"You didn't have to. But you don't understand. He takes care of me. We take care of each other. I'm not throwing that away."

"Okay."

"You think I'm making the wrong choices."

"You don't care what I think." Helen gave a sharp laugh. "You're so stuck on your ideas of what's supposed to happen, of how things are supposed to be. Life's not a fucking contest, Julia. It's actually okay to slow down, to change direction."

"You think I should have come down earlier. But I've worked so hard to get through this term. And the thought of seeing Gord in hospital..." Julia swallowed. "Plus, I knew you were here. All week, I've been saying that to Glenn: It's okay, Helen's there. They've got Helen. They'll be okay."

"They're not okay," Helen said. "That's what I'm telling you. Mom is not okay."

"It's not even just my classes. It's almost November; this stupid wedding is coming up so fast! I wish we'd just eloped. I wish I could cancel the whole thing. But I can never say no to Mom and she's planned this whole production and I can't back out, I can't take that away from her, but none of this is what we wanted! And now, with Gord..." Her voice rose hysterically. "Helen, what if he doesn't make it? How can we get married if he's not there?"

"He's here *now*," Helen snapped. "Mom needs you *now*. God, Julia. For once in your life, think about someone other than yourself."

"That's not—"

"Nobody's interfering with your life in the fast lane, okay? Go ahead and finish your semester. Get married to Mr. 'I'm the victim' Glenn Starkey. But you came down here to help, so fucking help! Mom is suffering. I'm asking you, her favourite child, to distract her. Is that really too much to ask?"

Julia stared at her. "I'm not her favourite," she said, after a minute.

"Of course you are!" Helen's heart was a ball of lead in her chest. "You're the superstar daughter who can do no wrong. So go back to St. Mike's, take her down to the cafeteria and talk about wedding favours until she eats something. Okay?"

"Okay." Julia's eyes welled up. She looked down, dipped her finger into her tea and drew a little spiral on the tabletop. "I can do that."

"I know you're scared," Helen said, touching her hand. "I'm scared too. We're all taking this one day at a time."

Julia nodded, silently. Then suddenly she was up on her feet, locking both arms around Helen's back, squeezing her so tightly she could barely breathe. They were both crying now. Helen's tears ran into Julia's sweaty hair as she hugged her sister close, her body so frail and thin that each of her ribs felt like a band of hot iron.

CHAPTER 25

Anna kicked her way through the piles of yellow leaves as she followed her father through Woodlawn Cemetery. The leaves had nearly all fallen now and the sunlight shone strangely bright through the bare branches of the maple trees. When they reached her grandparents' graves, Malcolm unwrapped the cellophane from his bouquet and arranged the flowers in the bronze vase at the base of the headstone.

Malcolm had given her the flowers to hold when he picked her up outside the apartment.

"Go on, give them a sniff."

Anna stuck her face in the pinky-orange roses and breathed in a surprising scent, intense and citrusy.

"Whoa. What are these?"

"Grandiflora," said Malcolm, pulling away from the curb. "My mother's favourite. She used to grow them in her garden. How was yesterday?"

"It was fine. Quiet." Yesterday had been Anna's birthday. She'd turned twenty-seven. "I stayed in. Ate some dumplings from the restaurant downstairs, watched TV. Helen's going to make me a cake next weekend, when she's back in Guelph."

"Frank didn't have you working, did he?"

"I've got weekends off."

Her father had gotten her a job working in his friend's warehouse. Eight hours a day, five days a week, Anna moved boxes, sorted files, shredded paper. She didn't have to talk to anyone. It was perfect.

When Malcolm finished arranging the flowers, he stepped back to Anna's side. The roses glowed in the

afternoon sunlight, reflecting orange on the pale gran-
ite monument. *Entered into Eternal Rest. Peter Leverett.
Annette Elizabeth McKenzie Leverett.*

"How well do you remember your grandfather?"
Malcolm asked.

"Only a little." Her grandfather had died when Anna
was four. When she tried to picture him, all she saw
were the pink starburst blood vessels in his cheeks, the
patches of grey stubble his shaking hands had missed.
"He smelled like peppermint."

"Did you know he had a tattoo? A swallow. On his
shoulder." Malcolm tapped his jacket's left shoulder.
"From his days in the Air Force."

"A swallow? Why?"

"Because swallows always come home. My mother
hated it. She wouldn't let him wear short-sleeved shirts."

"Grandma hated mine, too," Anna said. "Said they
made me look cheap."

When Anna was young, she had idolized her grandmother. Annette's high-waisted pantsuits, her brown hair
lacquered to a shine, her smile frosted in Barbie pink;
she'd been the epitome of feminine glamour. Grandma
Annette had brought her to annual performances of *The
Nutcracker*, taught her to mix and then appreciate a classic dirty martini.

The last time Anna saw her, Annette had seemed fine
for the first hour, firing off questions like heat-seeking
missiles: "What are you doing with your life, Annie?
When are you going back to school? Don't you know
your parents worry about you?" It was only as the visit
wore on that Annette's focus wandered, her gaze drifting away out the nursing home window. Anna could
still feel the fragility of Annette's arms, the way the

loose skin moved against the bones when she hugged her goodbye.

"She was a formidable woman," said Malcolm. He dug in his coat pocket. "Which reminds me. I know you said you didn't want anything for your birthday, but I thought…" He opened his hand to show a gold ring with an egg-shaped green stone. "This was my mother's."

Anna took the ring and slid it onto her index finger.

"It's an agate. I think it was her birthstone. We can have it resized, if—"

"No. It's good." Anna flexed her fingers, admiring the heavy stone. "It fits."

"It suits you." Malcolm looked down at the ring, then up into Anna's face. He took her hand. "I'm glad you're staying in Guelph, Annie."

"I don't know how long I'm sticking around."

"As long as you want."

She hitched her shoulders. "That's not what Mother said."

"I know you two don't always get along—"

"She hates me." Anna's throat was closing up. She tried to pull her hand out of Malcolm's grip, but he wouldn't let go. "She wanted that baby more than me."

"She was hurt. You know she hasn't had an easy time of it."

"Like anyone would believe it was hers. That was so fucked up."

"You're her daughter." Malcolm squeezed her hand. "She loves you."

Anna looked back at the gravestone, then down at her boots, which were covered in fragments of wet leaves. "Agree to disagree," she said.

*

"Where can I take you?" Malcolm asked, as they turned out of the cemetery. "You want to come back to the house for lunch? I think your mother's making quiche—"

"No, thanks."

As they turned onto Woolwich, Anna saw the floral clock that marked the entrance to Riverside Park. The clock's flowers were all dried out, its metal hands both stopped near the XII.

"I want to be outside," Anna said. "You can drop me off here."

Riverside Park was more crowded than she'd expected. She walked past the little scale model of the first log house in Guelph, through the parking lots overhung with willows, down towards the river where her grandmother used to bring her to feed the ducks, to ride the old-fashioned carousel and the miniature train. She flexed her hand with her grandmother's ring, feeling its weight, turning it to catch the light inside the agate's speckled depths. When Anna came out of the pine trees, a gust of wind made her shiver. She put her hands in her jacket pockets, feeling the sharp edges of the Polaroids.

She'd been planning to show them to her father. She wasn't sure what had stopped her, not her mother's threats, but some smaller, gentler impulse. *You make choices too,* Xuan had said. *Is this how you want to live?*

She cut across the grass, past a group of women in saris at an old-fashioned metal barbecue stuck into a concrete slab. Twenty feet away, near the busy playground, another barbecue was sending up a thin plume of smoke. Anna turned towards it, drawn by the smell of meat mingling with charcoal briquettes.

Anna picked up a stick and poked at the smouldering coals, watching a sullen orange flame flicker in and out of being. She stared into the little fire, then out over the Speed River. Then, as if in a dream, she reached into her pocket.

Anna burned the Polaroids one at a time. One by one, the square pictures curled, blackened and flared into bright chemical balls of flame. She leaned forward to watch them burn, breathing in caustic smoke until her throat felt scorched, her eyes hot and dry.

She was almost done when a sudden gust caught the last few photos and blew them out of her hand, sending them tumbling across the grass. Anna dropped her stick and rushed after them. She grabbed two, but the last one sailed over towards the parents standing by the climbing structure. With a quick sideways movement, a woman pinned it under her winter boot.

"Thanks," Anna panted, as she ran up. "I didn't—"

The words died in her throat as the woman pulled off her tuque, releasing a long red braid. Laura Sanders had a rounder face than Anna remembered. Her cheeks were pink and mottled as she looked at the picture in her gloved hand.

"What the fuck is this?" Laura looked at the Polaroid, then up at Anna, her freckled face appalled. "Is this you?"

Anna caught a side-on glimpse of the picture. Teenaged Annie had her eyes closed in this one, but sixteen-year-old Olly was grinning for the camera, his hands shoving her breasts against the pink mushroom of someone's erect penis. There was a discoloured mark in the middle of the Polaroid from Laura's boot.

"That's you without tattoos. With your old hair." Laura squinted, glanced at Anna, then looked closer at the picture. "Is that Olly Sutton?"

"Laura, we can't find Maddy's... Oh. Hey, Anna."

Mike Whitburg jogged up to them, pushing a stroller. "Have you seen this?"

Laura tore her gaze away from the picture and held it out.

"It's mine," said Anna, trying to keep her voice calm. "Can I get it back?"

Laura waved the Polaroid at Mike, lifting it higher when a small girl in a pink coat hurled herself against her jeans, wailing.

"Daddy can't find Elmo!"

"Just a minute, Maddy. Here, Mike. Take it!"

Mike Whitburg took the Polaroid, glanced at it and pushed it into Anna's hands.

"Jesus, thank you."

"I can't believe those are still kicking around," he said. "Olly had them."

"Did you see it?" Laura demanded. She'd picked up their daughter, who was batting mittened hands towards her face. "Maddy, just a minute!"

"He's seen it before," Anna said, suddenly. "Haven't you?"

"Mike?" Laura's green eyes swivelled to look at him. "Have you?"

He looked at his wife for a long moment.

"Give her to me." Mike leaned forward and lifted the toddler out of Laura's arms, then he leaned over and set his little girl on her feet. "Come on, Madison. Let's go look under the slide."

"They all saw it," Anna said, as Mike led his daughter away. "Everyone at Laurier. All the guys, anyway. They used to pass them around."

"What?" Laura looked queasy. "That's from high school?"

Anna turned the Polaroid over and slid it into her pocket.

"It's from Olly Sutton's New Year's party," Anna said. "In grade ten, remember? I passed out. A bunch of guys…took turns. Phil McKinley took the pictures. That's how all the rumours started."

Laura hissed in her breath. "But that looks…you weren't…God, Annie."

Anna kicked at the ground.

"Yeah."

Laura stared off towards the river. Her pale face contorted in a series of expressions: eyes widening, nose wrinkling, lips pursing. Anna wondered if she was going to cry.

After a long minute, Laura said: "I was at that party. Mike was too." The baby in the stroller let out a squall, making Anna jump. "Just a second. Do you mind?"

Laura hoisted up her sweater, revealing a surprisingly large nipple before her round-headed baby latched on, blocking the view.

Anna gave an abrupt laugh and pulled out the Polaroid.

"Times change, don't they?" She waved her naked teenage breasts towards Laura.

Laura looked scandalized. "What?"

"It's just…no, it's not that, it's not funny. But…" Anna felt on the verge of hysteria. "You just whipped it out, and…I can't…" She doubled over, trying to catch her breath. Finally, she stood up, wheezing. "Sorry. It's just…I don't know. The irony."

"It's disgusting," Laura said, flatly.

"Yeah." Anna sobered up in a rush. "No, of course it is."

"It ruined your life."

"Well, I wouldn't say…"

"*Ruined*," Laura emphasized, holding Anna's eyes until she nodded and looked away.

"I didn't know." Laura Sanders said. "Honestly. None of us did. Us girls, I mean. We wouldn't have…"

"Yeah. No, I figured."

"I'm so sorry that happened to you," Laura said. "It must have been terrible."

"I was blacked out." Anna swallowed. "I don't actually remember anything."

"Then they passed around photos." Laura was staring back out over the Speed River. "And we made it worse, didn't we? We thought you were such a slut."

"It was high school," said Anna. "None of us were making our best choices."

"You know," Laura said. "My cousin was raped, her first week at university. Frosh week. And Jennifer Nicholson, in… It happens everywhere." She pulled her baby away from her chest and tucked her sweater back over her shirt. When she looked up, her green eyes were angry. "Men are shit."

"Some of them are."

Anna turned her head to the playground, where Mike Whitburg was chasing Laura's daughter. Maddy had a red stuffed toy clutched to her chest and she laughed a high-pitched giggle as she ran.

"Do you know who else was there? At that party?"

"I've been hearing different stories," said Anna. "Different names."

"But those pictures. Olly Sutton."

"Him for sure. He was the ringleader."

"What a prick." said Laura, setting her child back in the stroller. There was a tiny bead of milk in the corner of the sleeping baby's mouth. Gently, Laura wiped it away, then tucked a blue fleece blanket around him. "What an asshole. He always thought he was so great, you know?"

"I think he still does."

"Guys like that don't change."

"No."

"Hey." Laura's head jerked up in alarm. "Wait, do you think he's done that to anyone else?"

"Do I…" Anna stared at her. "I don't know. I never thought about that."

"Nobody stopped him with you." Laura got to her feet. "He completely got away with it. We all let him get away with it." Her cheeks were going red again, her breath getting faster. "It's awful, when I think about it. Fucking awful. That he just…you know, people should know the truth about what happened. Everyone should know what he did."

"Yeah." Anna felt light-headed. "Yeah, they should."

"I'm going to tell them." Laura reared up like a grizzly, ferocious and tall. "I don't care what Mike says, what anyone says. I'm telling everyone I know. People should know the truth."

*

"So then I went and burned the last one," Anna said to Helen.

It was a week later, and they were sitting on the couch in their apartment, digging into slices of chocolate birthday cake.

"You didn't think about keeping it?" Helen asked. "As evidence? In case you ever want to go to the cops?"

Anna stuck her fork in her mouth and shook her head.

"I'm trying to move on."

"Well, it's done now," Helen said. "Laura Sanders. That's so crazy. You think she feels bad for how she treated you?"

"She was pretty fired up." Anna took another bite. "I hope she tells the whole fucking town. I hope Olly's girlfriend dumps his ass."

"Yeah." Helen hesitated. "Do you think she knows… never mind. Nothing."

"What?"

Helen looked down, brushing invisible crumbs off her lap.

"About you and Mike?"

"Me and—" Anna stopped, remembering the summer day when Mike Whitburg had taken her to *see some properties*. They'd barely got through the door of the first condo before she had him up against the laminate kitchen cabinets, panting into her ear as she unbuckled his leather belt. "I don't know what you're talking about."

"Uh-huh. Fine, I don't want to know." She took another forkful of cake and closed her eyes. "Do you think this icing is too sweet?"

"It's great," Anna said. "I can't remember the last time someone made me a cake. Honestly, I'm so glad you're back. I've been surviving on cereal and takeout."

Helen opened her eyes.

"The ice cream!" She set her plate on the coffee table, jumped to her feet and headed for the kitchen.

"It's fine. We don't need it."

Helen reappeared in the doorway with a funny look on her face, holding out an ice-filled stainless-steel bowl.

"Why is my mixing bowl in the freezer?"

"Oh. My credit cards are in there." Anna's face went warm. "The ones from my parents. I got my first pay cheque last week, and I didn't want to—"

"You froze them?" Helen laughed and rapped her knuckles against the ice in the bowl. "Anna. That's adorable."

Anna slid down the couch. "It was in one of your dumb magazines. *Ten ways to manage your spending.* I just thought…why do you have so many magazines, anyway? Don't they all say the same things?"

"*All the women who're independent, throw your hands up at me,*" Helen sang, as she sat down. She pried the lid off a carton of vanilla ice cream. "Good for you. Here, give me your plate. How's the job going?"

"It's fine. I mean, boring, obviously. But I think that's what I need right now."

"It was nice of your dad to set that up."

"Yeah. He's been great, actually."

"And your mom? She's still…?"

"Yeah."

They looked at each other, then Helen scooped ice cream onto her own plate.

"We both have one good parent and one…not."

"You also have Gord."

"Yes! Thank God for Gord, honestly."

"Thank God for Gord!" Anna laughed. "How's he doing? He's okay?"

"I think he will be. He's not going back to work until the New Year. Hey, did I tell you I quit my job?"

Anna swallowed too fast, making her throat go numb with cold. When she could speak again, she said, "You did?"

"I talked to Carmen a few days ago. We both agreed I should hand in my notice. I'm officially unemployed."

"So, you're out of the makeup business?"

"For now."

"Well, it's nice to see you without so much shit on your face."

Helen raised a hand to her cheek, where her birthmark was barely concealed by a thin film of tinted moisturizer.

"That's what Thom said, too."

Anna lifted her eyebrows. "Thom?"

"I saw him yesterday afternoon, before you got home from work." The faint outline of Helen's birthmark deepened as her cheeks went pink. "He thinks we should try dating. For real, I mean. But I don't know. I have to figure out what I want."

Anna nodded, thinking about Johnnie Campbell. *Give me a call when you're sober.*

"So, what's next? You want to come work in my warehouse?"

"Ha. No, thanks." Helen toyed with her fork, drawing furrows in her melting ice cream. "I think I'm moving."

"What?" Anna felt like she'd been kicked. "Where?"

"Somewhere that's not Guelph. Maybe Toronto. But not right away," Helen added hastily, putting a hand on Anna's arm. "In the New Year. After the wedding."

"Right." Anna's ribcage tightened. "Your sister's wedding. I keep forgetting."

She put a hand to her chest and closed her eyes, seeing Glenn Starkey, white-faced in the darkness in that Toronto park. *I never meant to hurt you.* She tapped her heavy ring against her breastbone, counting. When she got to ten, she looked up.

"It's fine. I'm okay," she said to Helen's concerned face. "I'm just not ready for details."

Helen reached out and took Anna's hand.

"It's a weird situation. I'm not choosing her over you, it's just—"

"She's your sister."

"And you're my best friend," said Helen. "Even if Julia and I somehow end up getting along—"

"You and Little Miss Perfect?"

Helen smiled. "She's been a bit less obnoxious lately. But we'll see. Anyway, no matter what, I'm choosing you, too."

CHAPTER 26

The night before the wedding, Glenn's family hosted a rehearsal dinner at the Shakespeare Arms, a British-style pub around the corner from the hotel. The South End of Guelph felt like a whole other city, with billboards announcing future housing developments and a new Tim Hortons where there used to be only cornfields.

As the plates were cleared away, Glenn's father climbed to his feet and clinked his spoon against his wineglass.

"I know I'm not supposed to make speeches tonight," he began, as his wife tugged at his sport jacket. "But I want to say how happy we are to be welcoming Julia to our family."

Helen looked over to where her sister sat perched on Glenn's lap. Helen had offered to do Julia's makeup tonight as well as for the wedding tomorrow, but Julia had shaken her head.

"It's just not me. You know I'm more comfortable without it."

"Not even some lip gloss? A little mascara?" Helen herself wasn't wearing much more, other than the concealer that still covered her birthmark.

"Tomorrow you can doll me up. Not tonight." Julia had lowered her voice. "By the way, Olly's not coming. At least not tonight. Glenn's pretty upset."

"I thought they weren't friends anymore."

"It's not that simple." Julia shook her head. "Did you hear he quit teaching?"

"What? When?"

"He gave notice before the holidays. I guess there were lots of rumours going around. He's going to work at his dad's office for a while. Maybe take the LSAT this spring."

Now, as Julia beamed around the room, short hair mussed and pink cheeks showing the effect of several glasses of wine, Helen had to admit that her sister looked radiant, even without makeup. Glenn clearly thought so too: his arms were clasped around her and he gazed adoringly up at her face, like he was the luckiest guy in the world.

"To the happy couple." Glenn's father lifted his glass. "To Glenn and Julia!"

"To Julia," Helen echoed, draining her merlot.

She could feel her own father looking at her from across the room, trying to catch her eye. Shane Wright and his wife had flown in from Calgary that afternoon. They sat at a table in the back, barely mixing with the other guests. Shane had gone fully bald since the last time Helen had seen him, but he looked trim and successful in a blue jacket over a white shirt. His wife Karen was in a green pantsuit, her black hair cut in a stylish asymmetrical bob. So far, Helen had managed to avoid talking to either of them.

A cheerful hubbub broke out at the back of the room as the dessert buffet appeared. Helen's East-coast cousins lined up for the assortment of Nanaimo bars, brownies, coconut bars…and were those date squares? Helen stood up and joined the back of the line.

"Gosh, they're a cute couple," said the woman behind her.

Helen turned, nodding, and found herself facing her stepmother. Fine lines radiated from her dark eyes but

Karen Chang's makeup was flawless, with classic red lipstick and thick black eyeliner.

"I hear you're moving to Toronto?" Karen reached for a Nanaimo bar. Her nails were short and rounded, shiny with dark polish. "Have you found an apartment?"

"I'm going to stay with my parents for the first few weeks." Helen stressed the word *parents*. "Help out, while Gord gets back on his feet."

"We were so shocked to hear about his heart attack. How's his recovery going?"

"He's getting stronger." Helen glanced at Gord. The fluorescent lighting brought out the dark circles under his eyes, but he was smiling, deep in conversation with Glenn's parents. "He's going back to work part-time, starting next week."

"Will you look for a place near them?"

"I don't know." Helen took a date square. "Anyway—"

"Wait." Karen placed a hand on her arm. "I hope you'll spend some time with your father, while we're here. He'd really like that. We both would."

Helen raised her eyebrows until Karen took the hint and dropped her hand.

"We're heading back to the hotel. But we'll see you tomorrow."

Her black stilettos were soundless in the carpet as she walked away.

Helen took a bite of date square and chewed without tasting anything, the oat topping powdery in her dry mouth. When her sister appeared beside her, she put down her plate.

"Can you talk to Mom?" Julia said. "She's freaking out about our pictures."

"Freaking out?"

"Come and see."

Helen followed her sister to the side table displaying the collage of family photos. The two sides of the display showed Julia and Glenn growing from infants to children to teens, meeting in the middle with photos of the smiling couple. Helen had looked at the display before dinner, lingering over her favourites: herself and Julia holding hands on a Nova Scotia beach; three-year-old Julia running down the street, half her face covered in red marker to mimic Helen's birthmark.

Now there were conspicuous holes in the collage. As Helen approached, Linda pulled down a fifth-grade class picture that showed Helen in front of blond, boyish Glenn. Helen understood why Julia had included it, but she couldn't look at it too closely, not when it also featured Olly Sutton grinning from the back row. For a moment, Helen wondered if her mother had somehow heard about Anna and Olly. But no, Linda was reaching out for a picture of her two daughters smiling in the red velvet lap of a mall Santa.

"Mom," she said. "What are you doing?"

Linda's wooden necklace bounced against the front of her turtleneck as she turned around.

"Julia can't use these." Linda held out the Santa photo, tapping little Helen's port wine stain. "Look at your poor face!"

Helen and Julia exchanged glances.

"It's just pigment," Julia said. "It's not a disease."

Linda clutched the photos to her chest.

"Glenn's good with computers," she said. "Couldn't he scan these, fix them somehow?"

"You mean Photoshop?" Julia turned to Helen. "Can you believe this?"

"Mom." Something inside Helen hardened. "Nobody cares about my birthmark."

"I won't have you embarrassed! Not when you've worked so hard to cover it up."

"What do you think they'll do, point and laugh? At my baby pictures?"

"I'm trying to protect you!"

"But it's my face! It's who I am! My whole life, you've made me feel like I have to hide myself away. I'm sick of it!" Helen could feel people turning towards them. "You know what? Maybe I won't even cover it anymore. Then nobody's going to be shocked by the pictures. They can see the real thing."

Helen plucked a napkin from the table, dipped it into a glass of water and dragged it down her face, again and again, until it was a wet crumbling wad covered in tan foundation. She looked around, then glared at her mother.

"Oh, look," she said. "No one cares."

Linda's own napkin was pressed to her face, her shoulders shaking.

"It's okay, Mom," said Julia, as she slid the photos out of her hand. "Here. Let me put those back."

*

The morning of the wedding, Helen swiped on eyeliner, mascara, and lip gloss, but she left her face bare, her birthmark emblazoned across her cheek. She'd shared a hotel room with her sister, and she left Julia singing in the shower as she pushed her bobbed hair behind her ears and marched downstairs. In the hotel restaurant, she intercepted a few looks, but most people didn't give her a second glance.

Helen was choosing a yogurt at the breakfast buffet when she felt a touch on her arm and looked up into her father's face.

"Good morning," Shane said. "Karen and I have got a table by the window, if you want to join us."

Helen glanced over, looked around at the other tables, then turned back at her father. Shane was holding a plate with two blueberry muffins. She hesitated, then shrugged.

"Lead the way."

Helen's stepmother looked up as they approached. "Good morning, Helen."

"Good morning, Karen."

Her stepmother blinked, just as Helen realized she'd never used her first name before. An awkward silence settled over the table. Helen set down her plate, wondering what she was thinking by joining them. She picked up a knife to butter her toast and glanced at Shane, who was looking at Karen, panic-stricken. This close, she could see the faint scar of an old piercing on her father's earlobe, as well as the tiny hairs starting to grow back between his bushy eyebrows.

Helen cleared her throat.

"Could you please pass the jam?"

"Of course!"

"So," Helen said, as Shane handed over the basket of condiments. "How's the jet lag?"

"Fine. It's only a two-hour difference," said Karen. She was watching Helen carefully. "We were in Hong Kong last year and that was another story."

There was another pause. Helen spread strawberry jam on top of the butter, scraping the knife to the edges of the toast.

"I've got to say," she said, setting her toast back on her plate. "It's kind of strange to be sitting here with you."

"We're happy to be here," Shane said, the words sounding automatic, formal. Then he shook his head. "No, really. Julia is glowing. They seem so happy, even if they're young to be getting married." He glanced at Karen again. "I bought a new suit for the occasion. Mine was getting a little shabby."

"A little tight, you mean," said Karen.

Helen laughed as Shane waved the comment away.

"I wanted something nice to walk Julia down the aisle. You know I'm doing that?"

"She told me."

"I'm so glad you two are talking more. There's nothing like family." He stopped, as if the word choked him.

Helen raised her eyebrows and peeled open her container of yogurt.

"I guess that's true," she said.

"And look, I don't know if this is the right time, but we don't get many opportunities to talk." He stopped again.

Helen put down her spoon and looked at him, her heart suddenly pounding. "I'm listening."

"Okay, well, I've been a shitty father. I know it, you know it, even Karen knows it." Shane squinted at his wife, who gazed back at him, her face placid. He turned back to Helen. "Your mother and I were very young when we got together. Too young, I guess. When I left, I didn't realize how much I'd be giving up, with you and your sister." He looked down at his plate. "I've certainly paid for that mistake."

Everyone makes mistakes. What if her father wasn't the cartoon villain she'd always rejected? Helen had a dizzying moment of longing, a vision of them all—Shane and

Karen and Gord and Linda—standing around her, the way they'd all stood in a smiling circle around Julia last night.

"Your mom worked her butt off raising you two," Shane said. "I'm so grateful to her, and to Gord, for being there when I wasn't. And I'm sorry. You should have been able to count on me too. Not just for money, but for everything."

Helen's father looked at her with eyes the same brown as her own.

"Man, I'm proud of you! So grown up, so independent. So beautiful."

"Beautiful?" Helen said. "Me?"

"You know that's where your name came from? I insisted, once we saw your birthmark. *The face that launched a thousand ships.*"

Helen stared at him, speechless.

"I never thought you needed all that makeup. But, of course, you wear it if you want. You're an adult, I won't tell you what to do. I just don't want to miss out anymore. Both me and Karen, we'd love to know you better. So, what's next for you, do you think? Any ideas?"

"I'm not sure." Helen's cheeks were burning. "I might take some classes in Toronto. George Brown has a culinary school that's close to Mom and Gord's condo."

"That's great! And you know, if you need any help, financially…if I can ever smooth the way…"

"I don't want your money," Helen said. "But I hear what you're saying. Maybe I could pick up the phone sometimes, give you a call."

"Or come out and see us in Calgary! You know we've got a spare bedroom. You're welcome anytime. Come for the Stampede! We could go up to Banff and Jasper, see the mountains. Do you ski?"

"Shane," said Karen, putting a hand on his arm. "No need to plan anything until you're ready, Helen. But we'd love to have you visit."

"Maybe. Thanks."

Shane reached out and touched Helen's hand.

"That's great. That's so great. And look who it is! The blushing bride!"

Julia walked up to the table, smiling. "You guys are talking. It's a miracle."

"Oh, stop." Helen pushed out a chair. "Here, sit with us."

Julia held out an arm and pushed up the sleeve of her sweater. "Look, goosebumps." She sat down, rubbing at her pale skin. "I'm so nervous. But everything's going to go fine, right?"

"Everything's going to be perfect," Helen said. "It's going to be a perfect day."

CHAPTER 27

March 2005

The day they went up in the balloon was cold and clear.

From where she stood with Helen by the truck, Anna watched Johnnie Campbell stride around the snow-covered field, spreading the parachute-like edges of the balloon—the envelope, he called it—before checking the ropes and the machinery. He'd been supposed to take Anna up in February; not Valentine's Day exactly, but near enough. Then a storm had blown in, and they'd had to cancel. Apparently, the weather had to be perfect. Anyway, Anna hadn't been sure, then, that she wanted to go up at all. But now, with Helen at her side, she felt ready.

They stood watching the green and blue nylon billow and expand, gradually taking shape and starting to float. The wicker basket lay sideways on the ground, with Johnnie's uncle standing in front of it, directing long jets of flame into the open balloon. Then, as the balloon rose overhead, Johnnie's uncle and the basket both tipped backwards.

"Whoa," said Helen, as Johnnie's uncle slid into the balloon, his hands still on the nozzle controlling the flame. "This is crazy."

Anna glanced at Helen, standing wide-eyed at her side, bundled in the freezing dawn air. Helen was living in Toronto now, working at a bakery. She'd cut her hair even shorter, the nut-brown waves poking out from under her knitted hat. Her birthmark was a distinct pink shape across her cheek.

"I still wear makeup," Helen had said, when she'd arrived at the apartment on Friday with a bare face and a basket of treats. "But I don't worry so much about covering it up, these days."

At 5:30 this morning, Johnnie had picked up Anna and Helen from the apartment.

"I was worried you wouldn't set your alarms," he'd said, holding open the door of his pickup truck.

Anna had laughed.

"We never went to bed!"

The snowy fields had glowed blue in the predawn light as he drove them to the launch site. None of them had talked much in the truck. Anna had mostly stared out the window, yawning, picking out constellations in the deep black sky.

"All right, girls," called Johnnie's uncle. "Come on over. Mind the lines, now."

Anna dropped her cigarette, since Johnnie had been clear that the "no smoking near the balloon" rule was set in stone. She and Helen ran over towards the basket. Overhead, the enormous balloon bobbed in the slight breeze, straining against the ropes like a dog eager to go for a walk.

Johnnie leaned out and offered his hand, but Anna grabbed the padded edge and scrambled in on her own, vaulting into the square wicker basket. She leaned back and looked up into the hollow nylon balloon. There was a click and a whoosh as Johnnie's uncle pulled on a lever with his gloved hand, releasing another tongue of flame as Helen clambered into the basket beside her.

Anna looked at Johnnie and he winked. He looked older out here, more in control, not at all the puppyish boy she thought she knew. Honestly, if she could press pause on this moment, Anna would pull him out of the basket and take him right there, in the van or even in the stand of evergreens over at the edge of this field. But that could wait.

Johnnie smiled and she grinned back, slapping the leather with both hands.

"Let's get this thing in the air!" Anna said.

"Which way are we going?" Helen asked. "And how far?"

"Wherever the wind takes us," said the uncle, reaching both hands up to grasp a metal lever. "Here we go!"

Anna expected a lurch, some kind of bump, but there was only a slow tilt as the basket left the ground. She'd flown more times than she could count, but this was not the fierce acceleration of a plane's engine fighting gravity; this was a lifting up, a letting go, a leaving behind. Around them, the ground crew in the field walked backwards, releasing their ropes.

Helen gasped as they started to rise, grabbing Anna's arm, pressing into her new tattoo. She'd had that done last week: a split-tailed swallow, its ink-black silhouette swooping up between the faded shapes of her older tattoos.

Wincing, Anna dislodged Helen's grip and found herself holding her hand, their fingers interlacing as the balloon rose steadily up and up, floating towards and then over the tops of the line of evergreens. Anna could see birds' nests and old branches in the tops of the trees before they moved past, floating higher. The burners flared on and off. Anna could hear distant traffic and the faint sound of crows calling, but mostly she was struck by the quiet, the stillness of the air as they rode with the wind.

Up and up they went, Helen clutching Anna's hand and breathing fast beside her. Anna's own breath came long and deep, pulling cold bright air into her lungs. She looked over the edge of the basket, watching the balloon's shadow follow them over the grey and white checkerboard of fields, over the meandering line of a frozen river, through the trees. Murmuring together, Johnnie and his uncle pointed up into the balloon's canopy overhead. The ropes creaked, the jets flared.

Johnnie turned to Anna, smiling at the exhilaration on her face.

"Do you want a photo?"

Anna shook her head.

"I'll remember this."

She squeezed Helen's hand, the two of them looking up over the flattened game board city of Guelph, towards the opening horizon. She looked up and up, as they rose and kept rising, into the limitless sky.

Acknowledgements

Thank you to Linda Leith, for seeing the potential in "Other Maps," to Elise Moser, mentor and editor extraordinaire, as well as the whole team at Linda Leith Publishing.

You can take the girl out of Guelph but apparently you can't take Guelph out of the girl. However, this novel takes plenty of liberties. The Guelph in this book is not on any maps.

Thanks to the Quebec Writers' Federation, le Conseil des arts et des lettres du Québec, the Banff Centre for Arts and Creativity, and Artscape Gibraltar Point.

Massive gratitude to those who read and gave feedback on early versions of this book: Sarah Turner, Jill Derby, Carly Vandergriendt, Katie Schwab, Sarah Lolley, Isobel Cunningham, Marc Boucher, Chloe Stuart-Ulin, Mahi Adsett and Joe Bongiorno. I'm deeply appreciative of your time, support and suggestions.

I've been privileged to know many wonderful writers as teachers and friends, from Montreal, Banff and beyond: Shannon Webb-Campbell, Rachel McCrum, Silmy Abdullah, Christy Ann Conlin, Cody Caetano, Julie Lalonde, Luciana Erregue, Ami Sands Brodoff, Cherie Dimaline, Paige Cooper, John Metcalf, Rachel Thompson, Moe Clark, Sivan Slapak, Ariela Freedman and Jen Sookfong Lee. I've learned so much from you all.

A few other friends whose support has sustained me through the long, long writing process: Emilie Coyle, Émilie Brière, Baptiste Pétré, Emilie Guillet,

Orla Wallace, Jenny Smith, Miriam Riches and Petra Niederhauser, who's also my brilliant photographer.

Thanks to family near and far, including my father Jim Atkinson and my aunt Irene Schwab, both gone too soon and deeply missed. My mother Susan Atkinson, a scientist who somehow produced an artist. My children Charlotte, Elijah and William, for inspiration and for patience as they learned to share their mother with the made-up people in her head. Infinite thanks to Eric Morris, for everything.